Benediction

Kelly Moran

Cover Art Design by: Kelly Moran
Photo Credit: Kruse Images & Photography
Cover Model: Baretta Vincent

ISBN-13: 978-1546763550
ISBN-10: 1546763554
Createspace Paperback Edition
Published in the United States of America

Praise for Kelly Moran's Books:

"Breathes life into an appealing story."
Publishers Weekly

"Readers will fall in love."
Romantic Times

"Great escape reading."
Library Journal

"Touching & gratifying."
Kirkus Reviews

"Sexy, heart-tugging fun."
USA Today HEA

"Emotional & totally engaging."
Carla Neggers

"A gem of a writer."
Sharon Sala

"I read in one sitting."
Carly Phillips

"Compelling characters."
Roxanne St. Claire

"A sexy, emotional romance."
Kim Karr

"An emotionally raw story. A compelling read."
Katie Ashley

Chapter One

Ribs screaming in agony, blood dripping from her nose and lip, and her right eye swollen almost shut, Amy Tarcher stumbled through the Cattenach Ranch iron gate onto her best friend's property. Her legs cramped, barely holding her up, and the vertigo was screwing with her balance. Loose gravel over the brick-laid driveway grated under her shuffling flip-flops, but they were all she'd been able to manage when she'd fled home.

Amy's own postage stamp of a house was in an older subdivision on the other side of Olivia's sprawling ranch. Which meant, somehow, she'd walked three miles to get here. Her car hadn't been an option. Before her husband had gone mental and put her in this current black and blue state, he'd slashed her tires, smashed her cell phone, and had taken a hammer to her photography equipment. That hurt almost worse than the beating he'd inflicted.

An end in sight, she forced her feet to keep moving and headed up the driveway at a drunken snail's pace. Squinting through the sun's glare, she eyed the three-story log cabin straight ahead, then the property. Since it was midday, no one but possibly Olivia's Aunt Mae would be at the main house. As Amy got closer, she veered right and focused on the barns. Three of them, side by side.

Salvation.

Damp grass shushed under her soles and cottonwood trees swayed with a slight breeze. The scent of hay and soil wafted in the air, so familiar she wanted to weep. Early spring had brought comfortable temperatures, but she couldn't get warm. Probably would never again.

Through the pain, she told herself over and over that this was it. She was done. As soon as she was able, she was filing for divorce from Chris and changing her last name back to Woods. Dejection and shame flowed through her veins and mingled with red blood cells. But that wasn't anything new. She would do something about it, though.

Finally. She'd made it.

On the brink of collapse, muscles contracting, she leaned against the entryway of the first barn, relief a tiny bud in her aching chest. The front and rear carriage doors were open, sunlight filtering down a long narrow path between horse stalls lining both sides. Her best friend Olivia stood on the far end of the aisle, checking a clipboard. Her auburn hair was up in a ponytail, jeans and flannel form-fitting to her slender frame. Amy had never seen anything so beautiful in her pathetic life.

"Liv?" She cleared the croak from her throat and tried again. "Liv, I need help." Her face must've been more swollen than she thought because her words were slurred.

Olivia's head jerked around. "Oh my God. Amy? What happened?" The clipboard clattered to the ground.

Amy stumbled forward and they met in the middle as she slid to the dirt floor in a painful heap. Her ribs let out a wail in protest. "Chris..."

Olivia sat beside her and gingerly set Amy's head in her lap, gently stroking the tangled hair from her face.

Amy closed her eyes at the comforting touch. "Little...banged up."

"Chris did this to you?"

She nodded, unable to do much else.

Olivia unclipped a walkie-talkie from her belt and spoke into it. "Nakos?" Her frantic wail demanding the foreman pierced the otherwise quiet space. "I need you up here. Now." She glanced down at Amy. "He's with Nate in the southern pasture repairing fence sections. It'll be about twenty minutes before they can get back. Why didn't you call me?"

"Couldn't. He...killed the...phone. And my car."

"Crap, Amy. You walked here?" Since she was too sore and exhausted to nod again, Olivia must've gotten the hint because she lifted the radio a second time. "I'll get Aunt Mae to call Doc Hank. And Rip, too."

The sheriff. Yes, good idea.

But before Olivia could utter a sound, a resounding click echoed and Amy's heart stopped at the telltale cocking of a gun.

6

From behind Olivia, a flash of metal appeared and pressed against her temple.

All Amy could make out from her prone position was a pant leg, but the sour stench of beer told her that her husband had decided to follow her here.

Chris staggered on his feet and came into full view beside them. "Give me the walkie-talkie, bitch."

Olivia's round blue eyes grew wider as she passed the radio over her shoulder to Chris with a trembling hand. Her gaze never left Amy's as oh-shit registered in her expression.

He tossed the device to the ground, stomped it to pieces, and kicked the fragments away. The horses whinnied and snorted, causing the scent of hay and fur to rise with dust motes.

God, this wasn't happening. It just...wasn't. Not even her luck could be this awful. She should've tried to keep going down the state highway to the police station instead of coming to the ranch. Now she'd brought her white-hot mess with her.

In her peripheral, she caught a flash of Aunt Mae's white hair as she emerged in the doorway behind Chris. A quick survey of the situation, and the elder woman ducked back out before Chris had a chance to turn and see her.

Thank you, Baby Jesus. Aunt Mae could get help.

Amy closed her eyes a brief beat, and the drugging pull of unconsciousness nearly consumed her. But she had to get her husband away from her friend. He was obviously drunk off his ass, more so than a couple hours before, and there was no telling what he might do.

When she lifted her lids, Chris had taken off his dirty cowboy hat and was scratching his head with the butt of the gun.

"Let Liv go. She didn't do anything. You're..." Dang, talking hurt. "You want me, not her."

He shoved his hat back on and aimed the 9mm at the ground. "You got us into this fucking mess, you selfish slut. Look at you. A waste of oxygen. Useless."

Nothing she hadn't heard before. A thousand times over. Still, the barb lanced.

His jogging pants were soiled and his sweatshirt didn't fare much better. She wondered where the hell he'd gone after he'd left her in a broken pile on the floor at home. He had a thin body, more

7

wiry than anything, and a gaunt-like face that rarely saw a razor. When they'd first met three years ago, she'd considered him rugged in a backdoor way. Taking in his brown greasy strands and bloodshot eyes now, she hadn't a clue what had ever attracted her.

He sneered and spit on the ground. "I should punish you some more in a way you'll never forget. But the thought of gettin' between your legs shrivels my balls. You deserved the back of my hand and worse. Had it comin' a long time, fat ass."

She didn't think it was possible to have more shame piled on this mortification heap, yet embarrassment stung her cheeks just the same. Olivia trembled against her and Amy wouldn't survive it if anything happened to her. She had to diffuse him, and attempted to summon the energy to try reasoning again.

Someone stepped into the entryway, gun aimed at Chris's back. Jeans and a black t-shirt molded to a...massive giant of a man. Tattoo sleeves rippled with thick muscle as he held the gun like it was an extension of him. Under his black baseball hat, he seemed to be bald, but light brown scruff darkened his jaw. Golden eyes dipped to Olivia, past Amy, and right back to Chris.

Mary Mother. This must be Nate. The soldier who'd shown up on Olivia's doorstep a couple weeks ago. He'd brought Justin's if-you're-reading-this letter to Olivia so she could read her brother's final words. Amy hadn't met the guy, but he'd served with Justin and had been there when he'd died. Olivia hadn't lied in her account to Amy, either. The man was a fortress of testosterone and bulge.

Silently, he stalked closer until only a few feet separated them.

Footsteps scraped behind her. "Drop it, Chris."

Nakos Hunt. Thank God. Amy would've known that low timbre anywhere.

Chris flinched and pressed the barrel to Olivia's forehead again. She closed her eyes on a whimper, a tear trickling down her too-pale cheek.

No! Not Liv. Panic clutched Amy's airway.

Nate lifted his revolver a fraction higher, bracing the bottom with his other hand, calculation in his eyes. "He said drop it."

Chris turned his head and stumbled to the side. "Who're you?"

"Lower the weapon or you'll never find out."

Nakos's boots shushed against dirt until he stopped by Amy's head and both men had Chris trapped. Nakos held a rifle, but he seemed to be taking Nate's lead.

"This is a private matter." Chris shoved the 9mm at Olivia so hard, her head snapped back.

Her friend sucked in a harsh breath, trembling. Her frantic gaze met Amy's.

Cold sweat broke out over her skin as her pulse skittered past stroke level.

Though he didn't so much as twitch, Nate looked ready to snap. "Private is what your jail cell will look like. Drop. It. Now."

If Olivia hadn't spoken so highly of the former soldier, his tone alone would've had Amy cowering in fear. Controlled. Deadly. Brooking no argument.

Nakos and Nate exchanged some kind of back-and-forth Amy didn't understand. After a pause, Nate said, "You sure?"

"Positive."

"What in the hell?" Chris spun, jerking the barrel away from Olivia.

Nate nodded once like he'd been waiting for just that opening. "Olivia, baby. Don't move."

A crack of a gunshot rang out, sending Amy's heart racing in her throat and causing Olivia to violently recoil.

Neighs rent the air. Hooves stomped dirt inside the stalls.

Terror took on a new name as Amy whipped her head around, ignoring the pain, seeking Nakos. Like Olivia, he'd been Amy's best friend since third grade. Thankfully, he appeared unhurt. Olivia, though? Another crane of Amy's neck to check. She let out a shallow sigh. No injury, either.

And then Amy realized what had happened. Nate had fired the shot, hitting the brim of Chris's tan cowboy hat and spinning it off his head.

Chris reeled and dropped the weapon.

Quick as lightning, Nate strode forward, shoved his revolver in his waistband, and planted Chris face-first in the dirt. With a knee between his shoulders and a firm hand on the back of his neck, Nate toed the gun farther from them.

He whipped his attention to Olivia. "Did he hurt you?" He scanned her for wounds as if he might expire on the spot if she had any.

She shook her head repeatedly, tears leaving tracks on her cheeks. Her gaze dropped to Amy. "She's pretty bad, though."

Amy opened her mouth to reassure her friend, but Nakos set his rifle behind him and squatted next to her. Familiar midnight eyes traced her face with frenetic concern in their depths. The dark skin of his Native American heritage grew ashen the longer he stared. Eyebrows wrenched in a frown and jaw tight, he reached for her with a shaking hand, but swiftly drew back.

"You've looked better, Ames." The tension cracking his voice nearly felled her.

She tried to smile, but it reopened her lip and sent blood trickling down her chin.

Panic and horror shoved the worry in his expression aside. He glanced over his shoulder. "Mae!" Nakos ran his hands down Amy's arms, her legs. "Do you think anything's broken?"

She did her best not to wince, shook her head, and closed her eyes. Every inhale was like a sharp poker to her lungs and the side of her face throbbed. With her adrenaline crashing now that she was safe, that her friends were okay, tears welled and her body trembled. Bone-jarring convulsions wracked her limbs.

"Doc Hank's here." Aunt Mae ran into the barn, quickly eyed her surroundings, and knelt beside Nakos. "Rip is just pulling in, too. We'll get you all fixed up, sweetheart."

Amy doubted it. Her life had been on a shit spiral long before today. There was no fixing the damage. She appreciated the warm sentiment in the elder woman's blue eyes, though. She'd always been so nice to Amy.

"Let me up!" Chris squirmed, but got nowhere for the effort.

Nate dug his knee deeper into his spine. "You ever want use of your legs again, you'll shut up and stay still."

Hank walked in carrying a doctor's bag circa the 1900s, one hand on her hip. She was a two-hundred pound, fifty-year-old woman with black hair down to her rearend. "Well, give the girl some room." She set the bag down, opened it, and settled on Amy's other side, shining a penlight in her eyes. "I'm guessing your sad

10

sack of a husband did this to you? Where'd he hit you and with what?"

"His fists." Amy struggled to draw a breath and hissed at the needling lick of pain. "Kicked...my side. Punched my face."

Beside her, Nakos growled low in his throat and went rigid.

"Nothing on the spine or neck? Did you fall at any time?"

"No." Amy closed her eyes, too tired to keep them open. Dizziness threatened to swallow her whole, her stomach somersaulting.

"She needs an ambulance." Nate's voice lacked the emotion of Nakos's, but the sharp order relayed his concern. Poor guy didn't know the isolation of these parts. One only went to the ER if a limb had been severed or there was no pulse.

"Closest hospital is in Casper. We've got it handled." Hank sighed. "Olivia, you got a room for her at the main house? I need to better examine her."

"Yes. We can put her in the extra guestroom."

"All right." Hank's feet shuffled as if she'd stood. "Nakos?"

Amy reopened her eyes, their voices no longer a faraway lull.

"Yeah. I've got her." Nakos offered a ghosted smile as if she were the one needing reassurance. With a tentative arm under her knees and behind her back, he gently lifted her and cradled her to his chest like she was made of glass.

Despite the caution, agony clawed at her from every angle and she yelped. Whimpered.

He froze, his eyes desperate and beseeching. "I'm sorry. I'll go slow."

God, he was such a good guy. Emotion clogged her airway, and she rested her head on his hard pec. His flannel was warm and smelled like him, earthy and sun-kissed.

Rip waddled into the barn, favoring the leg he'd injured in Desert Storm. His FuManchu and brown officer's uniform were out of place together, and he ran a hand over his thinning brown hair. "I apologize for the delay. The Hendersons decided it was a good idea to plow their minivan into the Garrison's ditch and take out a mailbox in the process." He glanced from Nate to Chris to Amy in Nakos's arms, then finally, Olivia. "Looks like you got it covered."

"I'm taking Ames up to the house." Nakos strode out, her limp in his arms, Aunt Mae and Hank on his heels.

She had a vague conception of floating through the yard, the house, and him climbing stairs before soft blankets cushioned her back and the safe, drifting sensation eased. The solid, warm, comforting arms that had been holding her slid away from her in retreat.

All of a sudden, and without any control of her own, the day's events slammed into her head and coagulated in her belly. A fist to her cheek and the popping which followed. Another to her mouth and the copper taste of blood coating her tongue. A boot to the ribs, stealing the wind from her lungs. The yelling. The stench of yeasty, sour alcohol.

Anxiety and dread shredded a path up her windpipe, seized her breath. Trembling, she threw her eyes open and latched onto Nakos's sleeve. "Don't let go... Please, Nakos. Just don't let go."

"Hey, it's all right." He eased a hip down to sit next to her on the bed.

A sob tore from her chest, and she would've hated herself for it if she were in her right mind. She just...needed him. For whatever reason, she needed only him. The stoic, sometimes brooding guy who would step in front of a moving train if it meant keeping Olivia and her safe. The shy boy who'd grown into a man and who was familiar to her as air.

He jerked a chin over his shoulder. "Give us a moment alone." When the door closed behind Aunt Mae and Doc Hank, he reset his focus on Amy. "Shh. I've got you. You're safe." He leaned over her, no part of him touching her but the warm press of his lips to her forehead. "Shh," he cooed again over her skin.

She sobbed harder, her ribs really angry now and tears burning the cuts on her face.

He threaded his shaking hands through the hair at her temples. "Let it out. Go ahead, we're alone. Let it out."

And that was enough to settle the terror. His soothing voice, his tender touch, the scent of him filling her nose and surrounding her.

Blowing out a careful breath, she got a grip. "I'm sorry."

"*Hihcebe*, Ames. Don't apologize." He lifted his head and, though dry, his eyes were red-rimmed as if he'd been battling emotion himself. He took off his customary black Stetson, revealing shoulder-length raven strands tied back in a low ponytail. Setting the hat aside, he dug his thumb and forefinger into his eye sockets. "Scared ten years off my life."

"I'm okay," she whispered, trying to reassure him as guilt morphed to consuming levels.

He shook his head like he didn't believe her and drilled her with a look of carnal fear bordering on desperation. "Did he..." He barked a sound of distress and clutched his stomach. "Did he do...anything else to you? Hurt you...in other ways?"

Oh God. "No. He just used his fists." As if that were okay. But she wanted to erase the image of possible sexual assault from Nakos's head right now. "Honest. Nothing else."

He nodded so adamantly she thought his noggin might roll off his shoulders. Then, he gingerly dropped his forehead to hers and slammed his eyes shut. "What happened? Please, tell me."

Knowing him, the only way to wind down was to have the details so his mind wouldn't fill in the blanks. That, at least, she could give him. "We argued over finances. He wanted to sell my camera equipment to pay off bills, but I said no. He...went ballistic. I walked here and I'm good now. All is well."

Lord, what a convincing liar she turned out to be.

He straightened and ran his slightly calmer gaze over her body. He ducked a glance behind him and returned it to her. "Is that the truth?"

"Yes." All but the being okay part.

"How long's he been doing this to you?" His wide, strong jaw ticked. "I don't recall seeing any bruises before today."

"First time." She may be a has-been with a future so dull it was black and white, but she wouldn't tolerate abuse. "Honest. First time."

Another nod, and he looked at the door again.

And it hit her. Painfully. He'd been in love with Olivia since they were teenagers. Amy wasn't the only one who'd had a gun aimed at her. Nakos must be going out of his mind with concern for Olivia, every instinct yelling for him to get back to her.

Though her shoulders sank and an all too familiar hollowness filled her chest cavity, Amy did what she always had—she accepted reality and ignored the loneliness. "Go ahead. I'm okay. Thank you for helping."

She would not cry again. She absolutely would not.

"You sure?" He studied her a moment. "Doc really should get a look at you."

"I'm positive. Go."

Of course, without further argument, he did.

Chapter Two

Three months later...

Today was going to suck. And not the good kind. Nope. The big, sweaty, hairy donkey balls variety. He thought he'd been prepared for this, but the shift in his gut said otherwise.

Biting back a sigh, Nakos Hunt glanced from the two men standing beside him to the wide open expanse of Cattenach Ranch. Two-thousand acres of rolling grasslands and high plains. The Laramie Mountains just to the south were little more than a bluish mirage in the distance, but a slightly cool breeze wafted across the basin to provide some relief from the heat.

A rare hot Wyoming sun beat down from a cloudless sky as prairie grass crackled in the wind. He shoved his index finger between his neck and the white collar of the button down shirt Olivia had forced him to wear, trying to get liberation from the upper eighties temperature. With his dark skin, courtesy of his native Arapaho tribe, he was roasting. At least she'd let him wear jeans and cowboy boots, but he felt naked without his Stetson. And she'd made him leave his hair down, too.

Only for her.

Olivia, sole owner of Cattenach Ranch where he'd served as her foreman for going on ten years, had him wrapped around her pinkie since age nine when his family had left the reservation to work for hers. As one of his best friends, she was the most stubborn, mule-headed woman in existence, but her heart was bigger than the damn state. No one deserved this happy day more than her, so he mentally got his shit together.

Again, only for her.

"Are you all right?" Nathan Roldan gave Nakos a quick head-to-toe sweep, his golden eyes glittering hard as if he'd seen the worst humanity had to offer and had fought it with his bare hands.

Then again, he truly had. Abandoned by a junkie mother, Nate had grown up in foster care, later joined a gang in his teens, and subsequently had enlisted in the Army to escape. It was there he'd met Olivia's brother. Except, after finally having found a genuine friend, Nate had watched Justin die overseas right in front of him.

Olivia wasn't the only one who deserved this bit of happiness. The guy was long overdue.

"I'm fine." Nakos shifted his weight to his other foot. "Shouldn't I be asking you? I'm not the one getting married."

"Exactly."

Right. This again. Because everyone in creation knew Nakos had a thing for Olivia.

He blamed it on culture shock. Having been raised with other Arapaho, catching sight of her red hair, fair skin, and freckles the first time as a kid had been like a gut-punch that never subsided. Even all these years later.

Yet, he thought he'd assuaged everyone's concerns. Was he attracted to her? Yes. Had he sometimes wished she'd look at him with something more than affection? Yes. But it hadn't happened and he was okay with that. Though he'd lie down and die for her, he wasn't the man she wanted. Somewhere in the back of his mind and in the underbelly of his heart, he'd known that all along. Thus, he'd never allowed himself to pine or permit hope to build.

Well, not much, anyway.

"I wouldn't be standing here as your best man if I wasn't one-hundred percent behind you." He'd said it before and he'd say it a million times more. "You're the right guy for her."

Another truth that had cemented in Nakos's brain since Nate had first rode up the driveway on his Harley. And the ex-soldier had stuck. Which, ultimately, was what Justin and Olivia wanted. And what they wanted, Nakos would do everything in his power to provide. He'd gone as far as to push Olivia and Nate together when they'd stumbled over their attraction.

If that had torn Nakos's insides to shreds like a dull, rusty blade...well, no one had to be the wiser.

Since Nate was still studying him in that assessing, silent way he was prone to do, Nakos looked him straight in the eye. "I love her. I always will. But I'm not *in love* with her." Much. "And since the Cattenachs care about you, I've grown fond of you, as well. At

16

the risk of you pulling out a gun and shooting me for being sentimental, I'll say one last thing, and then we're through with this. I'll stand beside you as a friend and a beacon of support while both the people I love get their happy ending. Okay? We done?"

Nate's eyes widened a fraction of a beat in surprise like they always did when someone claimed any sort of support on his behalf. Friendship, love, family...he'd never had any of those things until arriving in Meadowlark, so he was still adjusting. Nakos got that. Understood, even. And he'd meant every word. Nate, damn him, was as solid as they came.

"Thank you," Nate muttered and rubbed his hand over his shaved head as if uncomfortable. The camo fatigues Olivia insisted he wear stretched against the bulking muscles underneath. The guy was enormous and covered in ink. Buried under all that testosterone was a good heart with noble intentions. "That means a lot."

Rip, Nate's boss and the town sheriff who'd be presiding over the service, ran his tongue over his yellow teeth, causing his FuManchu to twitch. "I'm getting all misty." His sarcastic tone had Nakos rolling his eyes. "And my balls just shrank."

"Christ." Nate glanced heavenward. "You ever use the phrase *my balls* in a sentence again, I'll force you into medical retirement."

"I'll help." Expelling a breath, Nakos looked around.

Four rows of white folding chairs were set up on either side of a makeshift aisle with a lattice archway at the end. There were only roughly fifty people present, as the bride and groom wanted something small. Nakos and the two other men were waiting off to the side for the cue to start. And had been for forty-five minutes.

"What's taking them so long?"

"Women," Rip said by way of explanation.

As if reading Nakos's mind, Kyle jogged around the bend toward them. He worked as one of Olivia's ranch hands and was Amy's little brother. Amy was the maid of honor, but Nakos hadn't seen her today.

Kyle wiped his forehead with his arm. *He* didn't have to wear a dress shirt. "They're ready. I'm supposed to tell you to get into place." He glanced quickly at Nakos. "You doing okay, man? Holding up?"

At Nate's chuckle, Nakos narrowed his eyes at Kyle with a look that said he'd single-handedly put the *laugh* in *manslaughter*.

"Pretend I didn't ask." Kyle retreated the way he'd come, but made a hard right and claimed a chair next to Nakos's parents.

Nate rolled his lips over his teeth, which did nothing to hide his grin.

"Shut up."

Up went Nate's hands. "I didn't say a thing."

Would this day never end? "Are you nervous?" Nakos side-glanced the groom, wishing the dude had at least a bead of perspiration from anxiety. But no. A pillar, this one.

"Hell no. I can't wait."

Figured, not that Nakos could blame him.

They assumed their positions based on the pithy rehearsal the day before and waited for the music to start. If anyone thought having the nuptials right outside the wrought iron gate of the Cattenach's private cemetery was odd, they didn't know the family very well. Olivia's parents, along with three generations of relatives before, were buried there. As was Justin, someone who had meant the world to both the bride and groom. It was only fitting they'd want to be closer to him on their day, if merely to have his spirit nearby.

Situated off to the right, Meadowlark's high school band began to play, notes from guitar strings and flutes floating on the breeze. Moments later, Amy stepped into view at the base of the grassy aisle and paused.

Damn, but Nakos's airway seized. An occurrence that had been happening for a few months now in her presence.

He couldn't wrap his head around his body's reaction. He'd met Amy the day he'd been introduced to Olivia, and the three of them had been nearly inseparable. He knew her pretty oval face, long cocoa locks, and blue-green eyes that reminded him of a mermaid as well as he knew his own reflection. Lately, it was as if looking at her was like seeing her for the first time. Attraction and appreciation that had never been present before wrapped around his throat and squeezed.

Actually, if he were being honest, he could pinpoint exactly when the phenomena began. Three months ago, almost to the day.

Finding Amy mottled with bruises and bleeding on the dirt floor of the barn—courtesy of her ex-husband, who Nakos referred to as the Antichrist—had reset some kind of circuit in his brain.

18

He'd always been quick on his feet and able to control his temper. But that day? He'd been *this close* to a homicide charge and wearing an orange jumpsuit for twenty-five to life.

For whatever reason, Amy made him a little nervous. Had since they'd been kids. Before she'd wed the douchebag, she'd been a badass, take-no-prisoners woman. She didn't just chew men up for breakfast and spit them out. Oh, no. She'd had them for lunch and dinner, too. Nothing and no one scared her. She took life by the horns—or balls—and gave it her all.

Ergo, the way she'd clung to him the day of the assault after he'd carried her to the guestroom was like a horror movie reel on a continuous loop. He hadn't known whether to weep or pull her in his arms. And he'd been so frightened about internal bleeding or unseen injuries he had to make himself leave her side so Doc Hank could examine her. He'd spent hours outside that room in case Amy had called for help. Gutted from the inside out and crawling out of his skin.

Nakos hadn't seen a genuine smile pass her lush red lips in he couldn't remember how long. The realization had his stomach aching as she stepped forward and slowly made her way toward them.

That dress was designed to be a kill switch for rational thought. Blue as the cobalt sky and strapless, it hugged her generous breasts and narrow waist, flaring to a stop just above her knees. Amy Tarcher—no, Amy Woods since she'd gone back to her maiden name—had toned legs that went on for decades. Her hair was up in a girly complicated knot of curls, exposing her regal neck as she carried white lilies. Her skin was like porcelain, and there was *a lot* of it exposed. Silver dangly earrings matched her shoes and reflected in the sunlight.

God save him, those heels. Strappy and high enough to maybe bring her within an inch of his chin. If she ever made it to the altar. Time seemed to have paused to a drugging slow-motion in his head.

Nate grunted and leaned close to whisper out of the side of his mouth. "My bad. Guess you really are okay. You might want to start breathing, though, before you pass out."

Nakos slanted him an eat-shit glare. "What is this? You're getting hitched, so now everyone else needs to be bursting with fruit flavor in love, too?"

The jackass chuckled. "I'm not the one who looks like he just got a high-five to the face with a brick..." He expelled a wheeze and went still, eyes on the aisle. "Holy shit," he breathed.

Glancing in the same direction, Nakos suddenly understood the expletive.

And here came twenty-one years of his life in a bridal gown. Lovely as ever, Olivia's auburn hair was loose around her shoulders and her cornflower eyes were smiling. The simple dress matched Amy's, except it went to her ankles and was ivory-colored. Simple elegance.

Her aunt Mae, being Olivia's only remaining blood relative, walked her down the aisle wearing a peach suit, the soft white strands of her bob ruffling in the slight breeze. Pride and happiness gleaned in her wet eyes.

When they finally made it to the lattice arch, Olivia kissed Mae, hugged Amy, then took Nakos's hands and rose on her toes to speak into his ear. "Thank you for standing with me all these years and beside Nate now. It means so much to both of us." She kissed his cheek, causing her rain-like scent to swirl around him. "I love you."

He closed his eyes and drew a calming breath. Damn her. "Love you, too, little red." The nickname he'd given her at age nine. His stomach was in a riot and his sinuses burned. After a beat, he took her hands and set them in Nate's, clasping both sets before letting go.

And that's just what he did. He let go. Of her. The past. Everything. She had all she needed right beside her, and that was all he'd ever wanted for her. From this point on, it was sight ahead, future bound.

Which, as he turned his head, jarringly began with mermaid eyes locked on him from the other side of the altar. Amy studied him with a mix of understanding and something he couldn't name. Longing?

No. Couldn't be. Maybe she was feeling melancholy after her recent divorce. Weddings could do that...make people lonely.

Nevertheless, she held him captive for several moments, and the longer they stared, the more his heart kicked rhythm. A tingle of...awareness zipped up his spine, confusing the ever-living hell out of him.

Rip had to ask twice for the rings before Nakos heard him, and when he glanced back at Amy, she'd focused on the ceremony.

Leveled, he did the same.

Chapter Three

From a seat in the corner of Olivia's wide open barn, Amy tried to ignore the uncomfortable silence of her tablemates and watched her best friend and Nate share their first dance as a married couple. They looked so perfect and right together that Amy's teeth hurt. If she weren't so dang happy for them, she'd yak.

Longing tugged her midsection. No one had ever looked at her the way Nate did Olivia. Like she was his everything and nobody else existed. After thirty years of being the girl most guys skimmed past for a glance at her friend, Amy should be used to the shadows by now. Guess not, since her belly cramped.

Because this was the working barn for shearing sheep and grooming horses, there were no stalls in the generous hundred-by-hundred space, but everything had been cleared out. Amy's brother Kyle was in the far corner, running the stereo in lieu of a DJ. Ten or so round tables were covered in white tablecloths and votives. Both the front and rear carriage doors were open, letting a cross-breeze waft in. Strands of lights hung from the rafters to look like raining stars and, combined with the ethereal glow of the moon through the skylights, had the atmosphere cast in dreamy ambiance.

She would've loved something like this for her wedding. Simple, pretty. Rustic-chic. Instead, she'd gotten a fifteen minute service in the courthouse following a less than whirlwind three-month romance and takeout from the bar afterward.

Then again, it wasn't as if she'd ever been considered someone of great significance.

Nakos's father shifted in his seat to face her, a smile crinkling the corners of his mouth. "Our son says things are going well up at the main house. You're settling in, helping Mae with cooking." His voice was a deep, rich baritone. Between that, his leathery face, the dark skin of his Native American background, and eyes like impending midnight, he should've been scary or unapproachable. But he was the gentlest soul she'd ever met.

"Olivia's been very gracious." After her ordeal with her ex-husband, Amy had no options. He'd left her penniless when he'd been sentenced for assault and kidnapping, plus their house had been foreclosed. If Olivia hadn't taken her in and found some kind of work for her to do, Amy would've been screwed. "I enjoy cooking." It was relaxing and being productive felt good, so there was that.

Across the table, her mother snorted and her father bore an expression of banality.

Yep. Because Amy should be home cooking for her husband and perfecting the image of a devoted wife. Not embarrassing them with a divorce, ruining the sacrilege of marriage, and living in supposed sin with her BFF.

From beside her, Nakos winked in support, ignoring her folks. "Ames makes the best meatloaf this side of the Platte River."

Bless him.

His mother nodded. "That soup you sent to the reservation last month when I had the flu was delicious."

This earned another snort from Mom.

The Hunts stared at the table, clearly uncomfortable.

Guilt shifted in Amy's gut for her parents' bad manners. They were devout protestants and as narrow-minded as people could get. They'd never consider the Hunts their equals based on their skin color alone. Why the heck they'd chosen to sit at their table, she hadn't a clue. For that matter, why they'd come at all.

Oh, that's right. They loved Olivia, the daughter they wished they'd had.

Amy struggled to find something to fill the quiet. "Thank you for the compliments, but I'm afraid I'm going to need to find other living accommodations soon. I'll keep helping Mae in the kitchen, of course." She had no choice. Meadowlark was a small town with few job opportunities and her parents refused to hire her at their hardware store.

Nakos's gaze bore holes in her profile, but she ignored it. His concern, though appreciated, only added to her guilt. If not for him and Nate stopping Chris from turning kidnapping into something worse, she probably wouldn't be sitting here.

"Surely, Olivia wouldn't ask you to leave." Mrs. Hunt leaned forward, apprehension in her deep brown eyes. "You two have been friends since you were little girls."

"No, she wouldn't." And her friend had reiterated that countless times. Olivia would give Amy the shirt off her back and vice versa. They were closer than sisters. "But she's married now and they need space, time alone. I'm staying in Kyle's room tonight to give them privacy." Olivia's ten ranch hands lived in two cabins separate from the main house on the property, Amy's brother being one of them. "I'll figure out something permanent before they return from their honeymoon." Somehow.

Dad stiffened. "What do you mean, you're staying with Kyle?"

"As if you haven't embarrassed us or yourself enough, you want to bring your brother down, too?" Mom shook her head, disgust twisting her thin lips. "Living in a house with all those men." She'd all but left the word "whore" out of her statement, yet it was heavily implied.

Nakos inhaled. Hard. Nostrils flared, he clenched his fists on the table. "If you're so concerned, perhaps you should help your daughter by giving her somewhere to go instead of laying insults at her feet." The low timbre of his voice was barely above a whisper, but steel laid underneath, cutting in its intensity.

Frozen, Amy stared at him in shock while he and her parents had a glare-down.

Nakos wasn't a man of many words. Typically, he only spoke when it was absolutely necessary. Yes, they were the best of friends, and yes, he'd defended her before. Yet, in this case, he knew better. He wasn't going to change her parents' small minds by reminding them she was their blood. That had never mattered. Not when she'd been a girl and certainly not now.

A few years ago, she would've been the first person out of her seat and speaking her mind. But her I-can-handle-anything, tell-me-whose-ass-I-need-to-kick persona had died when she'd said *I do*. It wasn't coming back. That was the day her give-a-shit broke, the day hope began its slow suffocation. Up until that point, she'd been darn good at faking it. Except the age-old mantra hadn't worked because she never did make it.

"I will not allow her to step foot in our home after what she's done." Dad shook his head with finality.

Her first offense had been marrying outside of church. They'd had no money for anything more extravagant than the courthouse. Her second being the divorce. Yet she'd been a pariah long before either instance. And that was a memory she'd buried, where it would remain for all eternity.

Not for the first time, she studied them, wondering if they'd ever loved her. She'd inherited her dark hair and narrow face from her father, but her eyes were a more potent shade of her mother's. Curvy body type, too. Both their gazes cut to Amy as if Nakos wasn't worth the bother to further respond. And that nailed it home. The only thing she had in common with these people was a physical resemblance.

Dad sniffed. "You made your mistakes. Live with them."

Yeah. She'd asked for her husband to stop paying the mortgage and wrack up thousands in credit card debt. She'd asked for him to beat her to a pulp, then shove the barrel of a 9mm in her face. And she'd asked him to destroy the one thing she owned that brought her any pleasure—her photography equipment. It was just a silly hobby. Still, she'd saved for two years doing odd jobs to buy the camera. One swing of Chris's hammer had shattered it—and her—to pieces.

Nakos rose so fast his chair tipped over. "Dance with me, Ames." Not a question. A demand. And very unlike him. His gaze slid to hers, beseeching. Without words, he implored her to get him away from the table or he wouldn't be responsible for what came next.

She glanced around, realizing the first dance was over and other couples were on the floor. When she refocused on Nakos, she got hung up on the long lashes fanning his black eyes. They were the only thing offsetting the cavern of dark intensity, softening his features a smidgen.

"Please." He held out his arm, waiting, then lowered his voice to a whisper. "Nobody puts Baby in a corner."

Oh God. Only he would use a *Dirty Dancing* reference. The fact he even remembered the line from all the times she and Olivia had made him watch the movie was astounding.

Amy laughed, offering a quick smile of apology to his parents for deserting them, and took Nakos's hand.

He led her to a cleared area of the barn and pulled her to him. Close enough to draw his heat and breathe in his earthy scent, but not so their torsos touched. One warm palm settled low on her back as his fingers clutched hers in the other hand.

Suddenly nervous, she followed his lead to the ballad playing. After the service, he'd rolled the sleeves of his white shirt up to his elbows, revealing his corded forearms, and unbuttoned the first few notches by his neck. He'd also tied his long, silky hair in a low ponytail and reclaimed his black Stetson he rarely went without.

"I swear, Ames, if you weren't a product of those two idiots, I'd hate them more."

She breathed a laugh. "Don't let them get to you. They're judgmental and not worth the frustration."

"They hurt you, and that's uncalled for."

They'd been hurting her all her life. She'd grown used to it. "I'm fine."

Attempting to regulate oxygen exchange, she stared at his throat as they swayed. Stubble had grown on his jaw since this morning, adding a ruggedness to his olive skin. He was such a gorgeous man. Tall and lean, he wasn't built with bulges like Nate, but he had clear definition. Languid. Fluid. High cheekbones and a defined chin. Wide shoulders and a narrow waist.

She'd always had a bit of a crush on him. It had fizzled out over time, but being this close to him again made her hyperaware. Which was as stupid now as it had been back then. He'd only ever had eyes for Olivia. "We haven't danced together since prom."

Nakos had gone to school on the reservation, but for events like dances or homecomings, Olivia or Amy had brought him along in a friendship capacity. He'd been her date for senior prom. She'd ridiculously held out hope going with him would suddenly make her visible to him as the opposite sex, complete with breasts. She'd spent hours picking out the right dress and shoes and makeup.

He'd shown up at her door with the same pleasant smile, not a flicker of interest.

"It has been that long, huh?" He glanced down his nose at her, his gaze a fond caress. "In case I forgot to say it earlier, you look very pretty tonight."

"Thank you." If only he really meant the compliment and weren't being polite. Training her gaze over his shoulder, she smiled. She suspected it came off wan. "And you're very handsome all quasi-dressed up."

He grated a rough laugh, the one she figured he reserved for special occasions. "I'm just grateful I didn't have to wear a tie. You made me put one on for said prom."

"Twelve years and you're still not over it." She sighed. "Admit it. You clean up nice."

A grunt, and he spun her away from him, tugging her back. "No one paid attention to what I had on with you and Olivia present." He winked. "Cute as you were that night, you grew up into something special."

Dang. See, it was lines like that which made it hard for her to let go of foolish girly fantasies. "Ditto." She slid her hand from his shoulder to his bicep, straining against the cotton, and squeezed. "When did you develop guns?"

His mouth opened and closed, but nothing emerged. His brows furrowed in confusion.

"I'm not kidding. Do you ride the horses or just toss them for sport?" Because...dang.

He shook his head and stalled their motion. "Are you teasing me? I can never tell with you. That looks like female appreciation on your face."

"Why wouldn't I appreciate you? You're a very handsome man."

If possible, he grew even more still. Tick, tick, tick went the muscle in his jaw to the beat of her pulse. He stared at her with those fathomable, soulful eyes as if he'd never seen her before. He didn't seem to be breathing.

Had she made him uncomfortable? It wasn't as if she'd outright hit on him. She'd merely stated fact. Then again, his radar would've missed flirting on her part. In all their years as friends, not once had he noticed her as a woman. She could've stripped naked and made an arrow out of bacon on her stomach pointing to her goody zone. It wouldn't have earned so much as a blink from him.

And there was the issue. Her attention, however harmless, was unwanted. Of course, he'd be distressed, possibly even disgusted by her remarks. Today had probably been very hard for him having to watch Olivia marry someone else. Hurt lanced Amy's chest at the realization while remorse tightened her throat. After all this time, had life, her experiences, taught her nothing? She wasn't the object of desire in the great book of fairy tales. And she'd been damaged goods long before Chris had come into the picture.

The last thing, the *very last thing* she needed was to put a rift between them. She let out a quiet breath. "Sorry. Forget I said anything."

Nakos didn't move. Not an iota. Actually, if anything, his frame grew more rigid. Black eyes studied her intently, but his expression gave nothing away. When he desired, he could be stoic and mysterious. If Nakos Hunt didn't want someone to know what he was thinking, napalm couldn't get past his resolve.

An eternity later, his gaze jerked away and he set them in motion again. Just like that. As if the past few minutes hadn't happened. He was quiet long moments, then his fingers tightened in hers and the hand on her back twitched. Since he seemed lost in thought, it was probably involuntary.

Unable to take the silence, she chewed her lip. "I'm sure this hasn't been an easy day for you. I'm here if you want to talk." They were good at that. Conversation. It was the one thing he appeared to seek from her that he couldn't with Olivia. Not the heart-of-the-matter kind of diatribe, anyway. For whatever reason, he was more open and honest with Amy, and she clung to that tether.

He groaned. "Not you, too, Ames. Let a guy hold onto his pride, would you?"

She blinked up at him. "Don't ever be ashamed for loving someone, regardless of whether they return those feelings." He wouldn't understand how rare it was a man existed who was honest about his emotions, who made no attempts to hide them. "This isn't exactly the ending you were hoping for."

Features softening, he met her eyes. "No, it wasn't. I gave up on the idea of her and me a long time ago, though. Today, I merely closed the book. Did it hurt a little? Yeah. But not nearly as much as you'd think."

Surprised by the honesty in his gaze, in his tone, she nodded.

"What about you?" His thumb stroked her palm, but he didn't seem aware of the action. "This had to bring back memories of your wedding."

Not really. Just her failures. "I didn't have a wedding."

"I remember." His clipped tone gave her pause. He noticed her surprise because up went his brows. "You dated the guy for a few

29

months. The next thing I know, I'm hearing from Olivia you got hitched at the courthouse."

"I had no idea it bothered you so much."

Again, he stopped moving. "Should I turn around? Easier for you to pull out the knife that way."

"Nakos—"

"Damn right, it pissed me off. I hated the jerk. He was never nice to you. And to not tell me? To assume I wouldn't want to be there for you? It was a sucky thing to do."

Closing her eyes, she expelled a shaky breath. "You're right. I'm sorry. It's just..."

She'd been embarrassed. About everything. That she'd married the first guy who'd shown any sort of interest in her, no matter if it had been the wrong kind. That she'd agreed so quickly, without so much as him offering an engagement ring. That they didn't have the money for anything, not even a bouquet.

Shaking her head, she focused on Nakos's shirt, her cheeks hot. The mere thought of having him at the courthouse brought a level of shame she couldn't escape. Which was why she hadn't told him. Olivia, either. Kyle had been the only one to attend the service on Amy's side, Chris's brother Mark on the groom's. Just recalling the impersonal room and empty vows she'd recited had misery taking up space in her chest.

Loneliness and desperation made people do stupid things. Like marry a man who didn't love her, wouldn't allow her to work, refused to support her interest in photography, or acknowledge her presence unless he was drunk enough to get it up.

"It's just what?" Nakos's soothing tone snapped her gaze to his. "Finish that sentence."

Not on his life would she admit the whole truth. "I figured you'd try to stop me."

Irritation, hurt, and determination crossed his features in rapid succession. "Looking back on it, would that have been such a bad thing?"

"I really don't need your I-told-you-so's."

A lazy blink, and he sighed. "I wouldn't have interfered, Ames. I would have, however, been there to support you. But you took the option away from me."

Darn him. "I said I was sorry."

30

His dark gaze swept across her face as if picking her apart. A caressing exploration over her hair, her cheeks, her lips, then back to her eyes. She had no idea what he found, but frustration tightened his full mouth. Like his lashes, his lips were a criminal waste on a man. So erringly seductive.

"Why did you do it?" His voice was a low rumble and barely heard over the music. "Why the hell did you marry that asshole?"

Unable to take it anymore, she wrenched away from him, causing his arms to fall limp at his sides. This topic had been off the table. For whatever reason, they hadn't talked about it, and she was grateful. To bring it up now, to dissect and pick at the scab, wouldn't allow for healing. A girl could only take so much before she shattered.

"Why, Ames?"

Screw it. It wasn't like she had any confidence left. "He was the best I was going to get."

Nakos flinched. "What the hell does that mean?"

Turning her back to his wide eyes and shocked, gutted expression, she started for the door. One tequila, two tequila, three tequila...floor. That was the only plan for the rest of the evening. She'd grab a bottle of Cuervo from the main house, walk forever and a day to the staff ranch cabins, and crawl in her brother's room to get plastered.

Except a muscled arm wrapped around her middle from behind and lifted her off her feet, crushing her spine against a solid chest wall. "This discussion is not over, *anim*."

Anim. He'd never used the word in her presence. She had no idea what it translated to in his native Arapaho tongue, but she suspected it was a curse.

With her toes hovering above the floor, he stalked toward the exit as if she weighed nothing. "We're going to have a chat."

"No, we're not."

"Yes, we are." Stomp, stomp. "I've dealt with your particular brand of stubborn all my life. You think I don't know how to handle you?"

Why was she getting turned-on? As in, she couldn't draw air and heat coiled in her belly and her girly bits clenched. Alpha Nakos was hot.

31

Several heads swiveled toward them, trekking their progress across the room, around tables, and out the open doorway.

Her heel slipped off her foot. "I lost my shoe."

"We'll get it later, Cinderella."

"You're causing a scene." She squirmed, but his hold was unrelenting.

"Don't care." He marched over the pebble-strewn grass, ducked around the corner, and deposited her on the ground out of sight from the celebration. Backing her against the barn's wooden slats, he glared down at her, inches from bringing them in contact. "Explain."

Dark shadows encased them. Crickets chirped. A warm breeze ruffled her hair. Fireflies winked in the distance. An owl hooted.

She. Said. Nothing.

He crossed his arms. "I can do this all night."

Yeah, she was afraid of that.

Chapter Four

He was the best I was going to get.

With that statement rolling around in his skull, irritation pounding his temples, Nakos stared at Amy, waiting for her to break. He knew her better than anyone. Too much tense silence, and she'd crack. It was just a matter of time.

Shadows from the trees created havoc with the moonlight on her alabaster skin. Her dark cocoa hair swept past her shoulders, and he had the damnedest itch to shove his hands in the strands and force her to look at him. Since dancing with her inside, she'd yet to glance at him more than fleetingly and that, more than what she'd said, had concern sinking its claws deep.

Arms crossed, he shook his head. This wasn't her. The defeat in her shoulders, the sad curve of her lips, the lack of spark in her mermaid eyes...Not his Ames. Where was her fire? Where was the woman who could argue him into a corner and make him heel? She exuded confidence like most people did pheromones.

Except... No. Not lately. Ever since the incident with the Antichrist, she'd been a sunken version of the pistol he recognized. Actually, her behavior dated farther back to when Chris had come onto the scene. But not to this extent. Hell, Nakos swore she had no fight left.

Having been raised by two nurturing, attentive parents, combined with the fact both his best friends were females, he'd learned a thing or fifty. Foremost, how to love. Not to shy away from sentiment or attachment, but to embrace it. He only had one shot at this fragile thing called life and he wasn't going to spend it steeped in regret, too afraid to tell the people he cared about how he felt.

He'd also figured out how to read every nuance and gauge what the girls needed because what they said with their bodies often contradicted their words. Being close to them had cultivated his protective gene until it encompassed his DNA. Olivia and Amy. Them first, always. And those instincts were coming out of temporary dormancy to rattle his already frail cage.

She stood in front of him, so near he could breathe in her light perfume, and didn't open her pretty little mouth. How many times had he wished for her to shut up, and fate chose right this second to listen?

One of them needed to cave. May as well be him.

"You didn't really mean that, did you?" Please, *Hihcebe*, let that be the case. If not, that bastard had done more damage than Nakos thought. "You deserve so much better than him."

Her only response was to wearily close her eyes.

Something was very wrong. Realization bristled his skin, dropped a heavy ball of ice in his gut. If she thought all she deserved was that...guy, then there had been an issue prior to her dating and subsequently marrying him. What the hell was Nakos missing? Because he was at a loss.

"Look at me." He waited until her lids lifted and resisted the urge to hug her. They didn't touch often, didn't have that kind of relationship. "There is no convincing me the best person to spend your life with was him. A man who spoke to you as if you were a thing, who dared to raise a..." Mercy, he could kill just thinking about it. Amy had sworn up and down that one instance was the only time Chris had hit her. "I can't erase that day from my memory."

"I know." She nodded. Finally, a flicker of anger infused her eyes. "Because Olivia was in danger."

Hell to the no. His body went so rigid he thought he'd snap. No way, no how did she think she didn't matter as much to him. The notion had never crossed his consciousness. But...shit.

"Yes, Olivia was in danger. You *both* were." He slammed his palms to the wall above her head, trying and failing to dial back the assault of conflicting emotion. Anger for what that asshole had done. Fear that something terrible would happen to two people he loved. And, most shocking, grief that he hadn't suspected Amy doubted that love.

"Denial is not just a river in Egypt, Nakos."

He needed a stiff drink. With a side of straightjacket. "Do you have any idea what seeing you like that did to me?" His fingers curled against the boards, paint digging under his nails. "Finding you on the ground, mottled with bruises, barely able to open your eyes..."

Don't let go... Please, Nakos. Just don't let go.

A growl raked his throat.

Her eyes narrowed suspiciously as if attempting to make up her mind whether she believed him. And a bone-deep, narcissistic cold settled so deep inside him that the frozen tendrils wove around muscle and penetrated his veins.

The fact she doubted him in any capacity was a death blow. Somewhere along the way, he'd failed her. Completely unacceptable. Especially considering the source. Olivia had nearly her whole family wiped out, but she was trusting. Caring. A light in the dark. Amy was the total opposite. She had blood relations, right here in town, yet they discarded her time and time again. She didn't let just anyone in and her first instincts were to erect walls. She *was* the darkness.

Since this conversation was getting him nowhere, he tried a different approach. "Why are you staying with Kyle? Olivia won't like it. And you don't belong there." Which had nothing to do with the workers who lived in the cabins and everything to do with comfort. Not only was there no room, but no privacy.

"I don't belong anywhere." Though she held his gaze with determination and she'd used her I-eat-cute-and-fuzzy-bunnies-for-breakfast tone, the ever so slight tremble of her lower lip gave her away.

Before he could even think to counter that, shoes crunched over gravel to their right. Kyle strode around the corner and gave them the hairy eyeball. "There a problem?"

Several. Hell, problems were accumulating by the bucketful and their ship was going down. Regardless, Nakos took a breath. "We're fine. Give us a minute."

"No can do. Olivia's looking for you inside." His gaze darted between them like he'd interrupted a situation no brother wanted to find his sister in.

Exactly what Nakos didn't need right now. He shoved off the wall and pointed at Amy. "Don't go anywhere. We're not done."

In response, she bent over, slipped the remaining heel off her foot, and straightened. Brows raised in challenge, she dangled the shoe in a clear catch-me-if-you-can, and unceremoniously dropped it to the ground.

Hihcebe. There wasn't enough single malt in Wyoming to go toe-to-toe with her.

He followed her brother into the barn and stopped just inside the doorway, grabbing the guy's arm. "What does Olivia want me for?"

"Garter toss, I think."

What, in all creation, did he do to deserve this? "Amy said she's bunking with you tonight?"

"Yeah, though I have no idea where." Kyle crossed his arms, looking like a younger image of his sister with less 'tude. "Tupperware's bigger than my room and I only have a twin. Which, by the way, she refuses to take. I'm certain she's going to wind up *under* the bed."

Over Nakos's dead body. "Listen, grab two of the men and head up to the main house. I want everything in her room packed up in one hour and at my place." He dug in his jeans for the keys, passing them to Kyle. "Upstairs, second door on the right is the guestroom. Put all her stuff in there."

"Okay," Kyle said slowly. "You know, the parental units are gonna flip. They weren't exactly jumping for joy when they learned she was staying with—"

"I don't give a good goddamn. Do it. And," he leaned forward, hands on his hips, "you will not inform her of this little mission. Get in, get out, and return my keys."

"Whatever you say, man." The blasé response belied the appreciation in the guy's eyes. "Consider it done."

Taking a moment to breathe, Nakos glanced at his boots. Music and laughter echoed through the space, ricocheting around in his ears. Why the hell did it seem like his foundation had been leveled?

"Nakos."

He glanced at Olivia across the room, and her smile settled some of the riot in his head. "I'm coming." Begrudgingly.

Thirty minutes later, he wished he'd run the other way when he'd been summoned. With Olivia on Nakos's lap, Nate had taken off her garter with a flourish and, instead of making the single guys stand around to toss the thing, the soldier had just handed it to Nakos and nodded. Then came the bouquet what-the-heck-ever, for

36

which he had no clue why his presence was necessary. Back slaps and handshakes followed him to the barn exit.

No way had Amy waited for him, but he checked the spot anyhow. The only thing that remained was her shoe and the grating reminder of their conversation. Cinderella, indeed.

Since he didn't have his keys, taking his truck over to the staff cabins was out. Not unless he wanted to walk miles and eat up half the night. There was no guarantee that's where she'd headed, either. Hopefully, she hadn't wandered up to the main house. She didn't have much by way of possessions, but the men wouldn't be done packing her things yet. Then again, if she had gone that way, she might have them hog-tied and shaking with the fear of God.

He strode in the direction of Olivia's. It was as good a place to start as any. But halfway there, motion in his peripheral stopped him short.

Turning, he spotted Amy between the third barn and the cemetery. About fifty yards away, an oak crested a slight hill. Dangling from a sturdy branch was an old tire swing that had been there since they were kids. It was so dark he could barely make her out, but that blue dress she wore and her cocoa strands in the breeze were a dead giveaway.

Walking closer, he was struck by the past colliding with the present. The first time he'd met her, she'd been on that very swing and, just as she was now, leaning back while her soft hair cascaded in a waterfall, ends brushing the grass. She was alone at the moment, but that day Olivia had been standing beside her.

Funny, he'd forgotten he'd laid eyes on Amy first. Something about the fragile curve of her spine contradicted the hearty, almost sensual laugh she'd emitted. From the get-go, he'd been enamored by Olivia's auburn strands that were so unlike the characteristics of Arapaho on the reservation. Looking back on it, his reaction had been close to hypnotizing.

But Amy? She'd rendered a physical response that, even at age nine, he'd recognized as awareness. A cross between an improper heartbeat and tightness in his throat. Curiosity, he supposed. He had no idea what label to slap on it now.

Moonlight cast her skin in ethereal hues as she reclined on the tire, her slender fingers gripping the rope above it. The swell of her breasts and hips strained against the dress from her position, and damn if his heart didn't punch his ribs. Again. What the hell had she done to him three months ago? He hadn't been right since.

Climbing the hill, he smiled and stared at her upside-down face as he loomed over her. "You look like a nymph under the moon and dangling from a tree."

"Nah, nymphs get laid more than I do."

He wasn't going near that comment. "Know a lot about nymphs, do you?"

"Can't say I know any, but lore describes them as intensely sexual creatures who prefer nature and have an irresistible allure."

He wondered if she realized she'd just described herself. And, of course, she'd know something about mythical beings. Any topic at all, really. She had an intelligence about her that was neither condescending nor flaunting. A subtle quality that allowed her to carry on a conversation about nearly anything.

Why he suddenly found that hot was beyond him, but he ignored it. Hard as he could.

"I'm shocked you waited for me." He relaxed his shoulders as she straightened, relieved the tension was gone from her features. "You rarely, if ever, listen to me."

She shook her head in a clear case of pity. "I'm not waiting for you. Note I wasn't standing by the barn with bated breath for your return."

Her droll tone, phrasing, and verbiage weren't hot, either. It *wasn't*. "I'll scribble it on a post-it so I don't forget." Tongue in cheek, he debated how much he liked his head where it was at. Once she found out he'd had her items moved to his house, his skull was bound to roll off his neck. "A moment ago, I remembered we first met in this spot."

"Just remembered, huh? So memorable it was."

She had no idea. And he wasn't winning this one. "Recalled the details, I mean. Give me a break. We were nine."

In answer, she toed the grass and set her swing in a slow spin. "Feeling nostalgic, Nakos?"

Nostalgic, unnerved. Tomato, tomauto. "It was a good memory."

Her sudden grin depleted some of his brain cells. She was evil like that.

With the ball of her foot, she stopped the swing. "Know what I remember? You staring at Olivia like you'd swallowed your tongue."

Again, she had it all wrong. Olivia calmed the crazy. Amy stirred the pot. "And you stole my cowboy hat. One day maybe you'll give it back." He narrowed his eyes. "Why are you smiling sinister-like?"

Much to his dismay, she stood on the top of the tire, reached up, and swung her legs onto the overhead branch. Dress and all.

To avoid the possible peep show, he slapped a hand over his eyes. "Get down, Ames." When she didn't respond, he peeked between his fingers and found her standing on the limb, stretching toward a knot where the branches met the trunk. Damn, she was high. "Ames, down. Now."

"Just a sec."

He didn't know what made his heart jack harder—the concern she'd fall or the endless expanse of leg under her skirt. "Damn it. Amy, come on." No fear, this one. Always.

She pulled an item from the knot and—strike him dead—pirouetted on her toes. Something smacked him in the face and landed at his feet.

A glance down, and he glared at...his old hat. Smooshed, the black material had paled to a dull gray and had foliage stuck to it, but it was his hat nonetheless.

"What purpose did that serve?" Hands on his hips, he frowned up at her. "Putting it up there in the first place or choosing now to bring it down?"

"A girl doesn't need to explain herself, not to a boy or the man he grew into."

She needed to come with an instructional manual. And one not written in Spanish. "Fine. Don't tell me. Just come down."

But she was already making the descent. Legs wrapped around the branch, she twisted until she grabbed the rope and, limber as a circus performer, swung that lithe body of hers until her feet were on solid ground again.

"You're welcome." As if in afterthought, she smiled.

Screw instructions. She needed a warning label. *Caution: Incidental contact may cause mental and bodily harm.*

He swiped a hand down his face and refocused on her. As much as he wanted answers to their previous discussion, he didn't have it in him. She was acting more like her usual self, the one that made his left eye tick, and he was exhausted.

She bent and retrieved the hat from the ground. After vigorously shaking it out, it retained its crushed state. "Might want to just throw it away."

Unable to help it, he laughed. Rough, ragged, and with all the finesse of road kill. He swore, only she could drag one out most days. "What the hell am I going to do with you?"

"You could drive me to Kyle's so I don't have to walk. My feet were abused wearing those torture devices." She blinked at him. Tilted her head. "Not what you meant, though."

"No, not exactly." And yeah, about going to her brother's...

"Well, if it makes you feel any better, my parents used to say that to me all the time growing up, and they never did discover a solution."

Precisely how was that supposed to make him feel better? "They're assholes, and I'd prefer you not compare me to them or use us in the same sentence."

"Rawr, Nakos."

He did not appreciate her making light of this, either. Especially not this. After tonight, it was blatantly apparent they'd been mind-fucking her on a level he hadn't known existed. "She all but called you a whore, Ames." Never mind the variety of other issues. He clenched his fists at his sides.

She shrugged as if he'd said it was supposed to rain tomorrow. "I'm not disagreeing with you. I'm just wondering where all the aggressive alphaness is coming from. You act like you've never met them before."

Exhibit A. She'd just proved his point.

With a gentleness he almost never saw, her features softened and she stepped forward. "Hey, calm down. You're vibrating with fury. This is so unlike you. I said it before. Don't let them bother you, okay?"

Not. Okay. Parents were supposed to love and support their children, however many mistakes they made. Not deem them a slut, throw them out of the house, or not so much as pay one visit while they were broken and bruised in bed after a beating. A beating rendered by someone else who was supposed to love her.

He was so over tonight it was tomorrow already. "I need to get my stuff from the barn before we head home." His home. She was going to kill him. Hopefully, Kyle was back with his keys. "Come on. We can fetch your shoes, too."

"Or we could just feed them to the horses."

He huffed a laugh. "I like the horses. We'll toss 'em in the fire pit."

Her brother was, in fact, waiting for them when they made their way across the grass. "All set." Kyle nodded to his sister and took off deeper into the barn.

A quick glance proved Nakos's folks had left. He'd call them later. Snatching his coat off a chair, he led Amy to his truck, parked in Olivia's driveway.

Once they were settled inside the dim interior, he sighed. Long and loud. Turned over the engine. "You know I care about you, right?" He could feel her gaze on him, but he didn't meet it with his own. "Just remember that when we get to where we're going."

Chapter Five

Nakos's two-story rustic cabin had been built by Olivia's parents a few years before they'd died, and was intended to be living quarters for the active foreman. It was set on Cattenach Ranch, deep in the southern pasture, with a clear view of the Laramie Mountains on one side, sprawling prairie on the back end, and a copse of cottonwoods to the north.

Amy hadn't been inside since they were children. Yet here she was, standing in the second floor guestroom, just a sheet of drywall separating her from where Nakos slept. He'd...taken her home with him. Had arranged for all her things to be brought over. It was just like him to pull a move like this.

And it didn't feel right. He was no more responsible for her wellbeing than Kyle. The sheer loss of independence since her divorce had been jarring, but being utterly displaced was worse. Like dandelion fluff caught in a stiff wind. Rootless. Helpless. She hated not being able to stand on her own two feet.

She had no options, though. Olivia needed privacy with Nate, not Amy lurking around to disrupt their wedded bliss. Kyle's room in the staff quarters barely had space for him. Her parents sure wouldn't be of assistance. Though she was earning a salary helping Aunt Mae cook for Olivia's ranch hands at the main house, Amy was barely making a dent in the credit card bills Chris had wracked up. Last month, she'd consolidated them into one loan, which had helped, but there wasn't enough left over to pay rent elsewhere. And there were very few accommodations in Meadowlark. Their small town was mostly a ranching community. Plus, her credit rating was in the crapper.

Stuck between wanting to scream at the top of her lungs or cry herself into dehydration, she'd been standing in the center of the bedroom, unmoving, since they'd arrived. Still wearing her bridesmaid dress.

Two duffel bags containing the few articles of clothing she owned were on the center of the full-size bed atop a yellow and green quilt. A box of her cosmetics sat on a long dresser along the opposite wall. And her photography equipment had been carefully piled beside a trunk under the window facing south. Yellow curtains billowed in the breeze off the mountains.

She curled her toes against the hardwood floor and glanced from the prints on the white walls to her equipment. Two weeks after she'd gone to live with Olivia, a package had arrived for Amy. Inside had been a brand new camera, printer, and laptop. What had to be thousands of dollars in replacements for what Chris had destroyed. There had been no note and she had no clue who'd sent the gift. Until a few days later when Nakos had confessed.

Why? Not that the gesture wasn't exactly like his compassionate personality, but he'd never given her the impression he'd liked her pictures. Because he'd said very little when she'd shown him new images before, she'd quit altogether, not wanting to make him feel like he had to offer false praise.

Except...three of her originals were hung in the guestroom—a beam of sunlight streaking through a hole in an old piece of wood, a shot of a cowboy boot next to a horse hoof, and a large gloved hand holding reins. Downstairs, over the mantle, was another of her prints. Bones—Olivia's sheepdog—running a herd of steer.

Thing was, Nakos had no other art donning the walls. Not that she'd seen. They hadn't lingered downstairs due to the hour but, best she could tell, only her photos graced his home. She just...didn't know what to make of it.

Her gaze landed near the trunk again. She hadn't taken the stuff he'd gifted her out of their boxes. Accepting the present had felt wrong, just like being here now sent a sliver of guilt through her bloodstream.

This was not how she'd envisioned her life turning out.

Footsteps shuffled in the hallway, but she kept her profile to the open door, unable to glance away from the entities that encompassed what used to be her only joy. The weight of a camera in her hands. Playing with the focus to get a shot just right. Waiting for the perfect light or angle to capture a fragment of time forever.

Everything was prettier through a lens. No rejection or hurtful words or disappointment. Most people thought photography was a brutally honest portrayal of something—whether it be a person or an object or event. Not to her. Taking pictures was the only time she was free from harsh reality.

"Hey, you're still awake." Nakos leaned against the doorframe, arms crossed, but she remained unmoving, catching his form in the corner of her eye.

"Yep."

"And still dressed."

"Yep."

"And in the exact same spot I left you two hours ago."

"Yep." That was her in a nutshell. Stagnant. Going nowhere. She would've laughed at the irony if her sinuses weren't prickling with the threat of tears.

Silence.

His hesitation was either a Nakos-ism to get her to talk first or he was gathering his wits on how to proceed. Always cautious, her friend. He typically didn't say much, and when he did, it was usually not without thought first. If only other people were as considerate as him.

A rustle of clothing, and he stepped into the room. Barefoot, wearing a loose pair of sweats and a white tee, he strode to the window. He'd taken his ponytail out and his raven strands brushed his wide shoulders. He was so darn beautifully built. Lean grace and subtle muscular tone. Olive skin. He looked...yummy.

Something about the intimacy of the situation had her breath short. It was...casual in a way they hadn't been in a long time. The same bedroom. Only a dim lamp and moonlight to chase away the shadows. His every exhalation and shift was a shout to his presence. Although he was across the room, he took up all the available space. Even his unspoken thoughts were an entity.

He bent and lifted the camera box from the trunk's surface, staring intently at the packaging in his huge hands. "Why haven't you opened these? It's been months."

She was undeserving, that's why. "Why did you do it? Buy them for me?"

"I asked you first."

"Answer my question and I'll answer yours."

Contemplative, he ran his thumb across the box. "I didn't buy them. Nate did." When she frowned, he shrugged. "He went with

45

Olivia to your old house, helped her pack your things after Chris was put away. Nate had seen some of your work at Olivia's place and was impressed. He told me he had a lot of savings built up and no idea what to do with it."

"Why lie, then? Why say they were from you?" That was very unlike him. He didn't have a distrustful bone in his body, was always honest.

"He was a virtual stranger to you at the time. He figured you'd be more likely to accept them if they were from me." Lips pursed, he returned the camera to where it had been. "I guess he was mistaken since you haven't opened the stuff." With a solemn expression, he studied her. "I thought about doing the same thing, but he beat me to it."

"Why?" Dang, she sounded like a parrot, but her heart was thumping and she didn't know what to glean from his admission.

An air of frustration wrinkled his brows. "Because it makes you happy." His tone was matter of fact and indicative of a no-brainer response.

Yet... "So it had nothing to do with whether you thought I had talent." And they say women were hard to understand. Why spend—or think about spending—thousands of dollars on a gift like that if...

"It doesn't matter to me your level of talent. For all I care, you could take pictures of steaming piles of manure that are half out of focus." His hands fell to his hips as he cocked a foot to the side, clearly getting impatient. "All that concerns me is whether you enjoy what you're doing. And that," he jerked a thumb over his shoulder to the trunk, "brings you joy."

"How would you know?" Her body didn't understand how to react to him any more than her mind. On one hand, that was the sweetest darn thing she'd heard in a long time. But on the other, his opinion mattered to her. And he hadn't exactly claimed to love her photos.

Expelling a hearty sigh, he glanced at the ceiling as if praying for guidance from On High. "Because I know *you*, Ames." Those sinful midnight eyes leveled on her. His biceps bulged and knotted against the sleeves of his tee.

And scratch that. Her mind knew just what to do. It derailed straight to the gutter. Thoughts of being wrapped in those arms, her

46

breasts crushed against his wall of a chest, her fingers trailing over the dips and grooves of his abs...

"Let's forget for a second that you have the ability to stop time and bring a tear to the eye with every click of the lens." He took a step forward, but stopped. "That each picture tells a unique story and I have a hard time looking away. What I give a shit about is what it does to you."

She yelped a flabbergasted laugh. If she hadn't, she might've wound up fetal and sobbing. He...he...loved her work. In all her years playing with the hobby, no one had ever used such pretty words to describe the result. Unbidden, her eyes began to water.

He pressed a hand to his chest. "You are a walking, talking natural disaster."

Another sharp laugh. "You mean like, if someone pisses me off, naturally there will be a disaster? You say the sweetest things."

He froze. Blinked. Swiped a hand down his face. "I meant," he ground through a clenched jaw, "that you always seem to be in a state of chaos. The crazy quiets when you're behind the camera. The calm is written all over your face." He looked at her once more, all tension evaporating from his features and, when he spoke again, his voice was rough. Low. "Honestly, Ames, it's about the only time I don't worry half to death about you."

She opened her mouth. Closed it. And wondered what it would take to restart her heart. Her lungs were good, though. Yep, she was panting like she'd outrun the hounds of hell.

"Why are you looking at me like that?"

"Like what?" She hoped the floor wouldn't leave a mark when she face-planted any second from now.

His frown deepened. "Like I ripped out your jugular with my teeth."

Actually, that was kinda accurate after hearing him... Gah.

"You..." She rubbed her forehead to stop the room from spinning and cleared her raw throat. "You don't have to worry about me."

"Yeah, *anim*. I don't have to eat, sleep, or breathe, either."

She ignored his dry tone and focused on that term. "What does that word mean?" He'd used it earlier tonight, too.

"*Anim?* It means angel."

Angel. *Angel?* He had a nickname for her and it... God save her from this gentle, endearing man. She couldn't take it. He'd been calling Olivia "little red" since they were kids, and sure, he called Amy "Ames," but never a term of endearment.

"Angel," she breathed. She was the farthest thing as one could get.

"Now what's the matter?"

She gave her head a violent shake to clear it. His behavior had been off all night. She'd chalked it up to his distress about the wedding, but she wondered if it wasn't more.

"You've never been this..." She waved her hand to conjure the right term. "Territorial before. Protective, yes. Especially toward Olivia. But not overly so like lately. And certainly not in my case."

"I've been as protective of you as I have been of her. I just hide it better in regards to you. You can handle yourself just fine and I like my nose where it is, thank you very much." He scratched his jaw. Studied her. "What's really wrong? Why are you still dressed and standing in the middle of the room? Furthermore, you didn't go feral when we got here. I half-expected you to kill me. What gives?"

She'd been too numb with shock, then overwrought by relief. And that was before crippling guilt had set in. "This is wrong, me being here."

His eyes narrowed to slits. "What?" When she didn't answer, he stepped closer until they were nearly touching. "Earlier you said you didn't belong anywhere. You're wrong. I have plenty of room and you'll have privacy. You belong here just fine."

And he called her the angel? "I'm not your responsibility. This feels an awful lot like you're...taking care of me."

His nostrils flared and heat blasted his eyes, dilating his pupils. "Call yourself a responsibility or a burden one more time and see what happens, Ames. Even I have my limit when it comes to patience." He snapped his lids shut and inhaled. When he opened his eyes, affection stared back at her once more. "There's nothing wrong with taking care of you, of each other. That's what friends do."

But what would he get out of it besides her being constantly underfoot in his home? "I can't repay you for this." Her pride was already dust. "Our friendship always seems one-sided."

48

"I don't know whether to hug you or throttle you sometimes." He stalked away, came halfway back. "You're kidding me with this, right?"

She hated her insecurity more than the pity she sometimes found in Olivia's eyes. But there it was. Through the years, Amy had shown not one trace of the emotion in Nakos's presence. He'd just slap himself with remorse if he knew he, above all others, had made her this way. Juvenile and pathetic as it sounded, if given the choice, he'd always take Olivia over Amy. Hell, everyone would. She was lucky enough to have them in her life, so she'd accepted her lot and hadn't let it bother her. Much. Why now she was suddenly so...weak, she hadn't a clue.

"You make me laugh."

His quiet declaration had her whipping her gaze to his, but he was hands-on-hips, head bowed as if talking to the floor.

"You do. You make me laugh." He rubbed the back of his neck and lifted his wide-open gaze to hers. "A trivial thing to most people, but I've always been self-conscious about it. Maybe because I was different than others around me growing up. I think becoming the ranch foreman and being responsible for all these men made me more serious later on, too. I don't know." His gaze swept over her face. "With you, I don't hesitate. I...let go."

Unsure what to say, she stared at him. They'd always had a kind of bond between them. Able to say just about anything. Yet this seemed deeper than where they'd ventured before.

"And this?" He waved his hand between them. "I don't have this connection with anyone else, don't have to censer myself. Flipping from Arapaho to English and back again as a kid taught me to think before speaking. But for some reason, you shut off that habit. The most irreplaceable thing about you is that never, not once, did you judge me. Even now, who else could I say these things to?"

Glancing away, he expelled an uneven breath. "One-sided, my ass," he mumbled in disbelief. "I spent the first nine years of my life on the reservation with people who looked and sounded just like me. Do you have any idea the culture shock in coming to live here? Outside looking in, Ames. All the time. And to make it worse, I still attended school with the tribe."

His gaze leveled on hers, determined. Steady. "How many mundane rites of passage in the white man's world would I have missed if not for you including me?" He raised his hand to cut her off. "And before you say it was Olivia, too, I know." He checked items off on his fingers. "Bonfires, football games, movies with friends, school dances, or just hanging out. Yes, Olivia was there. But you made me a part of the action instead of an observer. Thing is, had you not been there next to me, I never would've gone. Because from day one, you got me. You understood without a word or a look or any indication from me just how different I felt. I don't even think you were aware you were doing it, which makes everything I just said ten times more important."

A tick of anger wove into his expression again, tightening his full mouth. "That's who you are, Ames. That's what makes you special. I should be repaying you. If you want to start keeping tabs on our friendship, I've got twenty-one years accumulated." He froze as if realizing his tangent, then rolled his head to stretch his neck. "You're also infuriating. Perhaps I need to reexamine the talking freely part. I stand by everything else—"

She launched herself at him, wrapping her arms around his waist and burying her face in his chest. He *oomphed* and took a step to steady them before enfolding her in a return embrace.

They stood together long moments, her breathing in his earthy scent and him idly stroking her hair.

God, she had no idea he'd thought of himself as an outsider growing up. He'd been a little shy but, as they'd gotten older, he'd seemed more vigilant than introverted. It had been second nature for her to include him.

Maybe that had been the invisible connection tethering them all along. Other than her brother, she'd never felt welcomed anywhere but with him and Olivia. Something in him must've called to a part of her. Displaced souls.

Though he made no attempt to move, she wondered if he was uncomfortable. They didn't do a lot of touchy-feely. But there was such a sense of safety, of relief, being held by him. "I know you don't like hugs, but thanks for tolerating mine."

He dropped his chin to the top of her head and spoke against her hair. "I don't mind them." The thump, thump of his heart against her cheek increased. "One last time, and hear me this go-around. You do belong here, for however long you want or need to stay.

50

There's no time limit. Hell, stick around until we're both ghosts, *anim*. I'm good with whatever."

Mercy, this man. "Perhaps you could, I don't know, lead with that next time?"

He stilled for a beat as if stunned, then...he laughed. That low, hoarse rumble she adored that filled the cold places inside her. His chest shook and his arms cinched tighter. Heaven.

She fisted his shirt at his back and closed her eyes, relishing the brief blip of intimacy before he would inevitably pull away. "Getting to see you in your habitat? The sweats and bare feet? Totally worth listening to you yammer."

Another ragged laugh. He eased away, tucking hair behind her ears. "I don't get it, but okay."

"You only ever wear jeans and flannels. Except in summer. Then it's jeans and a t-shirt. No deviation."

"I didn't realize my wardrobe was of significance." His amused gaze swept her face, but a tiny wrinkle formed between his brows as if his mind had gone somewhere else. "Answer me something. Why wouldn't you use the camera when you thought it was from me?"

"You won't like my response and we just got to the make-up huggy portion of the evening."

He rolled his eyes. "Will you use it now that you know it's from Nate?"

"Yes." At the hurt in his gaze, she explained. "I lost my mojo or something after the Chris thing. I'll get it back. But Nate owes me nothing. There's no history. He purchased the items because he genuinely likes my work, not out of obligation. Something about that makes it sit right in my conscience."

A slow shake of his head, and he cupped her jaw in warm, callused hands. "You're not, nor have you ever been, an obligation." He muttered something unintelligible and kissed her forehead, then stepped away. He walked to the door and paused. "Get some sleep. Tomorrow, unpack your things, and that includes the equipment."

As he retreated down the hall and out of sight, she said, "Are you going to be this bossy now that we're roomies?"

"What difference does it make? You won't listen."

True. Shrugging, she turned for her bags on the bed.

51

Chapter Six

Cursing his internal alarm clock, Nakos padded down the hallway before the buttcrack of dawn, his sole focus to get coffee. Lots of coffee. Until his blood type was Folgers. Once a caffeine blast hit his system, he could better determine the cause for the tension in his neck and why the hell he woke in a zombie state. Not that he normally popped out of bed raring to go, but *Hihcebe,* he felt like he was crashing from a week-long bourbon bender.

Rubbing his eyes, he rounded the landing, descended the stairs, and headed for the kitchen. And stopped short. Blinked. Scratched his chest.

Amy, facing away from him, poured coffee from a carafe into a mug at the counter. Long cocoa strands trailed halfway down her back, and she wore a pair of frayed skinny jeans that molded to her round, luscious ass. Blue polish peeked from her toes as she curled them on the checkered linoleum. As she reached for the sugar dish, her hips wiggled like she was grooving to an internal beat, and...

He grew semi-hard in less time than it took her to dump two spoonfuls into her cup.

Morning wood. Had to be. Because the sight of Ames had never blasted this kind of reaction in him. At least, not to this extent. Then again, he'd never woken to her in his kitchen, either. Domestic. Intimate.

Heat furled in his chest, part warmth from appreciating the view and part boil over from...loving the idea she was here. In his space. Her light perfume filled the kitchen like the scent had moved in, too. Semi-hard became all-systems-go, but in his confusion, he just stared. Processing. For a guy who was used to privacy and space, the response seemed crazy.

He skimmed his gaze over her curvy, lithe frame to test his first reaction a second time. Yep. His pulse kicked rhythm and some barbaric instinct to claim her rose.

A rip-roaring case of WTF shoved through his foggy state. Barely.

She glanced over her shoulder and, just like that, he was... Stone. Cold. Sober.

The wedding. The look of her in that dress. Dancing with her. Their fight. Insane things she'd said. His unending concern. Bringing her home. Finding her in the guestroom later. Their talk. His unfettered admissions. Her warm supple curves against him when they'd hugged.

Across the small distance, her mermaid eyes met his. Bluish-green and framed by dark lashes. The few feet between them shrank to inches without either of them moving. Short of air, he parted his lips, which only made him think to dip his gaze to her pouty red mouth.

And that was of no help to his aroused state. She didn't just take his breath away. She stole it. Violently.

Damnation. What the hell was happening to him?

Then her gaze trailed over him. Chest, abs. *Lower.* A smile curved her lips in amusement.

He glanced down at himself. Black boxer-briefs. Nothing else. Because he normally didn't have guests and was used to walking around however he pleased. Nearly naked, in this case.

Cursing a wicked streak, he pivoted on his heels and strode back the way he'd come. Her musical laugher faded as he hit the stairs at a jog. He stormed into his bedroom and kicked the door shut, pressing his forehead to the panel.

He swore, it was as if someone else had taken over his body the past few months, rendering him a puppet at the whim of a madman wielding the strings. Nothing made sense or properly clicked.

Not used to having someone else in the house was no excuse for forgetting to get dressed. He pushed off the door and grabbed pants from a chair, then got more pissed off as he shoved his legs into jeans because Amy wasn't an easily forgettable woman. And what had he done? He'd flashed her the morning after her first night in the cabin. With an erection. Her amused smile sprang to mind, and he groaned.

Hands on his hips, breaths rasping, he stared down at his crotch. Still. Hard. "Knock it off. Right now."

Retrieving a t-shirt from a dresser drawer, he pulled it over his head and was eternally grateful his littler head behind his zipper had listened. Taking a moment, he scrubbed his hands over his face, then made his way back downstairs.

Amy sat at the scarred two-seater table with a mug in her hands. Her knees were drawn up to her chest, bare feet at the edge of the chair. Out the window behind her, the sun was rising in pink and orange hues. In front of the opposite place was another steaming cup.

"It's black, just how you like it."

He claimed the other chair with a grunt of thanks. After downing half the coffee, he sighed. "I'm sorry. About, you know. My state of undress."

A quiet chuckle, and she smiled over the rim at him. "You're not exactly an eyesore, Nakos, and it's your house. Walk around all day in your skivvies for all I care."

Okay. That was twice now she'd made a reference to his body. She'd done it last night at the wedding when they'd danced, too. Once he could pass off as Amy-ness. Twice was the beginning of a pattern. Not that he was upset by the comments. He just didn't know if he should take them with a grain of salt or a silo. Though he knew her better than the back of his own hand, he never could tell when she was goading him.

And damn, but the...appreciation was back in her eyes. She'd pulled the rug out from under him last night and he was still recovering. Twenty-one years, and she'd never looked at him. Not like she was now. He sure as hell would've noticed.

Or perhaps he needed more caffeine.

He ran his thumb up and down the handle on his mug. "Are you flirting with me?" Because the four horsemen had just been released, if that were the case.

Her grin widened. Sucker. Punch. "You'd know. Trust me."

Nope. No, he wouldn't. "How so?"

"There's a difference between a statement of fact, flirting, and a come-on." When he just stared, she set her cup aside. "I'll demonstrate. Fact. Nakos, you have a great body." She said the phrase like explaining the sky was blue. "Flirting." She walked her fingers up his forearm and raised her voice an octave. Her smile amped a notch, as well. "Nakos, you have—" slow perusal of him

"—a great body." Then—sweet *Hihcebe*—she leaned forward over his chair. "This is a come-on." Her full breasts pressed against his chest, her hair teased his jaw, and her warm breath fanned the shell of his ear. "Nakos, you have a great body," she murmured in a clear I-want-you-horizontal-and-naked voice.

While oxygen vacated his lungs and every nerve under his skin misfired, she sat back and held up her palm. She lifted her brows as if to say, *understand?*

He'd never loved his kitchen table so much. He was hard. Again.

Twelve hours, and he was already losing his mind having her under his roof. At this rate, he wasn't going to make it twelve more minutes. Because fuck. He was attracted to Amy. Of all people. Amy don't-you-dare-go-there Woods.

An apocalypse wasn't merely coming. Oh no, no. It had arrived. He should just put his own balls in a vise. It would save time.

"Do you want more coffee?"

He shook his head. Didn't help clear the holy-shit, though. "What?"

"Coffee. Do you want more?"

Only if it was laced with a psychotropic medication. "I'm good, thanks."

She tilted her head. "It's really bothering you, isn't it?" He thought she'd read his filthy, filthy mind until she elaborated. "Your peep show, I mean. Seriously, it's not as if I'm a virgin. If it makes you feel better, I'll come downstairs tomorrow in just my panties. We'll call it even."

He choked. On his tongue.

A vision of her in some lacey bra and panty set the same color of her irises filtered to mind. He closed his eyes. Fast. He may have groaned for good measure.

"Well, jeez. No need to lose your stomach contents. I was only kidding."

Her chair scraped the floor, and he opened his eyes.

Had that been...hurt in her tone? Surely not. Except her posture was deflated as she rinsed dishes, her back to him. He wanted a good look at her face for clarification he hadn't insulted her, but he couldn't trust himself to move.

Wait. Why was she doing dishes? "Quit that."

She put another plate in the dishwasher. "What?"

"That's my mess. Leave it." He ate so often up at the main house that, typically, it took him a week to accumulate enough to start a load.

Of course, she ignored him. "I'm almost done."

"You're not my maid." He was about to rise and force her to stop when she closed the dishwasher door and pushed Start.

"I'm going to find my shoes. Make a grocery list." She jerked her chin at a pad of paper and pen by an empty fruit bowl next to his elbow.

"Why?"

Her expression dialed straight to *duh*. "So I can go shopping."

Right. He was low on items and she'd need her own food. "I'll go with you."

"No. When was the last time you had a day off?"

"It's Saturday. I'm working."

She gave him a withering glance. "Everyone is on a mini vacation with Olivia gone."

Not him. "The barns need to be done, regardless." He strummed his fingers on the table, growing defensive. "I have every Sunday off, just like all the guys."

"Yet you're going over to the barns to feed horses and muck stalls anyway."

"So? I'm the foreman." His job was never done. Olivia and Nate were on their honeymoon. He wasn't leaving chores for Mae to do. Besides, it wouldn't take him long and he'd have the rest of the day to lose his mind.

"Relax for once. Make a list. I'll head to the store. You will not argue." And with that, she left the room.

Wasn't that like the pot calling the kettle black? She wasn't exactly taking a load off, either. She'd cleaned his damn kitchen before he'd crawled out of bed. He was a pretty organized person, but she'd obviously tidied up.

Then again, getting her out of the house would allow him time to light a fire under what they'd discussed last night. His dad had left an old drafting desk in the basement when he and Mom had moved back to the reservation. It was the perfect size for Amy's laptop and printer. Which, he was willing to bet, were still in their boxes.

Sliding the pad closer, he scribbled a couple things down for her to pick up and tapped his pen on the table. He stripped the conversation they'd just had to the studs, replaying it in his mind, but he still couldn't figure her out. There had never been any sexual connotation between them, and though she'd claimed she had just been stating fact, he had to wonder.

Or he was simply excusing his own sudden shift by putting it on her. She'd been married to the Antichrist the past three years, and the divorce had been finalized but months ago. She probably wasn't ready to date or move on. Even tossing their lifelong friendship aside as a factor in the no column, Nakos didn't think Amy would go for him.

Just the thought of crossing that line had disaster written all over it. Yet lately, his feelings for her had been all over the map. Tumultuous and wild.

This morning had brought those scattered emotions into focus. Gave them a name.

Desire.

He didn't get it. At all. As far back as he could recall, he'd had a thing for Olivia. A quiet ache of longing. He hadn't dwelled on it, acted on it, and it hadn't taken over his life. It was just there, hovering in the distance. An awareness, of sorts. Something that floated in a tranquil sea of could-have-been.

Amy, however? She was a tsunami. Completely unable to ignore, surrounding him all the time, and capsizing any shred of rational behavior. He thought about her when she was around, when she wasn't, and almost every second in between. She kept him up at night, was almost his first thought upon waking.

There had been no relief since the barn incident, and now...she was under his roof. A constant physical presence. Leaving her scent and imprint in every room and...

"What kind of lunch meat?"

He flinched and jerked his attention to her, standing beside his chair. When the hell had she returned from upstairs?

And there was his point. So lost in thought about—what else?—her, he'd been completely unaware of his surroundings. "What?"

58

She held up the notepad. "You wrote lunch meat on the list. What kind?"

He could've penned a rendition of Moby Dick in Pig Latin and he wouldn't have been the wiser.

Rising, he walked to the hooks by the back door. "It doesn't matter. Whatever you prefer works for me." He removed his truck keys from a peg and held them out for her. "I have a tab at the grocer's. Get what you need, too, and place it on my bill."

Shadows darkened her eyes, very similar to the ones he'd seen last night when he'd found her still awake. Slowly, she took the keys and moved around him for the door.

"What's wrong, Ames?"

"Nothing. I'll be back soon."

He didn't care for the flat tone of her response and turned to face her. "Try not to mow down any animals or small children."

"Nah. I save that for rainy days to cheer myself up."

And, yeah. She was fine. He must've been mistaken.

The door quietly shut behind her. He ran a hand through his hair, staring after her. When the engine of his truck turned over and tires crunched on the driveway, he headed down the basement steps.

Distractions were good. Pivotal.

Locating the drafting table just inside the utility room, he hefted it with a grunt and muscled the thing all the way to the second floor. It had been stored for quite some time, so he grabbed a wet cloth from the bathroom, wiped the thing down, and placed it against an open wall near the closet in Amy's bedroom.

While it dried, he took the laptop and printer out of the packaging and tossed the manuals in her trunk. He plugged in the computer and played with the setup. Since he'd done the same thing with her first set of equipment two years prior, it was second nature to do it again. He installed the printer info, then the three photo editing programs she liked to use, for which she had discs in the trunk.

Finished, he arranged the stuff on the drafting desk and moved on to the camera. A quick glance at his watch, and he knew she'd be back any minute. Quickly, he shoved the boxes into the closet in the third bedroom he used as an office, put the new camera into the old camera case, snatched a couple memory cards, and headed downstairs.

He had just put the case on the kitchen table when she strode in carrying four shopping bags. She nudged the door closed with her hip and dropped the items on the butcher block island.

"I'll get the rest." Turning, he walked to the door.

"This is all of it." She set her purse on the counter and started unpacking.

Frowning, he eyed her, then the packages. Okay, his list hadn't been that big, but she didn't have anything she preferred to eat in the house. Her purchases alone should've filled the bags.

Sidling up to the island, he took stock. Confused, he checked his original list she'd set aside. Everything she'd bought was for him. Well, everything besides a half gallon of skim milk and a box of Special K. Not that he minded sharing. Hell, he was all for it. What's his was hers. But each item in front of him was single serving and he hadn't been joking when he'd said he was low on food.

"Did you leave a bag at the register by accident?"

"No, that should be everything you wanted." She stored the bags under the sink. "Why? Did I forget something?"

"Yeah, your food."

She held up the measly box with a giant K and put it in the cabinet. "I'm good."

With a box of cereal? The contents of which were...rice? "What gives, Ames?"

Like an expert, she avoided his gaze, telling him plenty and raising warning bells. "I eat mostly at the main house while I'm working."

Maybe so, but they were off all weekend. She couldn't live on cereal. Again, he was fine with making joint meals or whatever, but she'd purchased only enough for one. As if she...didn't matter.

His gut clenched watching her arrange fruit in a bowl at the table. One apple. One orange. One peach. One kiwi. One pear. One...everything. Oh, wait. There was a small bunch of grapes and three bananas. His mistake.

"Ames—"

"Are you heading up to the barn to feed the horses soon?" She moved over to the island. She put *one* steak, *one* brown package of what he assumed was *one* ground beef patty or *one* chicken breast in the fridge.

"Yes," he answered through gravel, his gut sinking. "In a few minutes." Had she eaten this morning? She'd barely touched dinner at the wedding.

"Since you took my new camera out, I think I'll screw around outside while you're gone." A can of corn, green beans, and peas went into the cabinet. "Is that okay with you?"

He was going to be sick. The dread filling him was that heavy. "Sure. Or you could come with me and take pictures there."

"Works for me."

Before jumping to any more conclusions, he cleared his throat. "I can swing by the store and grab hotdogs on my way back. Grill some for lunch?" *Say yes. Please, say...*

"Nah, I'm good. Thanks, though."

He shook his head as she turned away and fiddled with the camera. He tried and failed to recall a time he actually saw her sit down and consume a whole meal since she'd moved in with Olivia. Granted, the workers didn't head up to the house for lunch. They typically brought their own. But he usually arrived for breakfast and, at least a few times a week, stayed for dinner. She'd been at the counter with Mae. Cooking. Chopping. Talking. Nibbling, perhaps, but not eating, per se.

This time, when he looked at her, he did so with an eagle eye. She'd always been curvy. He wouldn't ever have said plump or heavy, but she was full-figured. Healthy. Her clothes were loose on her now and she'd definitely dropped weight. She still had her hourglass shape and, to anyone else, would appear normal.

"Oh, here's your receipt." She passed it over with a smile.

He waited for her to turn back to the table, then studied the slip. All his items were there, put on his tab as he'd asked. Her cereal and the milk were not. He scrubbed a hand down his face, fighting nausea.

This was her pride at work. He'd barely gotten her to accept the offer of his guestroom, never mind throwing groceries on top of it. But why hadn't she bought more than those two things? Was money that tight or was she dieting? Neither were any of his business, but he sure as hell was going to watch her this weekend.

And if she didn't consume something besides rice cereal, he was going to lay into her. Let her go feral. He couldn't care less. On this, he'd fight her. She was too important to him to ignore healthy eating habits. No way would he let her all but starve herself, no matter the reason.

Hihcebe, it was so damn good to see her holding a camera again, though. Chest tight, he studied her while she screwed with something in the digital settings, her focus on nothing else. Her expression held none of the grief or tension he'd witnessed as of late. A peace, *her* peace, however brief, settled inside him and latched on.

"Can I watch you?" he asked roughly.

She turned her head and blinked at him. "Take pictures?"

"Yeah. Do you mind?" Call it curiosity, but after the hell she'd endured, he just wanted to see her...happy again. Even if it was just an afternoon snapping photos.

By the look on her face, he couldn't have surprised her more. Her brows wrinkled and her pretty mouth pursed. "Sure, if you really want to."

"I do."

Chapter Seven

As Nakos pulled his truck up to the main house, Bones came barreling around the corner and stopped to sit on his haunches. Though the sheepdog's tongue lolled, his postured deflated as if disappointed in the visitors.

Amy released her seatbelt from the passenger side. "Looks like someone misses Olivia."

Nakos grunted. "Or Nate. The dog follows him everywhere."

They climbed out and warm, humid air tinged with the scent of pine and soil bathed her face. Hot sun beat down and created the perfect lighting for some shots she had in mind.

Nakos bent to rub the dog's black and white fur. "Just a honeymoon, boy. They'll be back before you know it." He straightened and glanced around. "Do me a favor. Check on Mae before you wander off to take pictures?"

She'd planned on it anyway. "Sure."

Leaving Nakos to care for the horses, Amy made her way to the mudroom and inside the spacious kitchen. Huge and airy, it held stainless steel appliances, granite countertops, and white distressed cabinets. Aunt Mae was reading at the small table, a cup of tea beside her.

She glanced up and set her warm blue eyes on Amy, smoothing her chin-length white strands. "Hi, sweetheart. Do you want some lunch?"

Poor woman was probably going nuts not having to cook since the men were off duty. "Have *you* eaten?"

"I was just about to make a sandwich." She rose, but Amy waved her back into place.

"I'll do it." She went to the fridge to retrieve items and got to work at the island. "How are you faring up here by yourself?" Amy didn't like the idea of her alone in this big ole house, but Mae could handle herself.

"Oh, fine." Aunt Mae smiled. "How is your new living situation?" She waggled her brows as if expecting a raunchy recant.

Amy laughed, shaking her head. "You should've been a romance novelist or something. You could turn anything into a sordid tale." She slathered mayo on wheat bread, then added turkey. "I'm trying to stay out of his way, but it's hard." She topped the sandwiches with lettuce and tomato, set one aside for Nakos, and brought the other two to the table.

"Why would you need to stay out of Nakos's way?"

With a shrug, she took a seat. "His house. I'm an invasion."

"That's ridiculous." Aunt Mae bit into her sandwich, studying Amy. "He wouldn't have offered if he didn't want you around."

She totally disagreed. White knight complex. He'd always had one. She kept silent, though, while she chewed.

Their conversation from this morning ping-ponged in her head. As did the image of him in nothing but a pair of boxer-briefs. All that tan olive skin. Ridges of abs. Hard pecs. Strong, muscular thighs. Her imagination hadn't done him justice. Tall, lean, and corded with sinew, Nakos was a prime specimen. He'd obviously fallen into habit and forgotten she was there. She'd tried to joke about the encounter, but clearly he'd been disgusted by her mere teasing, to the point he hadn't glanced at her since.

"Did he cook you a big breakfast?" Aunt Mae nodded at Amy's plate. "You only made yourself a half, not that you've even finished that much."

"Oh, no. I'm not hungry, I guess." Not a total lie. Her appetite had been for crap lately. Which she supposed was helping her count calories.

"You're getting thin, sweetheart."

"I'm trying to drop a couple pounds." She'd only managed ten and was going for twenty more.

"All right. Just so long as you understand there's nothing wrong with the way you are."

Hardly. Due to the number of times Chris had called her "fat ass" the past few years, Amy could've resembled a toothpick and she still would've heard her ex's insults. Believed them. Every single one. To think, he'd once liked her curves. Or pretended he had. Apparently, that hadn't been the case. And it wasn't as if other men had looked her way since the divorce, proving him right.

Nakos's reactions shoved to mind, cementing Chris's claim. Not just how he'd closed his eyes and gone pale in the kitchen as if nauseated by the thought of her in her underwear, but his rigid frame at her compliments, too. Both at the wedding and this morning. From now on, she'd just shut the hell up and pretend he didn't make her body come alive.

Ache. Want. Burn.

God, would she never learn?

Because Aunt Mae was still watching her, Amy forced herself to finish the turkey and stood to collect their empty plates. "Do you need anything while I'm here?" She wrapped the sandwich for Nakos in cellophane to take with her and moved to the door.

"Yes. I need you to enjoy your weekend off. It's Saturday. Go do something fun." Again with the eyebrow waggle. "Like a sweaty, naked activity with a certain tall, quiet cowboy."

She almost laughed. "I'm not the one he's in love with, Aunt Mae. Remember?"

Amy wasn't even the woman guys fell in like with, never mind lust or love. She'd fallen for the lie once before from Chris. Look where stupid, fruitless hope had gotten her. In debt up to her eyeballs, a residual pang in her ribs from a beating, not a shred of self-esteem left, and forced to rely on her friends or live on the street. Plus, her parents had disowned her, not that they hadn't been slowly doing that since birth.

"He's not in love with Olivia." Aunt Mae rose and met Amy in the doorway. "He might think he is, or was, but he's mistaken."

The woman was so very wrong on that account. Olivia stopped traffic. Always had. Auburn hair, shocking blue eyes, regally thin body. Plus, she was the sweetest person with a heck of a funny bone. And she'd had Nakos around her finger forever. Amy would've been jealous if she didn't love her best friend to the moon and back.

Aunt Mae cupped Amy's cheeks. "Go for it, sweetheart. I know you want to."

She stilled, staring into knowing eyes while her sinuses burned. Her whole life, the only kindness she could recall had been a product of this house. A large part of that had been from this woman. But that didn't make Aunt Mae right, just intuitive.

"Doesn't matter what I want. He doesn't and never will." She hugged Mae because the woman meant well. Relishing the brief

65

embrace since Amy so rarely got it elsewhere, she closed her eyes to savor before pulling away. God, she missed being touched. "Besides, I'm not..." Unable to finish the thought, she shook her head.

"Not what?"

Good enough, she almost said. That was the brutal truth. Even if Chris hadn't come into her life and broken the last of her will, she was still tarnished. Dirty. Had been since she was twelve years old. Amy had no right even being in the presence of a man like Nakos. His beautiful heart and gorgeous body belonged with a woman way more deserving than Amy could ever try to emulate.

She swallowed past the pain clamping her throat. "I'm not looking for a relationship." At least there was honesty in that answer, too. "I'll check on you tomorrow."

The temperature and humidity had risen to nearly unbearable when she stepped out. Making her way across the yard, she headed for the open carriage doors on the second barn. Nakos had put all the horses out to pasture on the rear side. A wheelbarrow next to him, he used a pitchfork to arrange hay in the farthest stall. He'd obviously already cleaned them and was almost finished.

Hail Mary, but he'd taken off his shirt. Sweat gleaned on his dark skin as muscles rippled and corded tendons strained. His jeans were hung low on his narrow hips and his black Stetson shadowed most of his face. He moved with fluid grace, the perfect symmetry of sinew and bone at work.

She wanted her camera so badly her fingers itched, but she'd left it in the truck.

Bones noticed her first and trotted over. She petted his soft ears and glanced at Nakos. "I brought you a sandwich."

Setting the pitchfork aside, he strode over looking like a bronze god. "You should eat that. I can get something at home." He wiped his face with a bandana and shoved it in his back pocket.

"I ate with Aunt Mae."

He eyed her as if he didn't believe her, but took the sandwich. "You sure?"

"Yep. I'm going to grab my camera and wander around. Do you want any help in here first?"

Shaking his head, he unwrapped the cellophane. "If you give me a minute, I can go with you. The horses need to walk around. I'll put 'em away before we leave."

Nodding, she pivoted for the driveway. "Be right back."

She grabbed her bag from the truck, took the camera out, and slung the strap over her shoulder. When she turned, Nakos was leaning against the doorway of the barn as if holding the structure up himself. Legs crossed, Bones at his feet, he bowed his head.

On instinct, she brought the camera to her face and zoomed to get a better shot from a distance. The contrast of his blue jeans, bright green grass, and red from the barn were an eyegasm, even if the striking man weren't shirtless and lickable. The lazy pose of him, expression hidden by his hat, and the dog by his feet, were breathtakingly captivating. Told a story.

Excitement zinged in her bloodstream and her breasts ached watching him. She got two clean shots before Nakos crouched and rubbed the dog's flank. Perfection. Dark shadows from inside the barn to his left and sunlight bathing him from the right. She snapped several clicks and sighed in utter contentment.

God, she missed this. Getting lost in a frame, the camera in her hands, the blank slate it created in her mind.

She made her way back to him and, without a word, he followed her across the pasture. Not sure where she was headed, she just kept her eyes open until something jumped out at her. Before long, they wound up on the hill by the tire swing. Bones followed and stretched out in a shady patch.

Nakos put his tee back on—a crying shame—and plopped his butt on the grass by the base of the tree. He rested his forearms on his bent knees and studied her as she laid on her back. Though he said nothing, she was ever aware of his presence. She could feel his gaze on her, heavy and potent, and wondered what his fascination was with her all of a sudden.

She glanced heavenward at the sunlight through the branches, highlighting the leaves, and brought the camera up again. *Click, click.* "What are you thinking about?"

Something was off with him. The shot, though? Awesome. Color and light blended together through the canopy. Summer days at their best.

When she realized he hadn't responded, she rolled on her side to face him. Setting the camera down, she propped her head in her hand. Mere inches separated them as he looked down at her. After a moment, he sighed and glanced away, his expression revealing nothing.

"If you don't tell me what's on your mind, I'll start my own dialogue. I can choose some very interesting topics on your behalf." She brushed a wayward strand of hair from her cheek and lowered her tone to mimic his voice. "Amy, I'm thinking of dyeing my hair pink and getting a butterfly tattoo. What do you think?" She brought her voice higher. "Well, Nakos, where would you get this tattoo? Somewhere forbidden?"

His gaze cut to hers, dark and irritated, even though there was the slightest quirk of his lips as if he were amused. "I'd shave my head before dyeing it pink."

"Travesty," she gasped. "Don't you ever chop off that hair. It's beautiful." Shoulder-length raven strands, which he usually had in a low ponytail, and looked as soft as his heart.

And there was the intense stare again, boring through her. "Beautiful?"

"You want a more manly word? There isn't one. That thick mane of yours is nothing short of beautiful." Darn. She was supposed to be shutting up in regards to the compliments. He hadn't reacted well to them before. Or, more precisely, to her attention.

Eyes narrowed, he reached out and touched her hair resting on the grass, his gaze following the movement. A barely there caress with his fingertips like he was curious about the texture but scared for the result. Shocked, she tried to keep still.

His jaw clenched, and he lifted a few strands, rubbing the ends between his thumb and index finger. "Can I ask you a question?"

She felt the touch through her whole system as if her hair had mysteriously grown nerve endings. "You can ask me anything."

His long lashes fluttered as he met her gaze. Seductive, that. "Have you...thought about dating again? Are you ready to, I mean?"

The breath seeped from her lungs. Slowly, she sat up and crossed her legs, causing him to let go of her hair and drop his hand. "Is this a ploy to remarry me off and get me out of your house?"

Not so much as a blink. He held her gaze, trapping her, and she couldn't figure out what was going on. His expression was locked down tight, and he wasn't caving to offer a clue.

"I guess so," she said slowly, answering his initial question. "I'm not hung up on Chris or anything. But there's not exactly a line of guys waiting to step up to the plate."

"Do you have someone in mind?"

Why couldn't she breathe? "I wouldn't say no if Charlie Hunnam asked me to dinner."

"Who?"

"The actor from *Sons of Anarchy*." She shrugged when he merely stared. "Blond hottie with an accent and—"

"I'm being serious right now and you're cracking jokes?"

She didn't like this entire conversation. Her Spidey sense was tingling, telling her to glue her mouth shut or bad things would happen. "I was being serious. If you saw him, you'd understand."

Growling, he dragged his hat off his head, tossed it next to her camera, and pressed his palms to his eyes. Long, long seconds ticked by. Cicadas buzzed and a whippoorwill cooed.

Finally, without looking at her, he mumbled, "Why can't you answer one question without turning it into a root canal?"

Growing irritated herself—and panicky—she shot to her feet, ready to bolt the second he backed her into a proverbial corner. And he would. The signs were all there. "Since when do you give a rat's ass about my sex life?"

He pulled his head away from his hands with such deliberation a chill shot up her spine. The glare he whipped her rendered her immobile. But when he lumbered to his feet, it numbed her to the bone.

"Just what in the hell do you mean by that?" His low, carefully controlled tone sliced like a blade.

Dang it. She should've just lied and said no. No, she wasn't ready to date again, and no, she didn't have anyone in mind. But she had a hard time not being truthful with him and a diversion had seemed the best course. Now what?

"Not once have you shown any interest, Nakos. Not who I spend time with, date, take to bed, or marry."

"Oh hell no, you didn't go there." Nostrils flaring, he vibrated where he stood. Muscles rippled and tendons strained—a panther ready to strike prey. "I—"

"Don't deny it." Yes. Anger was so much better than vulnerability. She let it boil in her bloodstream. "Name one instance, in our entire friendship, where you gave an opinion. You stood right in front of me on the dance floor last night and told me I'd hurt you by not having you at my wedding. But you didn't speak up about your contempt for Chris before or after we got married." Though it had been obvious, that was beside the point. "So explain to me how your sudden interest now isn't supposed to confuse me."

The color drained from his face, and he reeled. "Ames..." He swiped his brow and looked away. Distress etched across his features, in his posture. "I didn't..." He sighed. "You're right. It wasn't my place to say anything and I didn't. That doesn't mean..." He closed his eyes, hung his head. "Doesn't mean I didn't care."

Deflating, she let out the breath she'd been holding. "I know you care. It's this conversation I don't get."

He gazed at the horizon, but his glazed expression told her he wasn't seeing anything but the inside of his own head. Contemplation knitted his brows. "You've been different." His voice was so quiet she had to strain to hear him. He looked at her, concern and something else she couldn't place in the dark depths. "You've not been the same since the day he hurt you. Neither have I. Something got...shifted between us."

He strode closer and stopped mere inches from her, a pleading in his eyes. "Are you attracted to me?"

On a dime, her throat closed. Most likely, it was a defensive response because even her body knew answering was stupid.

His eyes darted back and forth between hers. Searching. Seeking. Imploring. "Out of nowhere, you started saying things to me you never have before and..." He grabbed the back of his neck. "I don't know what to think."

Ah. There was the root of the issue. Her comments about his body and light flirtation had disrupted his carefully construed view of their dynamic. He wanted a handle on her motives so he could deal with it. So he could make it end.

Rejection tore at her insides, regardless of how many instances she'd been dismissed in her life. Strange how it still hurt. Every.

Time. "I'll stop doing it. I'm sorry. You obviously hate the attention from me."

"I didn't say that. Don't put words in my mouth."

"You didn't have to. Your repulsion and uncomfortableness are apparent." She straightened. "Don't look at me like that. You know you were thinking it."

"I was?" He shook his head like he was baffled, then he blinked in clarity. "Knock it off. You're doing the Amy juju again and trying to derail me." He stepped flush against her and dipped to look in her eyes. "I want an answer and I want the truth. Are you attracted to me?"

"I already promised to stop—"

"Are you attracted to me?"

"Nakos, drop it. This is ridiculous. It doesn't matter what I feel. You don't have to worry about your delicate sensibilities and—"

"Quit avoiding." He grabbed her shoulders. "Are. You. Attracted. To. Me?"

She clamped her mouth shut. Hard. How, she hadn't a clue. But as her respirations flew into the triple digits and she trembled from the urge to escape one more epic pain she'd never recover from, he got his answer without her speaking a syllable.

A barely perceptible shake of his head, and he'd read her loud and clear. One by one, his fingers retracted from her shoulders and he stepped back. Arms splayed at his sides in shocked surrender, he stared at her. Lost. Bewildered. Dazed.

Teutonic plates shifted and the earth rotated the sun in the amount of time he attempted to get a grip. He tore his eyes away, gaze darting to the ground like he couldn't believe he was still standing. It would've broken her had she not known this would've been his response all along. Once, just once, could fate be on her side? Luck? Something, at least?

If she didn't play this moment off as nothing, didn't show him it was no big deal, she was going to lose him. She knew it as adamantly as she understood she'd never get her feelings reciprocated.

And because she was a total idiot, she said the first thing that came to mind. "Welcome to season three of my life. The writers are instilling outrageous antics just to keep it interesting." Please, God, keep him in the script. "A demon will be riding a unicorn next episode if you want to tune in."

His gaze whipped to hers with a what-the-hell. Once he appeared to digest her statement, his hands fisted and he held them to his forehead in a display of utter helplessness. He closed his eyes. Breathed heavily. Groaned.

"Nakos, I—"

One second he was a few feet away and the next he was pressed against her. He cupped the sides of her head with both hands, his jaw set in determination. With the distance evaporated, they shared air. Brushed noses. Blasted heat.

"What are you doing?" she whispered, heart pounding. Because his gaze was darting between her mouth and her eyes like he might...

"Getting you to shut up so I can think."

Oh. "Is it working?"

"No." His throat formed a swallow. "I'm trying hard to get myself together to do the right thing, but I have no idea what that is at the moment."

Heat wove through her bloodstream and her head swam like she'd slammed ten shots of whiskey in the same amount of time. She was probably dreaming anyway. In reality, Nakos wouldn't be holding her, emanating sexual waves of frustration, and giving off want-to-kiss-her vibes.

Carefully, to not spook the beast, she set her hands on his waist. "If it makes things any clearer for you, about every other day I feel like I've got my life under control and headed in the right direction. Then, I pat myself on the back and say, that was a really great two minute effort."

He muttered something in his native tongue and...well, he did shut her up, after all.

With his lips.

Chapter Eight

The second Nakos's lips met Amy's, he knew he was in trouble. The deep kind that drown a person where they stood and left no recourse for salvation. He'd cupped her face, dipped his head, and planted one right on her never-shut-up, poutier-than-hell mouth.

And blew logic right out of the water.

They barely touched, were suspended in a shocked-immobile pause in time, but moving wouldn't have mattered. He felt the feather-light press of her lips in every molecule of his body.

Hihcebe, she drove him batshit mad. The constant arguing and assumptions and distractions. It was enough to make a man crazy. Proven by their current position.

In all the years he was attracted to Olivia, not once had he lost it. He'd never had the urge to push boundaries, cross the line, or act on the hovering desire. Amy, though? She wound around his control so adamantly she'd snapped him off at the root. Rendered thought a cloud of dust in her wake. Burrowed under his skin until nothing made sense.

The light signature of her perfume wove around him, carried on a gentle wind, familiar but somehow new. He couldn't put a name to the sultry scent if he tried. It reminded him of summer nights and moonlight and warm breezes. Atmospheric, elemental, and sensual in the same breath. Distinctly her. The first time he remembered noticing it was back in high school at her prom. On and off since then, he'd catch a trace of it and a punch of recognition would slam into him, halting whatever he'd been thinking or doing.

She made a noise in her throat, part mewl and completely feminine. Her fingers flexed against his hips, bunching his shirt in her fists. Yet, she made no attempt to shove him away. Or bring them closer.

The hell with it. If he was going to screw up everything, he may as well do it right.

Threading his fingers through her soft strands, he held her to him while wrapping his other arm around her waist. He backed her to the tree, pinning her body in place with his, and rough bark bit into his skin. Heart thundering, he slanted his mouth over hers for a tighter fit.

Two things hit him at once. First, how her supple curves cushioned his hard frame. It was as if she were designed exactly for him. For this. Perfect alignment. Despite their height difference, they synced like one unit clicking into place. Her full breasts crushed against his chest and the way she'd spread her legs so he could stand between them had her cradling his throbbing shaft just right. And second, he'd always known her mouth was a weapon. Whether it was her sharp tongue or her stop traffic grin, the military should have it in their possession. But he'd underestimated the damage it could inflict.

Because he was leveled. She'd stormed his castle and invaded. At least, he'd thought so, until she parted her lips and their tongues met. Hot, slow swipes that shifted from a trial of caution to languid caresses in a blink. Detonation. Forget the castle. She obliterated his entire existence.

He had no idea she could be submissive. In fact, had anyone claimed such a thing, he would've died laughing. Twice. Yet, here she was, up against him and compliant, letting him do whatever he damn well wanted.

And want her he did. With everything in him.

Didn't it figure the only time she'd follow his commands and allow him the upper hand was when he couldn't remember his own name. Liquid heat poured through his veins. His heart couldn't decide between shifting organs or cracking ribs. He took advantage of the rarity and dove deeper, thrust into her warm, wet cavern of a mouth and explored. She tasted like lemonade, the sweetness of it blending with a barely stoked fire. Lungs seizing, he rocked against her.

She arched toward him, her hands tracing up his spine and back down as if she was unsure what or how much to touch. Her breathing accelerated, the hard peaks of her nipples begging for attention as they grazed his chest. His fingers flexed against her back, thumb stroking the material of her shirt. He'd rather be under it. Have her skin against his.

He'd always considered himself a patient man. With previous partners, he'd preferred a gentle mating and a slow climb. Savoring. Unhurried. But his body was having none of that with Amy. A primal need to dominate surged within his entire system. Barbaric in its intensity and shocking him to his marrow. Damn, but he wanted to climb inside her.

Urges. Mercy, the urges.

The kiss became frantic, desperate, and he growled low in his throat. As if needing proof he'd made the noise, she ran her fingertips across his chest and he did it again. More. He needed more of her touch. It was too much and not enough. Her other hand latched onto the back of his neck, her nails lightly raking his nape. The contact followed a nerve path straight to his erection, and he jerked.

A sharp cry, and he tore his mouth away. Resting his cheek against hers, he stared at the bark on the tree trunk, mere inches from his face, and siphoned air.

Long moments passed, neither of them moving, and he couldn't risk looking at her. She'd responded, had been right there with him, but he had no clue what he'd find in her bluish-green depths. The uncertainty was unnerving. The way he was still vibrating—from a kiss, no less—was like an exclamation point to the holy shit.

Nothing like that had ever happened to him before. Attraction, desire, affection? Sure. Animalistic need? Untamed passion? A soul-jarring, control-clawing connection? No. Never.

After he didn't know how long, her throat clicked with a swallow and she took a breath like she was going to say something.

Please, no. He couldn't handle one of her Amy-isms or her potentially blowing this off. Worse, her gutting him with another truth.

Removing his hand from the back of her head, he placed it over her mouth instead. "Don't speak." Closing his eyes, he turned his face toward hers and rested his forehead to her temple. His nose brushed her cheek and his heart turned over in his chest. "Give me five seconds to wrap my mind around what just happened. Please."

She was always quick with a joke or comeback or witty insight, but he wasn't as clever. His thought process took much longer to engage. Half the time, he had no clue how to respond to her.

Considering she'd just blown his gray matter into the ether, he was screwed.

They'd just flipped twenty-one years of friendship onto its side. And he was still hard in the aftermath.

She mumbled something against his palm.

Knowing he'd regret it, he lowered his hand.

"It's been five minutes, not seconds." She inhaled slowly and ran her fingers through his ponytail. "Not that I'm complaining or anything, but do you plan on saying something soon?"

The uncertainty in her voice leveled him a second time. Or third. Fifth? Whatever. If Amy was unsure, there was no hope at all for him.

How he reacted to this moment could make or break everything they'd been to one another. She'd been hurt before, unimaginably and by a man who was supposed to love her. Self-esteem was such a fragile thing, and though Amy never struck him as delicate, he'd learned that even she was breakable.

Three months ago, his heart had stopped dead at finding her on that barn floor, and he realized, shockingly, that it had just started beating again. Nothing he said would encompass what he was feeling since he didn't even know himself. And until he did, no way would he be another in a long line inflicting her harm. He'd die first.

He skimmed his hand down her hair, smoothing the strands, and let out a careful breath. "We'll talk later. Give me an hour to get the horses situated, then we can head back to the cabin."

Without waiting for a response, he bent and picked up his hat, then strode down the hill toward the barns. On autopilot, he groomed the horses, put them back in their stalls, and fed them.

His legs were still weak and his mind numb when he went in search of Amy again, finding her in the same spot he'd left her. Legs sprawled in front of her, she leaned against the tree with the dog's head in her lap.

Staring into space, she didn't seem to notice his approach and her expression was void of any emotion. Since he couldn't read her, he had no way of knowing what to say any more than he had right after the kiss. His body hummed just being in her vicinity, though.

"You ready?" He cleared the rasp from his voice. "Figured we'd swing by the store to grab something for dinner."

She nodded and rose, grabbing her camera. She said zilch on the way to the store and waited in the truck for him instead of going inside. She then said even more nothing on the ride back to the cabin. He barely had the door shut behind them and she headed upstairs. Where she remained the rest of the afternoon.

Concern took on a new name while he fired up the grill. Not knowing if her food quirks were a diet thing, he'd bought two chicken breasts and veggies, figuring she'd eat that. He turned the foil packet of broccoli, carrots, and red peppers over and watched the meat, trying to figure out how to approach the subject of what had happened by the tree.

After plating the food and bringing it inside to the table, he was no wiser for the contemplation. He climbed the stairs and knocked on her open bedroom door. She was sitting on the bed, laptop in front of her, and pictures scattered by her hip.

"Can I come in?"

Type, type. "It's your house, Nakos."

He ground his teeth. One step forward, three backward with her. "But it's your room."

She gave him a baleful glance. "Yes, you don't need to ask."

He swore, it was like someone showing her common courtesy was unheard of. "Dinner's done." At her look of confusion, he elaborated. "I grilled some chicken." She may have only bought his grocery items earlier, but he'd countered. This kitchen split she'd tried to instill was ending here.

She didn't even deign to glance up from the screen. "I'm not very hungry, thanks."

He bit back a weary sigh and tried to remember strangling her would solve squat. "I haven't seen you eat all day. I made enough for two. Please join me?"

Lip chewing. Staring. Blinking. Finally, after the longest pause in the history of womankind, she climbed off the bed. "Sure. Lead on."

Praise *Hihcebe*. Progress. He pointed to the photos. "Are those from today?" She nodded. "Can you bring them down so I can see?"

And there she went with the stunned stupid expression again. "Okay." She gathered the pictures and preceded him out. In the kitchen, she eyed the plates. "It looks really good. Thank you."

Taking a seat across from her, he said nothing. No sense in rocking the boat. He waited for her to cut into the chicken before starting himself, and an overwhelming sense of relief hit him when she chewed.

Strong and independent and fiery as she always appeared, he'd had a different impression of her through the years. Especially recently. Nothing specific had triggered the sensation, but it was there just the same. Her bravado seemed like a front. Without a word, she screamed a contradiction of *take me* and *take care of me*.

And an ingrained instinct to suddenly do both was too overpowering to ignore.

In the silence, he reached for the photos and sifted through them. Damn, but she was good. The undershot of the tree and filtered sunlight was amazing. He chuckled at another of Bones with a ladybug on his nose. She must've snapped it after Nakos left to tend to the horses.

He turned it around to show her. "Olivia's going to love this."

She smiled. "I'm printing a larger one for her tomorrow."

Nodding, he kept flipping while they ate. There was a close-up of a dandelion, blades of grass surrounding it. Simple, yet it spoke volumes between the colors and the background blur.

At the last batch, he paused over his own image. Two of him leaning against the barn and three of him crouched by the dog. He'd never been comfortable having his picture taken, but these were artistic more than candid. And...emotional, if that made sense.

Amy was the first person to complement or boost another's ego. Forever honest and supportive, too. But if her actions were a sentence, her words a page, then her photos were the whole book. They relayed a tale through her eyes and it always intrigued him.

Yet these? Of him? For the first time in memory, he was getting the unfiltered version of how she viewed him. Strong. Pensive. Gallant. There was something oddly romantic about the shots, as well. His chest swelled the longer he stared.

Unsure whether to get choked up or nervous, he turned them around. "Didn't know you had the camera on me."

Her grin stalled his lungs. "I'm sneaky like that. Don't worry. I won't show anyone. Which is a crying shame. You belong in a magazine ad."

"What?"

"I'm serious." She set her fork on her empty plate. "There's a ton of stock photo sites where advertizing people and others go to buy pictures. Some just purchase for private use. Authors and cover designers are the biggest pull, though. I could make a mint on you alone."

He placed the stack between them on the table, shocked his hand wasn't shaking. "Do you have accounts on the sites?" How many others of him did she have?

"No, but I'm thinking about it. Might earn me some decent additional income." Her lips twisted. "It would take awhile to build an audience, but the right tags would draw people to my stuff. The real bank is shots like these." She tapped the one of him. "Private shoots with models or exclusive rights to certain pictures."

Huh. He didn't know what the hell she'd meant by tags and whatnot, but she should set up accounts and plow forward if she could make a profit from the sites. Besides, he'd love nothing more than for her to get her work in the public eye.

Picking up the pictures of himself, he glanced at them again. He hated attention and the very idea of being slapped on book covers or something made him shudder. But, if it would help her, he wouldn't hesitate. "You can use these, if you like."

She froze, pretty mermaid eyes bugging. "Say what?"

"None of these show my face. That would be my hard limit. I don't want to be recognized. As long as you get my permission and let me see the shots first, you can upload and sell them." He paused. "Why are you looking at me like that?"

Expelling a ragged breath, she rubbed her temple. "Why, he says." She shook her head like he'd sprouted wings and said he was the Tooth Fairy. "I mean, the better question is, why would you let me do that?"

There was very little he wouldn't do for her, and he was more than a lot pissed off she didn't know that. Obviously, he'd done a crappy job of showing her how much he cared. "Because 'Woods Photography' has a nice ring to it."

She tilted her head in thought, then dropped her chin in her hand. "It kinda does." Her gaze slid to his. "Are you sure? I can go forward without your pictures."

"I'm sure." He rose and grabbed their plates, rinsing them in the sink. "Do it, Ames. Put yourself out there." Drying his hands, he turned to face her and leaned on the counter.

She studied him with a mix of awe and disbelief. Not unlike the state in which he'd spent his day. And that brought him back to a conversation they needed to have.

"About what happened earlier..."

A slow blink, and she turned her head away. "Let's not."

"We need to talk about it."

"No, we don't." She looked at him, and the somnolent hollowness in her eyes killed him. "It happened. It's over. Let's ignore the whole thing."

Why? And he didn't want to ignore it. Hell, he didn't think he could. For that matter, how could she? It wasn't as if she hadn't participated. Willingly. Eagerly.

Damn, the reminder had his blood heating.

Rubbing his jaw, he chose his words with care. He had no clue where her head was at. "That was one hell of a kiss. Pretending it didn't happen is begging for trouble." He fought for divine wisdom because he was at a loss. "I..."

She raised her hand to stop him and stood. "You didn't mean it and putting focus on the situation will only upset you more."

Didn't mean it? Was she joking? He'd meant it so fiercely his shaft was going to have a permanent zipper impression. "You're confusing me to no end."

"Am I? Think about it, Nakos. Really think."

He didn't need to rehash the kiss. It was playing in a constant loop before his eyes. Heaven help him, but he wanted to do it again. Repeatedly. He'd asked her, begged her, to answer the question of whether she was attracted to him. Her utter refusal and the deflection in her eyes was all the reply he'd needed. So what, exactly, was she trying to do by getting him to ignore the elephant in the room?

"I'm not sorry, *anim*. I'm not," he insisted after she shook her head.

"We're not going there, not doing this."

He shoved his hands in his pockets, lest he use them to throttle her. "Why not?" Nothing. Not a syllable. Fine. He'd try something else. "What do you want?"

"Doesn't matter."

"Of course, it matters."

Hands on her hips, she huffed. "Did it matter what you wanted when Olivia didn't return your feelings?"

Damn her. She should've been a lawyer. "This situation is entirely different." Like night and day. Oil and water. Politics and integrity...

"How?"

"Because you kissed me back." Olivia never would've done that, even if he'd been stupid enough to try. Amy, though? He nearly groaned. He was not alone in this attraction.

The brutally open gaze she cut him was jarring. "Your body responded to our kiss. Yes?"

Hell yes. He nodded, not sure he could speak. Or should.

"Your body was into it. That's basic. Visceral. But your mind and heart don't want me. No." She lifted her palm to stop his argument. "Don't lie to me. Can you honestly say the first thought running through your head wasn't *Oh, shit. I just kissed Amy? What the hell am I going to do?*"

Okay, she had him there.

But that didn't mean he didn't want her. Physically or emotionally. He simply needed to discuss the matter with her. Explore possibilities. Conversation had never been a problem for them, and he despised the way she refused to talk now. This was too important to brush off, damn it. How were either of them supposed to know if there was any potential if she put up walls around the event?

She crossed her arms, her head bowed and shoulders deflating. "That's what I thought. Here's your out, Nakos. Take it. Don't beat yourself up over a simple mistake." She turned away. "Thank you for dinner. It was delicious."

While he picked his jaw up off the floor, she quietly left the room.

Chapter Nine

Amy leaned against the headboard in Olivia's bedroom at the main house and stretched her legs out in front of her. "So, how many hot men in kilts did you see? Be honest."

Laughing, Olivia folded a shirt from the laundry basket. "A few guys, but none you'd want to test the theory of whether they go commando under the kilt, if you know what I mean." She put the shirt away in the dresser and grabbed another. "Scotland was amazing, though. Nate looked up a few of my ancestors and we found this old cemetery where some were buried. I've always wanted to go, but I'm glad I waited to see it first with him."

Considering Amy had never been outside of Wyoming, she'd be happy going anywhere. "At least you did some tourist things. Being your honeymoon and all. What a wasted trip that would've been only seeing the inside of a hotel room."

"Ha. We saw plenty of that, too." Olivia winked, a flush in her pale cheeks. She brushed a strand of auburn hair from her face and set the empty basket aside. "We were only gone ten days. I don't know how we amassed so much laundry." She sat at the foot of the bed. "There was one disappointment. I didn't get a Nessie sighting."

Amy rolled her eyes. "The nerve of mythical creatures. So inconsiderate." Her BFF's obsession with the Loch Ness Monster was adorable. And weird.

"Right? I did bring you back a present, however." Olivia rose and dragged her suitcase out of the closet. "There was this shop we visited and the stuff in there was incredible. The couple who owns the place makes trinkets out of things others throw away." She set three picture frames on the bed—two eight-by-tens and an eleven-by-seven. "I thought you could put your photos in them."

"Wow. How cool." The larger frame was made up of various scraps of denim, some ripped and faded, others newer and dark navy. The two smaller frames were wood. The first looked like driftwood and had broken glass embossed on it. The second was rough planks with rusted nails. "I love them. Thank you." She placed them up against the nightstand next to her so she could take them back to the cabin later.

Olivia plopped on the bed and crossed her legs, her knees bumping Amy's. "Anything good happen while I was gone?"

"It rained." She shrugged. "Otherwise it was same old, same old." Except, that wasn't true, but she debated how much to spill. She wasn't sure what Nakos would think of Olivia knowing what had happened. "I applied for a LLC license this week."

"What for?"

"I started my own photography company. Sort of."

"No. Really?" Olivia grabbed her shoulders. "That's fabulous, and about time. Grats!"

"Thanks. I did the license to protect me from being personally liable for the company's debts. Just in case." After what had happened with her ex, Amy wasn't taking chances. She told Olivia about the stock photo sites. "I played with a website, too. Thinking I might not put all the pictures on the accounts. Maybe reserve some to sell exclusively on my own at a higher price."

"Look at you, an honest to God artist. You're acting like it's no big deal." Olivia slapped her arm. "I'm so proud of you."

Happiness bubbled in Amy's chest. "Thank you. I probably won't make much from it, but it'll bring me a little closer to paying off debts."

"You're going to be uber successful. I know it. You're too talented to fail." Olivia sighed. "I leave for a few days and everything is different when I get back. You moved in with Nakos."

Yeah, about that...

Olivia wrapped her arms around Amy and flopped sideways on the mattress. They lay facing each other like they used to as little girls, noses nearly touching. There was something intimately reassuring in the position, that a few precious things hadn't changed over time or been warped by reality's cruel light of day. Though completely non-sexual in nature, Amy cherished the closeness. How she'd wished, feverishly as a child, to have Olivia as her true sister.

"How are you doing? You know, since Chris went to jail and everything. We never talked about it much. I worry about you."

Olivia took Amy's hands in hers and squeezed. "Never mind the beating, but he said some really awful things to you."

Olivia hadn't heard the half of it. And never would, if Amy had any say.

"I'm fine." She smiled to soften the lie and reassure her friend. One day, she would be okay. She'd been waiting for that someday all her life. Yet to give up hope it would ever come would mean quitting altogether. "You know me. I'm a boomerang. I always come right back."

A low chuckle, and Olivia sighed. "Yes, you do. I wish I had half your strength."

Amy wasn't strong. She was just that good at faking it. "That's what you've got Nate for. The guy bench-presses cars before breakfast." At Olivia's grin, Amy pushed the slight twinge of jealousy into a hidey hole. "He adores you so darn much. I'm happy for you."

"I never knew love could be like this." Her glassy blue gaze drifted away. "I can't breathe without him. All I can think about is making sure he knows that he's my world, assuring him I'll always be here. Lord, the things he's been through. And even after getting past all the ugly, he's still so...gentle."

"I'm pretty sure that's the way it should be." Not that Amy had any clue what she was talking about. Love, in any form, had never knocked on her door. "You're the perfect person for him. The one to tame the beast and show him he's worth loving. Thing is, Liv, you needed him right back."

She scrunched her nose at Amy's nickname. Olivia wasn't fond of it, but too bad. "Very true." Olivia let out a quiet breath. "I'm sad you're not staying here anymore. Remember when we were kids? We said we'd live together forever and do anything we wanted, whenever we wanted."

Amy laughed. "Three months was a good run. Besides, you're married and living your ever-after." One of them should, at least. She would've sworn fairy tales didn't exist if the proof weren't right in front of her. "I expect nieces and nephews soon. Note the plural there."

"I have no problem with that." Olivia propped her head in her hand, wide grin slipping. "I'm glad you're staying with Nakos. I worry about him, too. He's reclusive, never goes out anymore. It'll be good for him to have you around."

"Well, he likes his solitude." Amy mimicked Olivia's pose. "I'm not so sure me being there is a good thing, though."

"Why?"

Where to start? "He's tense. We drive up here to the main house together every morning and back in the evening, pass each other in the cabin, eat beside one another, but we don't say anything. Like ghosts occupying the same space." It had been that way for a week, ever since she'd put a stop to the romantic complication they were about to weave. She'd been right to do it, knew it was necessary to save their relationship, but it had the opposite effect. The friendship was decaying before her eyes.

Slowly, Olivia sat up. "That's not like you guys at all. He's much more open with you than he ever was with me. We're close, sure, but you two click without effort." She ran a trembling hand over her forehead. "You don't think...it's about the wedding, do you? He seemed okay with Nate and I, stood up as—"

"It's not you, Liv." She clasped Olivia's hand and let go to sit up, as well. "He's happy for you."

"Then what's going on? It's not like him to behave that way."

Amy closed her lids a beat and pressed her finger to the throbbing between her eyes. "Nakos kissed me."

"He did what?" Olivia reared.

"Yeah, a week ago. The day after the wedding. Take your surprise, multiply it by infinity, and you'll have my response."

"Like, as in, *kissed you*, kissed you, or a quick peck? Mouth? Cheek?"

"Mouth, tongue, tonsils." Full body press. She sighed fondly, remembering. "I could barely stand afterward."

"Jeez. So it was good?"

Amy's laugh was so dry she was stunned sand granules didn't spit from her mouth. "Let's put it this way. Our pensive, broody guy pal has got an animal under all that stoicism."

A nod, and Olivia's grin morphed from shock to interest. "Well, then." She tilted her head. "I guess I can see that. He is quite observant, can be commanding when he wants to be, and has the patience of a saint. Those traits would make for a great kisser."

"Don't forget thorough." Or the hot as sin body.

86

"Wait." Olivia waved her hand. "What brought this on? You two never hooked up before."

"Duh. He was into you."

Olivia's gaze traveled away, mouth twisted in thought. "I don't think he was, to be honest. I know everyone thinks so, and maybe there was attraction on his end, but I..." She blew out a breath. "This will sound stupid, but I think I was a safe bet."

"You're right." Amy narrowed her eyes. "That does sound stupid."

"Hear me out." Olivia leaned back on her hands. "When we met, I was different than what he was used to encountering, right? My hair, my skin...not like his heritage. He took that first initial pang of wonder and built upon it. Add in the friendship, and feelings got muddled."

Amy thought that over, picked the reasoning apart. There was merit to the theory, but a guy didn't spend half his life pining if something beyond affection wasn't hovering under the surface.

"You know him as well as I do." Olivia brushed a strand of hair from her face. "He typically goes after what he wants. He might take his sweet ass time, think it to death, lurk on the fringes to calculate odds, but he doesn't sit idle." She eased forward, forearms resting on her thighs. "Not once did he ever make a move. A few times, he told me he wasn't the right man for me. He had plenty of opportunities before Nate came into the picture to act on his feelings. Deep down, he knows it wasn't real. The kicker? He didn't fight Nate for me. In fact, he pushed us together. If he was truly in love with me, really wanted me, you know he wouldn't have stood for that."

Okay, her friend had a point. And Amy couldn't argue the logic. Still, Nakos believed, regardless of why, that he loved Olivia and had for years.

"He never kissed me."

Amy's gaze jerked to Olivia's.

"Never kissed me, but he did kiss you." Olivia's brows rose. "That says something."

Yeah, it said the woman he wanted was permanently out of reach, so he went after the next best thing. Amy had no doubt Nakos was attracted to her. That much was evident. But, like she'd told him, it was a physical response. Lust faded, given time.

Speaking of... "I find the timing awfully convenient." Heck, for all Amy knew, this was boredom or desperation on his part.

"Emotions don't flip that quick, Amy. He wouldn't have made a move on you twenty-four hours after I said 'I do' if it was me on his mind. And he doesn't play games." When Amy said nothing, Olivia plowed on. "What happened afterward? You mentioned some tension."

Amy puffed a laugh. There was tension and then there was *t-e-n-s-i-o-n*. "He walked away after the longest *oh crap, what have I done* in the history of mankind. Later, he tried talking to me about it, but I shut it down. Told him we weren't doing this."

"Why?"

"Come on, Liv." Anger and frustration pounded her temples. "His first reaction spoke volumes. I'm not the one he wanted, and I'm not screwing up a lifelong friendship over temporary insanity masked as desire."

Up went Olivia's brows. "So, it's not because you're letting him down easy, not because you don't have feelings for him?"

Sneaky. Real sneaky. Amy expelled a hearty sigh toward the heavens, keeping mum.

"We talked about Nakos, but what about you? What do you want?"

Him. She wanted him. And the longer she let the notion fester, the more she realized he was what she'd wanted all along. But wanting and having weren't the same thing. Even if Olivia had been right about everything, Amy didn't belong with him in any capacity. Period.

"All right." Olivia huffed. "What led up to the kiss?"

"A fight. Or a disagreement, really. He tried calling me out on my feelings and I evaded. He grew irritated and...well, you know."

"Let me get this straight." Olivia ticked off points on her fingers. "He lost control and kissed you. By the way, when was the last time Nakos didn't have all his faculties? Never," she answered without waiting for a response. "He attempted to talk to you about it, but you wouldn't let him. And only after you shut him down did things get weird and the silent treatment began. Do I have the gist?"

Amy rolled her eyes until they thunked the back of her skull. "Yep."

"He said maybe three words in my presence once I discovered he had a thing for me. We eventually worked it out, of course. Almost two weeks, though, and all I got was three words. Five, tops."

Slowly, Amy slid her gaze to Olivia, wondering what she was up to now. "That's more than he's given me."

"No, no, and no. Unlike in my case, he went straight to you when he could've outright ignored the situation. He tried to talk to you, discuss what happened. It was you who put a stop to it. He didn't avoid or deflect. You did." Olivia put her face right in Amy's, her smile wicked. "He's fighting for you. Granted, it's in his warped, slower-than-molasses Nakos kind of way, but that's exactly what he's doing. Knowing him, he's pulling the gentleman card and maintaining space because, in his head, you said no."

Heart pounding, pulse tripping hope shoved into Amy's throat. Wedged there as if it planned on taking up permanent residence. Utterly dangerous to her wellbeing since optimism had rarely worked out for her. Actually, anticipation and wishes and dreams had been quashed so many dang times that she was shocked she was capable of triggering any.

Olivia reached up and tapped Amy's chin, her face still close. "What are you so afraid of? He's not Chris. Nakos is a great man. Why not try? You deserve something good, too."

He deserved the best, and Amy wasn't it. Maybe someday she would be, but she doubted it. Besides, somewhere down the line, she had to stop settling and start believing she could be more than the fallback woman. The leftovers.

A knock sounded, and she glanced over to find Nate in the doorway. Or rather, filling the doorway with his enormousness. Bulge and ink, this guy. And he was smiling with an easiness Amy hadn't witnessed often.

In jeans and a black tee, he leaned against the frame. "Don't tell me I'm missing girl-on-girl action."

Amy snorted. "We can make room for one more."

With a fond shake of her head, Olivia grinned. "Everything okay downstairs?"

He strode in and bent to give her a quick kiss, lingering. The sap was a total goner over her. "Just fine. Nakos is looking for you in the barn."

"Speak of the devil." She eyed Amy and rose from the bed. "Know what? We should go out tonight, the four of us. Nate doesn't have to be back at work at the sheriff's station until Monday, and you and Nakos haven't let loose in forever."

"Whatever you say, baby."

Amy wasn't as blindly compliant. "What are you up to?"

Olivia pressed a hand to her chest and feigned surprise. "Who? Me?" She patted Nate's shoulder on the way to the door. "I'll talk to Nakos about it. Seven? The tavern?" She didn't wait for an answer, just walked out.

"And then there were two. So much for a threesome." Amy sighed. "I heard your honeymoon was wonderful."

He dipped his chin in a nod, then eyed the picture frames by the nightstand. "We should've picked up more of these, but we were worried about getting 'em home."

"I love them. Thank you."

A grunt, and he fingered the copies of the photos on the dresser she'd taken this week. He spread them around, a faint smile lifting the corners of his mouth. "These new?"

"Yep. Took them with the camera you bought me."

He winced, his expression dialing straight to *busted*. "Nakos told you?"

"Yes." Her fingers itched for said camera. The way he stood in profile, all macho maleness while studying the photos with an engaging smile, triggered the contradictions she loved to capture. "I'm not sure what possessed you to do that, but thank you."

The smile flatlined. "It wasn't right, what that asshole did to your things." He looked at her. "Or what he did to you." His hard, golden brown eyes skimmed over her as if searching for physical injures that had long ago healed. "That's a day I wouldn't mind forgetting."

"Me, too." Nate wasn't responsible for Chris's actions any more than it was his job to replace what had been damaged. "At the risk of sounding like a broken record, thank you. For the equipment and for the rescue mission."

He glanced away, his expression indicating he'd gone somewhere else momentarily before drifting back to the dresser. He tapped the pictures. "That's all the thanks I need."

90

Be still her heart. No wonder Olivia was sunk. "She's lucky to have you."

A smile, and he shook his head as if to argue he was the lucky one.

"Hey." She waited for him to look at her. "There's almost no one I love as much as her, no one kinder or more genuine." But they'd broken the mold with Nate. That he could love as deeply as he did, considering not a soul had shown him how before Olivia, only proved his worth. "She's lucky to have you."

Chapter Ten

Nakos had under thirty minutes to shower before meeting everyone at the tavern. Why he'd agreed to go, he hadn't a clue. The very thought of sitting across a table from Amy with her silent treatment and wounded eyes on the menu was not his ideal Saturday evening.

Then again, another night in his house, sleeping in the room right next to hers, wasn't his version of a great time, either. They couldn't go on like this. He was this close to imploding.

At his wit's end, he planned on forcing her to talk to him when they were alone tomorrow and both off work. He rolled his head to stretch his neck as he climbed the stairs in his cabin. As if anyone could force Amy Woods to do anything. Especially him, considering she got him tongue-tied and made his head dizzier than a carousel on heroine just standing in front of him.

At least there would be alcohol involved tonight.

He turned the knob on his bathroom door and halted dead over the threshold. His lungs seized, despite the perfume-scented steam that hit face.

Damp cocoa hair up in a knot. Smooth, fair skin. Pert, pink nipples. Rivulets of water trailing over lush, sweet curves. A small triangle of dark curls between the juncture of...*Amy's thighs.* She turned fully to face him just outside the tub, a towel in her hand and gaze wide.

"Holy shit. I'm sorry." He slapped a hand over his eyes and turned away.

Hihcebe, she was naked. Completely, utterly, beautifully naked.

"I thought you were..." He reached blindly for the door handle, smacking his knuckles on the frame. "...getting ready..." Damn it. Where was the fucking knob? "...at Olivia's." *There.* Praise

Almighty. He slammed the door at his back and slumped against it in the hallway.

Leveled, he heaved air, his skin hot, his blood hotter. Thoroughbreds trampled inside his chest. Never. He'd never erase the image of her naked. Five seconds. That was all. For five seconds, he'd caught a glimpse of a literal wet dream, and he was ruined. Wrecked.

"Um, I was." A shuffle sounded behind the door. "But all my makeup and clothes are here, so she drove me back."

Clothes, she claimed. Yet she didn't...have...any...on. And he'd walked in on her. Because he'd been thinking about her and the mind fuck she'd given him this week, so he hadn't paid attention to the fact that the door had been closed, that she'd possibly be coming out of the shower. Dripping wet.

Mercy, he was hard.

Another shuffle as if she was drying off, and he slammed his lids closed a second time imagining that particular scenario. All that fair, perfect skin. Gorgeous curves and...

Shit. Like, really, *really* naked.

He groaned. "I'm so sorry, Ames."

"No biggie. I should've locked the door."

No biggie? He glanced down at his fly, disagreeing.

It was one thing to acknowledge his attraction, to kiss her and decimate good intentions or to fantasize about how far to take things. It was another entirely to be thrust within reaching distance of the object of his desire and smacked with reality. She was far better than anything he could've envisioned.

Heaven help him, she was achingly beautiful.

The door opened, and because he'd been leaning against it, he lost balance. Scrambling, he grabbed the jamb with both hands and righted himself.

"Can I get by?"

"Yes," he grated and side-stepped into the hall, shocked his legs worked. Keeping his gaze trained to the floorboards, he noted in his peripheral she was dressed. He cleared his throat. "I'm sorry. Again."

"They're just breasts. I'm sure you've seen them before."

Not hers, damn it. And the humor in her sultry voice wasn't calming his arrhythmia. A week with not a word out of her pretty mouth, and what was one of the first things she spouted? *Breasts.* In regards to hers. Because he'd seen them.

This was the sixth realm of hell.

"Give me ten minutes to shower, and we can go." He pivoted on his heels and stalked to his bedroom to get fresh clothes, then made his way back to the bathroom.

Which smelled like her. So did his truck as she rode shotgun. And, for reasons unclear to him, the tavern did, too. Among the scent of cheap beer, stale smoke, and leather, Amy's light perfume remained with him like a shadow. Teasing the crap out of him. Taunting.

He leaned back in his chair at a hightop table next to Nate and ran his fingers up and down the condensation on his glass. Olivia and Amy had taken off for a game of pool to his left, blessedly giving Nakos a semblance of breathing room.

Country blared from a jukebox and a few patrons he recognized from town were dancing on the makeshift stage against the back wall. Stools saddled up to the scarred pine bar were relatively empty for a Saturday, but Meadowlark wasn't that big and it was early.

He ran his gaze over the light wood paneling and neon signs, wishing he was at home. He didn't see the point in being here, nor the scene. Mader's could be any dive in any Podunk blip across the map. Even if Amy weren't front and center in his mind, half the women present were married, a quarter of them too old for his father, and the remainder he wouldn't touch after a full round of vaccines. When he did seek a partner, he typically met up with someone on the reservation, and his last encounter had been more than a year ago.

"Amy's finally using the new camera?" Nate leaned his forearms on the table. "She said you told her it was from me."

Nakos grunted and glanced at the girls by the pool table. A couple of Olivia's ranch hands had joined them. "Yeah, sorry about that. It got her to open the damn thing, though."

"Figure it would go over better coming from you. That's why we lied to her."

One would think. "Nope."

Amy bent over, cue in hand, lining up a shot. Her blue blouse dipped low enough for him to catch the swell of her breasts. *Hihcebe.* He couldn't win.

Refocusing on Nate, he sighed. "She fooled around with it while you and Olivia were gone." He mentioned some of her ideas. "She took a couple pictures of me when I wasn't paying attention. Something about book covers or ads."

Nate chuckled. "You?"

"Just wait. She'll hit you up, too." He took a sip of room temperature draft. "She got Rico to pose shirtless riding a horse at the end of Wednesday's workday. Lined up a couple of the other ranch hands for next week, as well."

"The other guys? Maybe. I can see that. Not you, though."

"I'm not exactly excited, but if it helps her out, I don't care." He shrugged. "Told her she had to keep my face hidden."

"Huh." Nate slowly shook his head, the implication of Nakos being crazy clearly implied. "You're sunk deeper than I thought."

"Remember back when you first got to town and we didn't like each other? Those were good times."

What passed for a smile twitched the ex-soldier's lips. "Calling it like I see it." He studied Nakos for a beat. "You should talk to her about it."

Been there, tried that. Got the t-shirt. And the resulting migraine. "I like my balls where they are."

Nate chuckled, gaze on his beer. "You told me to man up and go for it with Olivia. What's wrong with me returning the favor?"

Nothing, and Nakos was acting like a jackass. Maybe having someone else's input might help. Wasn't like he'd come up with any brilliant insights on his own. "I kissed her." When Nate's gaze shifted to his, he nodded. "I think she sucked my brain right out through my mouth."

Another laugh. "What's the problem?"

"She quit talking to me." Until tonight.

They're just breasts.

Okay, he needed something stronger than beer. ASAP.

At Nate's frown, Nakos elaborated. "She was into it. That much I know."

"Again, what's the problem? Sit her down. Work it out."

Nakos ran his tongue over his teeth. "If you knew her half as well as I do, you'd understand that's about as likely as me becoming leader of the United Nations. Amy only divulges what she deems fit. She has dodge, divide, and distract down to a science."

"Knew I liked her for a reason." Nate grinned. "Sorry. Okay, just kiss her again. Fry her brain cells in retaliation."

He wanted to. Badly. But her excuses kept freezing him immobile. The whole *only his body wanted her* diatribe was... He didn't know. Not exactly accurate, but food for thought. Truth was, he *had* freaked out and it *had been* because it was her he'd kissed. Years of friendship and memories hung in the balance.

The ladies made their way back to the table, and Olivia climbed in Nate's lap. She downed half his beer. "That's orgasmic. I was thirsty."

Nate's grin amped as he looked at her. "Orgasmic? It's watered down and lukewarm."

Claiming the seat next to Nakos, Amy snorted. "Orgasms are a myth. Like good credit scores." When everyone stared at her, stunned into silence, she didn't so much as blink. "What? They are. Only twenty-seven percent of women get off during intercourse. All that freaking hype over three measly seconds of trembling nervous system activity? Please."

After a very long pause, Nate pointed at her. "Someone's been giving it to you wrong."

Olivia nodded her agreement.

Nakos, unable to do much else, shook his head. Amy had been married to the Antichrist for three years, and he very much doubted her ex had been attentive. But Chris hadn't been her first lover. At least, Nakos didn't think so. She'd dated plenty before.

He wondered if this was just her in snark mode or if she truly hadn't had decent sex. Hard to tell with her. And hell if he didn't want to prove her wrong. Repeatedly. All damn night long. Until she couldn't even open her eyes, never mind move.

"Whatever." She hopped off her chair and dug her vibrating cell from her back pocket. "I don't..." Eyes on the screen, her face paled several shades and she went rigid.

Olivia frowned. "What's up?"

"My Uncle Clint is coming for a visit." Her hand trembled as her throat worked a swallow.

"Blech. When?" Olivia peered at the phone.

"I don't know. Kyle just texted." Amy's thumbs went to work in reply.

Nakos's gut bottomed out as her complexion slipped from an insipid shade of white to green. "I don't remember you mentioning him before." More over, why would the uncle elicit this kind of reaction from her?

"My mother's brother. He lives in Texas." Her voice shook almost as badly as her hands. "He doesn't come up very often. A couple times when we were kids and once when Chris and I were married. That was the only time my ex proved useful. He told my parents we wouldn't be around, that we were camping. Since Chris hates familial things, it worked for him."

Olivia shuddered. "Total creep. What were we, like thirteen when I had dinner at your place and he was there?"

"Twelve," Amy breathed, gaze still on her cell. "That was the last visit until the one two years ago."

Glancing between Nate and Nakos, Olivia scrunched her nose. "He reminds me of a used car salesman. Greased hair, too much cologne. He tells foul, lewd jokes. I swear, he spent the whole time staring at me like I was candy. Ugh." She shuddered again.

Nate's gaze hardened to cement. "He did what?" Teeth flashed as he growled.

"Relax. It was years ago. He never touched me. He's harmless, if not disgusting." Olivia looked at Amy. "Still needed a shower afterward."

Regardless of whether he'd laid a finger on Olivia, what kind of sick asshole looked at a little girl that way? Or told filthy jokes to them at their age? Nakos's own temper was reaching critical. No wonder Amy was shaken. Anyone would be uncomfortable as hell with that sort of person around.

"Next week Friday." Amy closed her eyes a beat and re-pocketed her phone. "He'll be up then and is staying with my parents."

"Well, at least there's one good thing about your folks disowning you." Olivia squeezed Amy's hand. "You don't have to play nice. Or see him at all."

"Very true." A deep breath, and her color returned. She resettled on her chair, and since she seemed all right, Nakos's stomach quieted down. "What did we miss while I kicked Liv's butt at pool?"

"Nothing much." Nate flicked Nakos a smirk. "What's this I hear you've taken up an interest in photographing cowboys?"

Her grin was wicked. "And leaning toward tatted ex-soldiers."

Nakos chuckled. "I told you." He gave it under five minutes before the guy said yes.

A shake of his head, and Nate zeroed back on Amy. "No."

"Come on." She wiggled her brows. "You need to be captured on film."

"No."

"Just try it out. One shoot." She batted her lashes. "You bought me the camera, after all. Plus, Olivia will enjoy it."

He glanced at his wife, and his shoulders sank at her nod of agreement. "Traitor." Mouth thin, he looked at Amy once more. Paused. "No showing my face, like you did with him." He jerked a thumb at Nakos.

"That can be arranged." Amy jived in her seat like she knew she had him.

"And I keep my shirt on."

"Off."

"On."

She strummed her fingers on the table. "Partially off. Open chest? Or a tight t-shirt to show that ink and your guns?"

Nate studied her a beat. "Fine. Deal."

"Yay." She did a fist pump and slid her gaze in a once-over as if imagining the shot now. "You're going to be so yummy through my lens."

"Yummy, huh?" Nate frowned and looked at Olivia for a reaction.

Olivia tipped her head. "I agree." She gave him a quick kiss, smiling, and focused on Amy. "Are you going to say yes to Sam?"

Amy shrugged. "Maybe."

Wait. What? "Sam our employee?" Nakos glanced between the ladies. These two switched topics faster than a brush fire got out of hand. "Yes to what?"

"Yep, our Sam. He asked Amy to dinner." Olivia pinned Nakos with a whatcha-gonna-do-about-it glare. "Unless you can think of a reason for her to decline."

Ah, so Amy had told Olivia about the kiss. Great. Perfect. Why didn't she just take up ad space? And no way was Amy dating the ranch hand. Sam was a great worker and nice enough, but hell to the no. Nakos wouldn't stand for it.

Hihcebe. He froze. Nate was right. He was sunk.

"Weird he's worked for you for five years and just now asked me out."

Olivia waved a dismissal. "You were married for three of those. He just broke up with that waitress from the diner."

"Yeah, I suppose." Amy dipped her chin as if considering.

As Nate rubbed his mouth at a poor attempt to hide a grin, Nakos sighed. He got the distinct impression they were trapping him. Which didn't matter because his first gut reaction wasn't something he could control any more than he could control Amy.

Resting his elbows on the table, he looked her dead on. "Do it. Go on a date and have fun." His left eye twitched, and he bit his tongue in order not to retract his statement the second it passed his lips.

Her irritated gaze narrowed while she measured him, but... *Yes.* Yes, yes, and hell yes. Finally, some confirmation. Hurt lay under her blue-green depths as if she despised his response. She clearly didn't want to date the guy and Nakos sure as hell hated the idea.

All week the situation between them had been driving him nuts. Questioning what she wanted. Dissecting his own feelings.

No more. This whirlwind stopped tonight, starting the moment he got her home. He might not come out alive, but it was a risk he was willing to take. It didn't matter how fast or slow he had to go, didn't matter what confusing thing flew out of her mouth.

This chemistry? The undeniable pull? Irrefutable.

The fact he'd never felt anything like it was enough of a green light. He had no idea why she'd thrown roadblocks or was running the opposite way. Her defense mechanisms had been in place from the beginning of their crazy shift. However, he was going to unearth the reasons if it took until his last breath to accomplish the feat.

Because she wanted him, too. And she might be the loose cannon in their pair, but he very much wanted to be the trigger that made her go boom.

"Totally didn't expect you to say that." Olivia glanced at Nakos, Amy, and back again, then did a double-take on Nate. "Why are you grinning?"

Nate scratched his jaw, his expression dialed to *should I or shouldn't I*. "Amy never listens to him. Ever. Actually, ninety-nine percent of the time, she does the opposite of what he says." His brows lifted in a *get-me*.

Digging his thumb and forefinger into his eye sockets, Nakos shook his head. So much for reverse psychology.

"Oh." Olivia straightened. "*Ohhh.*"

He leaned back in his seat, watching Amy's myriad of emotions. Annoyance. Relief. Confusion. Interest. Before she swept into plot mode or agreed to dinner with Sam or any other such thing to render his plan useless, Nakos cut her off. "You ready to head home?"

If the startled widening of her eyes was any indication, the answer was... "No."

He nodded, a smile teasing his lips. "I can wait, *anim*." Oh yeah. He'd wait her out however long she decided to take.

Chapter Eleven

Still rattled over learning her uncle was coming for a visit, Amy hopped out of Nakos's truck and waited for him to unlock the front door to his cabin. Ever since she'd gotten the text from her brother, her stomach had been a twisted, nauseous mess. Memories she'd worked hard to overcome kept shoving to the surface.

The smell of cigar breath and Old Spice.

Rough hands leaving punishing bruises.

Her screams muted by a palm over her mouth.

The pain. The tears. The shame.

She had to get herself under control before Nakos figured out something was wrong. She strode ahead of him and into the house, making a beeline for the stairs. She got over it once, she'd do it again. If she had to remind herself a million times she wasn't a weak, scared little girl anymore, then that's what she'd do. She was stronger than anything life had to dish out, proven by the fact she was still standing.

Dang, but she felt like crumbling.

"Ames." Nakos's feet shuffled behind her and she paused on the bottom step. "I miss you."

Her fingers tightened on the railing, and she slammed her eyes shut, unable to deal with him tonight. At the tavern, he'd watched her like a hawk in that measured way of his that always made it seem like he could read her mind.

Thank God, he couldn't. There were layers of shadows and refuse and hurt and humiliation he'd have to wade through to even get to the innocent person he'd first met that long ago summer day. What she wouldn't give to do it all again, to erase what she'd become in order to be worthy of the affection she often saw in his eyes.

But that was impossible and none of this was his fault. His needs came before hers, and if what he was seeking was her, an end to this rift, then that's what she'd give him.

Swallowing hard, she turned and offered her profile. "I haven't gone anywhere. I'm right here."

"No, you're not." He stepped forward until his boots met the step and they were eye level. "You checked out three months ago and have only offered brief intermittent appearances since. This week?" He pressed a hand to his chest. "This week killed me, *anim.* I miss you."

She closed her eyes a second time and fought the prickling in her sinuses. Tears would upset him more. "I'm sorry," she whispered brokenly. Her putting a stop to whatever had been brewing between them had erected a larger cataclysm instead. The reasons were valid and she wouldn't change her mind, but she would fix their friendship. Somehow. "I'm sorry."

"Don't be sorry. Talk to me." His midnight gaze searched hers. "Tell me whatever dark, horrible things he did so you can get past it and I can get my Ames back."

At first, she thought he *had* read her mind and was talking about her uncle, then realized he'd meant her ex. God. Chris wasn't the problem. At one point, she'd assumed he would be the solution, but she hadn't even been able to make that sham work.

"He didn't do anything to me." Except render her more insignificant, proved she was undeserving of the simplest things. Acknowledgment. Eye contact. Touch. Fidelity. Love. "You know what happened. I'm over it."

Nakos was right, though. This had started with the assault. Because that was the day she'd discovered no amount of backbone or regression or modification would alter reality. Every punch to her face and kick to her ribs and vile thing yelled at her had punctuated the truth.

She was a no one.

"You're not over it." He cupped her shoulders, his thumbs stroking her neck. "If not me, then talk to Nate. He knows about post traumatic stress. Perhaps he can help."

The issue wasn't PTSD, either. She shook her head to relay that to him, unsure what else to say. And he obviously wasn't going to leave it alone.

With a sigh, she wove around him and headed for the kitchen. Any longer under his gentle caress or tender gaze and she'd lose it. "Since you're feeling chatty, I need ice cream."

He muttered a sound of exasperation and followed her. "Since when do you need fortification to have a conversation with me?"

Since he'd started digging instead of observing, that's when. She pulled her emergency pint of mint chip from the freezer, a spoon from the drawer, and went out the kitchen door.

Plopping on the top step of his back deck, she pried the lid off her pint and stared at the horizon. The Laramie Mountains were black shadows against a navy sky littered with stars. The southern pasture stretched ahead, long grass swaying and crackling in a soft breeze. The scent of pine and ozone from the mountains clashed with soil, and she breathed deep.

Until the door behind her closed and the thunk of Nakos's boots drew closer. She dug into her mint chip and kept her eyes forward while he sat next to her. Avoidance, her best friend.

He took off his Stetson and slid the brim through his long, callused fingers, then set it aside. "I'm worried about you." He turned his head and looked at her as his low tone washed over her skin. "I care about you too goddamn much and I'm worried about you."

And...total deflation. He did it to her every time. "I'm all right." She stabbed at the contents of her pint. "I don't have nightmares and I'm not afraid of touch or anything. I'm just trying to get my feet back under me. That's all. I'm okay."

"Forgive me, but I don't believe you." He studied the land, his wide jaw tense and ticking to the beat of her pulse. Such a beautiful, masculine face.

She spooned a healthy serving and held it out for him. "Want a bite?"

He eyed the spoon, then her. "I don't like ice cream."

That's right. She'd forgotten. "I knew you had a flaw somewhere."

Rigidly, he glanced heavenward and then at her as if utterly confounded. "What does that even mean? I'm not perfect."

"No, not at all." She rolled her eyes. The stupid man. Sarcasm dripping, she held up her fingers as she ticked off points. "Your heart's not bigger than the universe. You wouldn't give up everything for someone you care about. You're not the most loyal person ever born. You're afraid to show your emotions. You don't work harder than everyone else." She ran out of fingers and started over since the other hand was occupied holding her melting ice cream. "Your eyes aren't the most perceptive or piercing things known to man, not to mention those thick lashes. Don't even get me started there. Your voice isn't low and coarse and tremble-inducing. The way you walk and carry yourself isn't confident or prey-like in hotness. And your bronzed Trojan body rippled with muscle doesn't scream sex-on-a-stick."

Darn it. She needed to take a page from his playbook and shut up. She jabbed her spoon into her pint repeatedly and stared down, avoiding him. "Totally correct, Nakos. You're not perfect. What was I thinking?"

Silence stretched. Crickets chirped.

He stared holes in her profile like he was burrowing in for the winter and planned to stay in her head indefinitely. She'd tell him not to bother because her mind was a trap of nightmares, but he wouldn't listen anyway.

After a heinous pause, he rubbed his jaw. The scratching of his short whiskers against his palm raked the space between them. "If that's truly how you view me, then why did you push me away when things started evolving?"

Evolving? Yeah, they were progressing right into the Stone Age. "We already discussed this."

"No. You talked circles around me and ran away."

She sighed in frustrated exhaustion. Despite their history, she might consider adapting to his version of evolution if not for two things—how he felt about Olivia and what Amy knew about herself. Olivia had some good theories about the first, but Amy was far from ready to climb aboard that sinking ship. And there was no getting around the second issue. Duct tape and superglue couldn't repair that crap.

Stupid hope threatened to strangle her, though. Time to cap it off. "Do you remember what color dress Olivia wore to prom?"

Amy needed the reminder she was never the one he wanted. If he answered correctly, and she had no doubt he would, she'd stop torturing herself with what-ifs. She'd shove friendship down their throats and ignore the chemistry until he moved on.

He glared at her like he couldn't fathom why she'd ask such a random question, then dug his fingertips into his eyes. "Blue. Dark blue and knee-length. Why?"

Bingo. However, verification only made her belly clench. She should be used to disappointment.

"Here." She passed him the ice cream and stood. "It'll only go straight to my ass." Turning, she forced one foot in front of the other.

"Your dress was green."

The quiet, determined timbre of his tone froze her in place. Facing the door, her back to him, she tried to catch her breath. The fine hairs on her arms rose.

Clothing rustled. His boots vibrated the planks and stopped behind her. "I don't know what name you females call it, but it was green. The color of grass. The material went down to your ankles. Every time you bent over, one of the thin straps fell off your shoulder and you spent half the night tugging it in place. Your shoes were black, your hair was up, and you wore a necklace with a yellow stone in the pendant."

Shit. Oh God, shit. He remembered. And in great detail. Which sent reason number one not to succumb straight out the window.

Trembling, her gaze remained locked onto the mesh screen of the door. Heat coursed through her system and her lungs were one declaration away from collapsing. His presence loomed, sent off its own gravitational pull, and it took everything she had not to turn around.

"Is this about Olivia? My feelings for her?" His feet shifted. "I couldn't help those back then any more than I can the ones for you now. It doesn't mean you were invisible, Ames."

Her eyes fluttered closed, and she couldn't take it. He was killing her with kindness. How many times over how many years had she prayed, hoped, or begged for just those words to escape his mouth? For him to see her as a woman? There had been safety in that, though. Dreams never to be fulfilled, so she didn't have to worry about regret or guilt.

And he'd spoken about his attraction to Olivia like it was past tense. No more.

"Ames, I—"

Whirling, she grabbed the pint from him and strode inside.

He cursed and followed. "What did you mean by the ice cream would go to your...ass? What's wrong with it the way it is?"

As if she'd discuss her weight problem. He of the abs and gluts and biceps wouldn't understand. Mortification knew no bounds.

Keeping herself busy, she rinsed the spoon and set it in the sink, then capped the mint chip and put it in the freezer. Hands on his hips, he watched her every move.

The sanctity of her bedroom in mind, she walked out of the kitchen on shaking legs and was determined to get to the stairs before he leveled her again. The footsteps trailing her said he wasn't near done with this discussion.

"You were right, *anim*."

Damn it, damn it, damn it.

Again, she halted on the bottom stair. Sighed. Struggled for guidance. She settled for turning to face him.

"This shift between us is physical. My body wants yours, and the magnetism is only getting stronger the longer we pretend it doesn't exist." Slowly, like he did everything else, he walked closer until he'd eaten half the distance with his long legs. "Accidentally walking in on you after your shower knocked me from in lust with those curves of yours to in love. The need is fierce. Is that what you want to hear?"

Her damp panties said yes. Her conscience yelled no. Wisely, her mouth kept mum.

"You're forgetting our friendship, though." He eyed her, jaw set. "My head and heart are a factor. We wouldn't be standing here otherwise. So no, this isn't just physical. And I don't get intimate without some kind of connection. I'm not wired that way."

At a loss, she bit her lip and looked at him. Really looked. It seemed he was taking some kind of stand, and the fact she was it rendered her mute.

All her life, she'd wanted this very thing. Acceptance. Notice. Someone to fight for her. She'd never gotten it. Not from her parents, who wanted a son and birthed a daughter instead. Had she been a boy, Kyle wouldn't have been conceived. They'd spent her entire childhood and teen years pointing out her faults, tossing bible verses at her, and skimming over her with contempt. She got the impression Kyle had stuck with her out of duty. None of her lovers, nor her ex-husband, had bothered to try. After all, she was disposable. A one-time use cluster of tissue and bones.

Aunt Mae, Olivia, and Nakos had been the exception. Yet, even with them, she often felt the odd one out. Like perhaps her remaining in their world stemmed from habit more than desire.

She'd learned to put up a great front and pretend she didn't need a warrior, that she could slay her own monsters, but the truth was in her failures. She was a walking, talking, breathing lie contrived of desperation and loneliness. And if Nakos kept this up, he'd be dragged into her pain vault with no hope of escape. That was her gift.

His dark eyes bore into hers, pleading, seeking, framed by long lashes that tended to flutter when emotional. The hard set of his jaw and thin lips bespoke his aggravation. Yet his stance remained open, relaxed, like he was simply waiting for her to come around. Change her mind and leap into his arms. Forget all the why-nots and press up against him.

Finally, his brow furrowed as if he'd reached a conclusion or snapped a piece into place. "You always make me nervous." The slight tilt of his head and unsure tone indicated he was trying the sentence on for size.

She reared. Blinked. "What? We've known each other since—"

"We were nine. Yeah, I know." He shook his head in disbelief. "Still, you do. You make me nervous. I felt it the first time I saw you on that tire swing as a kid. It got stronger in our teens and it's constant now." He let out a quick exhale. "There's this...flutter in my gut whenever you walk into a room or I catch you out of the corner of my eye in passing or even if someone mentions your name."

He stepped forward two paces and stopped. "There's almost no one I'm more comfortable around than you. Especially considering our open dialog. But there you have it. All these years between us and you can still make me nervous." His hand raised to adjust his hat in a common gesture, but he must've realized he'd taken it off and ran his fingers through the ponytail at his nape instead. "*Hihcebe*," he muttered. "It's been there all along."

His gaze flicked to hers and held. Midnight torment and dark passion. "It's been there all along," he firmly repeated. "Maybe I wasn't ready to acknowledge the sensation or perhaps, deep down, I knew this was significant. My bet is it took me this long because you tend to steamroll me with your witty comebacks and I can't ever think clearly."

He straightened suddenly and huffed. "But you're not speaking now, are you? You've been uncharacteristically quiet."

What the heck was she supposed to say? If she was reading him correctly, he'd just claimed an attraction had been present forever. Which couldn't be true.

Irrational happiness shuffled her synapses around and tried to take root. But she stomped that crap dead. Even if she trusted the emotion, it didn't matter. She would never—*could never*—be with him. She loved him too much, for too many years, to ever assume the day would come she deserved him.

"Say something, *anim*."

Angel. How she wished he'd stop calling her that. It only made the guilt churn harder and her hope refuse to go quietly into the good night where it belonged. Out of reach.

She rubbed her forehead. "I think I should've cut you off after the first beer."

Up went his brows. He huffed a rough laugh. "I only had one and didn't finish it. Try again."

To think, she'd gotten turned on by Alpha Nakos not two weeks ago. He was very dangerous when this side came out to play.

Fine. Abort, then. She turned on her heel and...made it nowhere. Fast.

One-hundred and ninety pounds of hot, hard male pressed against every inch of her from behind. He wrapped a solid arm around her waist, another banding her chest, and held her to him. His lips caressed the shell of her ear, his breath warm, and a full-body tremble tore through her. That amazing scent of outdoors and denim and earth she associated with him enveloped her at the same moment a strange sense of safety nailed her midsection.

She whimpered. Sweet baby Jesus in the manger. She used to chastise women who thought with their girly bits, letting lust rule over common sense. Having never experienced it herself, she'd assumed she was incapable and better off for it. But this carnal heat and sweet ache was addicting. Ten seconds, and she was already in need of rehab.

Turning her around, he backed her to the entry hall, palms planted beside her shoulders. He took a leisurely, drawn-out perusal of her face and nodded. "That's what I thought."

And, God save her. He aligned their bodies again by leaning in, this time from the front, and two toned biceps straining against the seams of his t-shirt caged her face. The cut muscle of his torso held her in place and her head thunked the wall.

"Your heart is pounding against my chest, your breathing is labored, and your mermaid eyes are dialed to gone, baby, gone. You want me, and I'm going mad with wanting you." He brushed his nose to hers and dipped his chin. His lips grazed her throat, and she trembled. Again. Or still. "I don't know what's going on in that gorgeous head of yours or what excuses you've compiled, but I'm done tiptoeing around. If it takes me until we're eighty and in side-by-side rocking chairs, I'm going to wear you down."

While her pulse went spastic, he looked at her, his lips hovering millimeters from hers. Watching her, he grabbed her thigh and brought her leg around his waist, then thrust into her. She gasped as his hard length ground against her core, and even through their jeans, it was better than any contact she'd had with anyone else.

He groaned, long and loud. "That's what you do to me. At night while I try to sleep, during work, driving my truck, riding the horses, or making a damn sandwich in my kitchen. One thought of you, one whiff of your lingering perfume, and that's all it takes, *anim.*"

His heavy gaze darted between her eyes, and the only thing keeping her upright was being trapped between the wall and a...hard place. Her brain cells went poof. Her breasts ached. Her core wept. Her organs puddled to goo. And he just stared, calm and controlled on the surface, but he pulsed as if the animal inside needed escape.

Another groan, and his mouth crashed against hers. He pried her lips apart with his and his tongue drove inside. Stroking. Swirling. Coaxing. Dominating. The patient side of his personality eked through with the unhurried caress and exploration, but his body was another matter. A contradiction. Shallow grinding and rigid muscles and ragged inhalations through his nose.

Putty. He'd turned her into putty.

Nipping her lower lip, he lifted his head, his sleepy gaze settling on hers once more. Ten distinct fingertips gripped her

111

backside, dug in, and retracted, only to have his palms cup her in their place. "Oh yeah. Prepare yourself. Tomorrow, it's on."

Chapter Twelve

A tray balanced on his forearm, Nakos paused outside Amy's bedroom. Unless she was changing, she always left the door open, even while sleeping. He would've thought living with a man, despite having known him all her life, would make her uncomfortable not having a measure of privacy. Yet every time he passed by, it remained open. He wondered if it had something to do with her attack, if enclosed places scared her.

He stared at her, asleep in bed under a mound of blankets. Only her face was uncovered, and early morning light bathed her profile. She had one hand tucked beneath her head and her dark lashes fanned her cheeks. At least when she slept the strain he often found in her expression finally eased. Peaceful, almost.

A shake of his head, and he stepped deeper into the room. He'd been in the habit of calling her angel lately. The word had flown out of his mouth the first time, unbidden, as if by no control of his own. It was accurate, though. She was a take-no-prisoners, hear-me-roar woman, but under all that backbone and attitude was a heart too big to measure. A side she rarely allowed others to witness and he swore she viewed as a weakness.

He hadn't realized it until last night, but she'd been taking care of him and Olivia a long time. In her typical twisted way and without either of them knowing it, but that's just what Amy had done. Put others' needs and desires before hers, seemingly in spite of her own personal contentment.

To him, she had been a kind of saving grace, so the angel moniker fit. Plus, she was gorgeous. Not that she didn't have a beautiful soul, too, but why she was so defensive left him at a loss. Half the night had been spent staring at his ceiling and calculating guesses. The twist in his gut and clamp around his windpipe were a testament to how much he hated the answers he'd assumed. Every action and reaction from her was as if she didn't trust happiness. Like she didn't deserve it.

Last evening, he'd chased her from the living room, outside, to the kitchen, and back again, shooting down her excuses for not acting on the attraction. Yet still, she'd stood there before him with wounded eyes wrapped in hope. And hadn't given in. It wasn't until he'd backed her against the wall and took the initiative that she'd responded.

Craziest part of all? Her submission. Just like she'd done the first time he'd kissed her by the tree, she'd handed him the reins and conceded. It was such a direct contrast to her temperament that he would've sworn she was messing with him if he hadn't been right there with her. Seen her flushed cheeks. Heard her ragged breaths. Felt her heart pounding. Tasted the desire on her tongue.

He didn't know what the hell was going on, what her reservations were, but he was going to find out. Based on how she'd behaved in the couple instances they'd been intimate, he knew his plan would work. He despised games, and if this was any other woman, he'd accept the loss and move on. However, there was no doubt in his mind she wanted him in return, and since this was Amy, he'd fight.

Setting the tray on the nightstand, he crouched and stared at her red lips, parted in sleep. An all too tempting mouth that was as lush as the sweet curves of her body. Her porcelain skin tone warmed in the morning light and her scent clung to the sheets, filled the room. He itched to run her cocoa strands through his fingers, but he denied the urge and left them spread over her pillow.

Hihcebe, the ache she instilled inside him. Insane. Potent. The revelation he'd gleaned last night hit him all over again. Had he been ready to accept it, he might've realized it sooner. This awareness, the desire, had been there all along, just like he'd told her. And denying it was no longer an option.

"Morning, Ames." He smiled. She was going to be mad. Confused, defensive, and mad as hell. "Hey, *anim*. Wake up."

A tiny wrinkle merged between her brows before she peeked one eye open. The other swiftly followed, and then all that blue-green landed on him. "It's Saturday. We're not working."

True. He and Olivia traded every other weekend tending to the horses, and unless they were in wheat harvest season or the steer and

114

sheep needing relocating to a new pasture, the guys typically had off. To think, he'd been nervous having two straight days alone with Amy. Now? Not so much. Anticipation clawed his gut.

"I know." He smiled wider, enjoying her bafflement and the husky tone of her morning voice. "It's time to wake up anyway. We have plans."

"No, we don't."

"Oh yes, we do."

Her eyes narrowed a fraction. "It's rude to confuse me before caffeine."

"I took care of that." He pointed to the tray on her nightstand. "Coffee."

Lifting her head, she eyed the plate of eggs, toast, and fruit beside the coffee. "What is that?"

"Breakfast in bed."

Slowly, her gaze dragged back to him, suspicion narrowing her lids to slits. "Why?"

"I told you last night, Ames. It's on." Damn, he wanted to kiss her. He settled for a quick one on her forehead.

She inhaled at the contact. Hard. "What do you mean, it's on? What is *it* and why is said *it* on?"

Shaking his head, he chuckled low in his throat. "Drink your coffee." He grabbed the file he'd brought up on her tray and rounded the bed. She trekked his movement until she had to roll on her back to follow him. He sat on the mattress beside her, back against the headboard, and opened the file. Pulling a pen from his pocket, he stuck it in his mouth while he read. Without glancing up, he mumbled, "It's going to get cold if you don't drink it soon."

"What are you doing?"

Tongue in cheek, he studied forms. "Olivia wants me to head to Casper and check out a horse we might buy. I'm reading the vet report and history before you and I go out there." He grinned around the pen, then put it aside lest she take it from him to use as a weapon.

"Me? Why would I go?"

"Because I'd like to spend the day with you and I intend to take you out to dinner afterward." He purposely left the term "date" from the equation. Better to mention that in a public setting where she couldn't kill him.

That got her to sit up. Impatiently, she shoved hair behind her ears. "We'll circle back to that firm no in a minute. I meant, what are you doing in my room?"

"Drink your coffee. You'll be less irritable and confused."

"Nakos." Her growl went straight to his balls and tugged.

He tossed the file on the blankets, straddled her hips, and palmed the headboard by her shoulders, trapping her. "I tried to get you in a caffeinated state first. Just remember that." He studied her wide, unblinking eyes and flushed cheeks, fighting the barbaric urge to deepen that blush. "The *it* I referred to is you and me, and the *on* is in reference to moving forward. Because we are, *anim*. From this point on, we're doing this. Period."

Shallow pants had her breasts rising and falling, her erect nipples poking his chest through their shirts. And the material of hers was very, *very* thin. Deer-in-headlights battled with oh-my-God in her expression.

There it was again. Surrender. Like she had zero idea what to do with the fact someone was interested in her. He wondered if that was target specific to him or in general.

"This is a really bad idea, Nakos."

Her whispered plea nearly did him in. Regardless, he didn't yield. "So you've said. But your body's response belies your words." He traced a path across her throat with his finger, gaze following the movement. He was going to spend an hour alone on that patch of skin right there in the not too distant future. "Your pulse is thumping hard." He lifted his gaze to hers. "Look me in the eye and tell me you don't want me."

She met his gaze all right, but she said nothing. Helpless desperation looked back at him, shone in her eyes, and he knew right then and there he'd do everything in his power to find out what made her so wary she couldn't trust even him.

Hell, he'd die before hurting her. After all these years, how did she not know that?

His instincts said claim, but he leaned forward and kissed her gently, taking her mouth in a sweep of his lips that had her uneven breath mingling with his.

Three times now he'd expected fire and brimstone, but was met with languid and fluid heat instead. Though she followed his commands, let him set the pace, she kissed with the side of her personality she tried to hide. Tender. Vulnerable. Compassionate. That she was letting him see that much only turned him on more.

He lifted his head, keeping his eyes closed while he lingered. "I think you get my point."

Before he became incapable of pulling away, he kissed the tip of her nose and rolled back to his side of the bed. Spine against the headboard, he reached for the file and forced himself to read the documents. Or pretended to.

It took her long moments, but she removed the coffee from the tray and studied the cup, then took a sip. She eventually worked her way up to the fruit, leaving the eggs and toast untouched.

He watched her out of the corner of his eye, hoping she'd say something. Yes, she drove him nuts with her sharp wit. Hell yes, she confused him nearly every second of the day with her tangents. That was what made her unique. Her snark and humor and gumption were all a part of her genetic makeup and as distinct as her. The quiet pensiveness was nice, too, but he didn't want to trade one for the other.

Maybe that was it. Other lovers or her ex had tried to tame her. Why, he hadn't a clue. She was perfect the way she was, kept him on his toes. Who'd want to switch animation for bottled placidness? The day he attempted to quash her spirit would be a cold one in hell.

She set her fork beside the plate. "Why did you bring me breakfast in bed?"

The better question was... "Why act like the notion's preposterous?"

Though she didn't look at him, the way she studied the comforter implied that was exactly what she thought. Instead of answering, she rose and collected the tray. "Are you sure you want me to go with you? I think it would be wiser if I didn't."

"I'm sure."

She bit her lip, gaze on her uneaten food. "How long before we have to leave?"

"An hour. There's no rush."

She nodded and headed for the door, but he called her name to stop her.

"Have you never had breakfast in bed before?" Three years of marriage, and not once on their anniversary? What about as a kid when she'd been sick or something?

"Let me shower. Give me thirty minutes and I'll be ready." She turned again, totally avoiding him.

"Amy, leave the tray." When she paused but didn't comply, he stood and met her in the doorway. He took the damn thing from her and placed it on the dresser, then tucked his finger under her chin to force her to look at him. "I'm allowed to do nice gestures, am I not?"

She blinked up at him like he'd spoken Vulcan and the word "nice" didn't compute.

Hihcebe. It really was a foreign concept for her. He didn't know whether to be pissed off or gutted.

Either way, he had the strongest urge to drive to the prison where the Antichrist was spending the next fifteen to twenty and relocate the bastard's teeth. Then again, her parents weren't exactly pleasant people, either. He hadn't spent all that much time with them, but their behavior at the wedding spoke volumes. He couldn't recall if he'd ever heard them utter a kind sentiment in her direction.

"I'm not them." He smoothed her hair with both hands. "I'm not the men you've dated, the asshole you married, or your tactless folks. I'm not them, Ames."

She stared at his chest, her throat working a swallow. "I know."

He ducked to meet her eyes. "Do you?"

A deep breath, and she looked away. As if an afterthought, she pointed toward the hallway. "I'm going to shower now. Just to be clear in case there was any misunderstanding and you planned to walk in on me again."

"Hilarious." He stepped back, though, glad she was acting somewhat normal.

After she'd disappeared into the bathroom, he remained where he was, thinking about the past hour. Since she'd ceded control in all things intimate, at least so far, he'd figured he'd just bowl her over and chip away at her reserve. Except her shock and awe this morning added a whole new element he hadn't anticipated.

It seemed no one had ever courted her. Archaic as the term was, respect and decency weren't altogether dead. He didn't do a lot of dating himself, but compliments and attention to his partner were his usual operandi. The way Amy had responded would imply she hadn't had even that much. He had to wonder how the Antichrist

118

had moved past first base, never mind gotten her to say yes to his marriage proposal.

He was the best I was going to get...

Her words from the night of the wedding came back to him, and he rubbed the twinge of pressure in his chest. He'd known her marriage had been mostly temperate, judging by the things she'd said, and it had ended in hostility. It never crossed his mind she'd been...neglected, though. Add in the fact she'd thought that asshole was her best option, and it proved the disregard predated Chris moving to Meadowlark. Going all the way back to her parents and previous boyfriends, no doubt.

Mind blown, Nakos grabbed the file and tray, then headed downstairs to the kitchen. He didn't know how, but he was going to fix this. Tossing the food she hadn't eaten, he rinsed the dishes, his mind a riot. With that task complete and hands on his hips, he glanced around, trying to conjure ideas. Solutions.

His gaze landed on the shallow windowsill above the sink and the flower she'd set there. A couple days ago, she'd spent thirty minutes taking pictures of it. Something about light and dust motes and color. The yellowish petals were wilted and the leaves on the stem were dried. But it gave him a starting point.

Snatching her camera bag off the table, he shoved his Stetson on his head and his feet into cowboy boots. He went outside and around the side of the house to a wildflower patch, the sun warm on his skin. Cicadas buzzed while he took stock.

The field had been around since his parents lived on the ranch and he'd never paid it much mind. Yellow, purple, pink, red, blue, and white petals in various shapes and sizes blew gently in the breeze. His mother would know their names, but the knowledge was wasted on him. He picked two of every color until he had a decent bunch, then strode to his truck. He set Amy's bag on the floor by the passenger seat and laid the flowers on top.

Leaning against the cab, he crossed his arms and waited for her. Letting the scent of grass and soil settle him, he tipped his face toward the sun and breathed deep. Cooped inside too long and he tended to go crazy. He'd worked the ranch yesterday, but last night had been tense and this morning an eye opener. Just stepping outside again calmed his errant thoughts and the incessant trip of his heart.

Damn, but Amy had him on edge. Every cell in his body wanted her. She called to him in a way no other woman had before, and it had hit him so fast, he couldn't grab a shred of focus if he attempted the task with both hands and a lasso. The lifelong friendship and how much he cared about her muddled the physical aspect with the emotional one. Every declaration from her or realization on his end was destroying him atom by atom.

He hadn't been joking when he'd admitted to her what it had been like for him growing up. Even in this day and age of equality, many of the Arapaho still viewed things as them versus the white man. Not an animosity, per se, but a subconscious tremor below the surface. History clashing against modern advances.

For him, the only time he'd felt safe, normal, or not judged had been with his folks or in Amy's presence. Olivia brought peace, sure, but Amy took that beyond a superficial level and made it a state of mind. A way of life. Day by day, month by month, year by year, she'd built upon that initial sensation. He was so accustomed to it, so submerged, he hadn't noticed the significance until other emotions rose up to suffocate him.

Truth was, he didn't think he'd be half as comfortable in his own skin or have a quarter of his confidence if he'd never met her. He'd been raised by two quiet, loving parents who'd taught him how to stand on his own. That had carried over when they'd left the reservation to work at Cattenach Ranch. Yet it was Amy who'd shown him there was more to the world than tending land, more to him than being a simple rancher.

Brave, broken Amy.

Guilt shoved around in his stomach. If he'd realized his feelings sooner, could he have stopped her before she'd made the mistake of getting married? Could he have done something earlier about this warped view she seemed to have of herself? Most of all, could they have been together all this time instead of wasting it in ignorance?

He'd never put much stock in what-ifs and could-have-beens. It served no purpose. He couldn't help but feel responsible, though. He was her friend. He'd go as far as to say she was his best friend, and the thought of her hurting in any way slashed his insides to shreds.

The porch door slammed with a clack and he watched her descend the steps toward him, his heart somewhere in the vicinity of his throat. She wore skinny jeans that molded to her interstate of legs and a loose yellow top that hung off one shoulder. Her hair was tied up in a knot, wisps framing her face, and she'd foregone makeup. He much preferred her natural than how she'd been done up at the tavern last night. She didn't need cosmetics.

Stopping in front of him, she gave him a once-over. "Are you okay?"

"No." Why lie? He widened his stance and grabbed her hips, drawing her to stand between his legs while he continued to lean against the truck.

"What's wrong?"

He didn't know where to start, or even if he should, so he brushed a wild strand of hair from her face and let his fingers linger on the ends. Soft. All of her was soft. Her voice, her skin, her body. Hard as she seemed, he knew the truth.

"Nakos?"

Letting out a breath, he met her gaze. Her mermaid eyes were a blow. Always. But in the sunlight and inches from him, he got sucked in by the potency of their color. Expressive, too. Typically, it was his first line of defense with her, checking her eyes. Sometimes it was the only way to gauge her at all. His gaze roamed her face, the fair tone and arched brows, before settling on her mouth. Her lips had a naturally dark hue and a pouty shape.

"You're beautiful." Distracted, he ran the pad of his thumb across her lower lip.

She caught his wrist, her expression implying he'd insulted her somehow.

Hihcebe. Don't tell him no one had ever said that to her before, either. "You are."

Her nostrils flared as she closed her eyes. Shook her head. When she opened them, torment thrummed from her and punched him with the aftershocks. She stepped away. "I'm staying home. I'll see you when—"

Fingers in her belt loops, he hauled her right back. "Have I ever lied to you?" He wasn't expecting a response, but he paused anyway. "You all but called me perfect last night, listed several admirable qualities you claimed I have. Am I not allowed to return the favor?" He tilted his head while she looked everywhere but at him. "I could give a shit what your folks or ex or anyone else has

121

drummed into you. I don't lie and I don't say things for the sake of filling silence. You're beautiful. To me, you're beautiful, Ames."

After a tense beat, she deflated and eyed him warily. "Thank you."

Thank Almighty. It was a start.

"You're welcome." However, his relief was short-lived after he straightened and opened the passenger door. She merely stared at him, unmoving. "Are you coming?"

"What are you doing?"

"Holding the door for you."

"Okay," she drew out slowly and stepped closer, only to freeze again. "What's that?"

He bit back a sigh. Barely. "Flowers."

"For what?"

Apparently, they'd landed back in kindergarten and were playing the "how come" game. He called upon all the patience he had in reserve. "For you, *anim*. They're for you."

Chapter Thirteen

The drive to Casper took just under ninety minutes. While Nakos spent quite a few hours with the prospective horse and talking to the breeders, Amy wandered around, snapping pictures. She'd gotten some great shots by the time Nakos was ready to head out.

"There's a family restaurant right up the road." He glanced at her from behind the wheel, then back to the two-lane highway. "We can do an early dinner. I'd rather take you somewhere nicer for our first date, but I've been stomping around a farm all day."

Date? There he went again. First, breakfast in bed, followed by the beautiful comment and flowers. Now, dinner out. She couldn't hack it, not this take charge side of him, nor the consideration. It was one thing when they were friends and the occasional slips could be chalked up to placating. Dating was entirely different.

Unsure how to respond, she glanced out the passenger window as trees and hills whizzed by in a blur. Dating led to sex. She'd been with other men before Chris, but she had zilch for experience. Intimacy was incredibly uncomfortable for her, and since it had rarely been pleasurable, she had no skills, either. Most of the time, she'd laid there, doing what she'd been told.

She had little strength when it came to Nakos. His kiss alone cindered her brain cells. A first in her book. She'd tried to summon the courage and wherewithal to tell him no, remember why them together was an epically bad idea, but she lost all sense near him. Worse, was his determination. He'd obviously made the decision they were going for it, and she'd never change his mind. He could be so hard-headed and obstinate when he wanted.

Halfway through the day, she'd come to the conclusion she'd just go along with whatever he had in mind, let this attraction run its course. Fighting him would only encourage him and give her a headache. If they ever got to the take-their-clothes-off stage and had sex, he'd quickly learn she'd never satisfy him. Even Chris had sought it elsewhere. Nakos's curiosity and desire would fizzle, peter out, and die a quick death.

Except, he kept trying to throw chivalry into the mix. Why couldn't he just strip her naked, get his jollies, and have a blinding morning-after insight like every other guy? It would speed things along and she'd be less likely to get more attached.

Dang, she was so worried their friendship would suffer, though. All she had was Kyle, Olivia, and Nakos. And really, her brother was family. If things went horribly south with Nakos, Amy would be the one abandoned. He wasn't the type to get ugly in a breakup, but their situation was unique. The uncomfortable tension alone would unnerve him. Not only did he work for Olivia, they were close, and he'd developed a bond with Nate, too. Olivia would side with Nakos if it came down to it, if forced to choose, and where would that leave Amy?

Almost no family and zero friends. Hell, nowhere to live.

"Does that work for you?" His hoarse, low tone filled the cab. "I'd really prefer to take you somewhere outside of Meadowlark for a change."

Definitely better for his reputation if he wasn't seen around town with her. Hanging out was a vast cry from a one-on-one meal. People would talk.

"That's fine." She pressed her temple to the window, sick to her stomach. Most of all, she didn't want to hurt him. Her love for him spanned almost two decades and there was nothing she wouldn't do to make him happy. She'd gladly live on the streets and dumpster dive for scraps after this relationship ended if eradicating her presence from his life was what he needed. "We skipped lunch. I bet you're hungry."

"All you've eaten today is fruit, and that was hours ago."

Yeah, well...she probably wasn't going to keep much down, regardless of what was on the menu.

Ten minutes later, he pulled into the parking lot of a nondescript restaurant and she almost laughed as they were seated by a hostess. Nakos had been worried about taking her somewhere nice. He'd be shocked to learn this place was several bars above anywhere Chris had taken her. Before him, she'd never been on a date. Not an official one. She'd hung out with previous boyfriends, but nothing that constituted an actual date.

124

"What can I get you to drink?"

Suddenly nervous, Amy smiled at the server. "Just water, please."

Nakos ordered a cola and eyed her over the menu when the waitress walked away. He'd taken his hat off and set it on the booth beside him, so his face wasn't partially in shadow anymore. Those black eyes studied her intensely and it amped her anxiety. It wasn't like he was a stranger, but she didn't know how to behave around him all of a sudden.

She glanced around for reprieve. Since it was only four o'clock, the place wasn't hopping, but several of the white lacquer tables and booths were occupied. Flower print wallpaper covered the walls and vague prints of roses were scattered about.

"You are going to order something, aren't you?" He jerked his chin at the laminated menu beside her silverware. "You haven't looked at it."

To appease him, she picked up the menu and skimmed the options. She had very little cash on her and she'd just made a loan payment, thus her account was low. Dinner out was not in her budget. He'd never let her pay anyway, and it wasn't like she was hungry. "You've been nosy about my meal habits lately."

"Because you don't eat enough."

Refusing to look at him, she stared as words blurred on the page. "I'm on a diet."

He slapped his menu on the table. "What the hell for?"

And this was why she'd tried skating around the conversation with him. "Typically, one diets to lose weight. If you must know, I'm trying to drop a few pounds. And it's rude for men to discuss such things with women."

"You've already lost more than a few the past couple months." His index finger curled around the top of her menu and tugged it down, forcing her to look at him. Irritation tightened his mouth. "You don't need to diet."

The waitress returned with their drinks and asked what they wanted. Nakos ordered a burger and fries, then zeroed in on Amy as if in challenge.

"I'll have a cobb salad, please." Once the waitress was gone again, Amy changed the previous subject before he could insert more of his two cents. "Are you going to buy the horse?"

He studied her for the longest time, dissecting and picking and invading. Finally, he sighed. "Probably. I have to talk to Olivia, but the horse has good lineage, a gentle temperament, and he's healthy. Young, too." The strain bracketing his eyes and mouth eased while he paused, gaze locked on hers. When he spoke again, his voice held a sad note. "You don't have to change, Ames. There's nothing wrong with your weight or anything else. Did he say something to you? Your ex? Because you shouldn't listen to a thing that flies out of his mouth. Believe me, not him."

"That's been my problem all along. I believed him." Not just Chris, but her parents and everyone who shouldn't matter. They didn't care about her. Her gaze drifted away, lost and unseeing. "I believed him when he said he loved me, wanted to marry me. When he claimed to pay the mortgage or bills on time. That he was just at a poker game with friends, even though he always came home smelling like perfume and his shirt was buttoned wrong. I fell for every lie and believed him. Such an idiot," she muttered. "That's the worst part. I fell for it, for him. I was stupid enough to think he truly wanted me."

In the odious silence that hung, she glanced at him. Fists clenched on the table, jaw working a grind, he stared out the window. Not a solitary muscle moved or twitched, but the tendons and veins in his neck bulged.

She swallowed. "What are you thinking about?"

"Murder." As if he had to force himself to do so, his gaze slid to hers. "I didn't know he cheated on you along with everything else."

That had been the least of Chris's offenses in her book. The rejection and betrayal had stung, but compared to his infidelity, the insults or ignoring her outright had lashed harder. She should've kept her mouth shut. Now Alpha Nakos was donning his metaphorical brass knuckles, in full protection mode.

"I don't blame him for that part." She shrugged when his midnight eyes narrowed to menacing slits. "I don't. Honestly, I suck at sex."

He blinked. Several times. "He tell you that lie, too?"

"No." Yes. She straightened her silverware. "I..." God. Talk about embarrassing, but it wasn't the worst idea to inform him of her inefficiencies. Maybe he'd get the hint and back off before damage was done to their friendship. "I'm incapable of having an orgasm."

There. Now it was out there, floating in the air and settling in his head. If her face got any hotter, she'd wind up with a third degree burn.

He flattened his hands on the table. "Ever?" His gaze bore into her, but she didn't respond. "You've never...?" He cleared his throat. "Not even by yourself?"

Great. They were going to discuss masturbation. "Not often. It takes a really long time for, well..." She never wanted to die so badly in all her life. And there had been a lot of instances when she'd wished to be swallowed up into nothing.

"Was he your first?"

A dry laugh scraped her throat. "No. I lost my virginity younger than most and—"

"How young?"

The clipped question caught her off guard. No way, no how was she having that conversation. "That's not the point. I've been with others and still nothing. Damaged goods, Nakos. Like I said, I don't blame Chris. You should walk also before we get any deeper."

He offered a slight shake of his head, but the move seemed more involuntary than argumentative. "Is that why you've been fighting the idea of us? Some misguided worry of not satisfying me?"

It definitely made the top ten list. Right above this-will-ruin-her-when-it-ends and just below she-wasn't-good-enough-for-her-ex, never-mind-Nakos.

"Why didn't you say something sooner?"

She rubbed her eyes, frustrated as shit. "When, Nakos? At sixteen when we went to the homecoming bonfire with the football team? Or how about during graduation with all fifty-five of my classmates around? I know. I should've done it at twenty-two when Olivia announced you as her foreman. Can't you picture it? *Hey, Nakos. Congratulations. By the way, I can't get off in bed.* Be serious. We were never a romantic option. Why bother?"

"We're an option now, and we've been alone countless times. If I had known—"

"You would have what? Pitied me much sooner? Fought the attraction harder?"

"Done everything in my power to prove you wrong." Elbows on the table, he leaned forward, fire darkening his already black eyes. "You responded to me. You're not damaged goods or defective. Obviously, your previous partners didn't have a lick of patience. Just because you take longer to get there doesn't mean you can't, *anim*."

Mary Mother, her girly bits wept. She clenched her thighs, desperately wanting to try, but history proved an orgasm was too much to hope for. Granted, none of her lovers had turned her on near as much as him, but hot and bothered didn't equate to *oh yes, please* while going at it.

"Here you go. A cobb salad and burger with fries." Plates were set in front of them. "Can I get you anything else?"

Since Nakos's heated glare was on Amy and he didn't appear interested in responding to the waitress, she smiled at the woman. "No, thank you. It looks wonderful."

"Enjoy."

She watched the server until the woman disappeared behind the counter, then Amy leveled her gaze back on Nakos.

His expression went from interested to carnal in one flutter of his impossibly thick lashes. "Those guys you were with? They missed out. There's nothing more rewarding than knowing a woman is satisfied when you're together. It heightens the experience. Challenge accepted." His gaze searched hers. "What?" he added when she lifted her brows in shock. "Were you expecting me to cut and run? I told you before. I'm not them."

Because she had no clue what to say, they ate in silence, then squared the bill and got in his truck. Halfway home, she couldn't stand the quiet anymore. Need battled with curiosity and coiled in her stomach, knotted her muscles.

God, she was just stupid enough to believe him. That all she required was patience and the right man to get there. Darn hope, anyway. It had never landed her anywhere pleasant.

She watched the picket fences and landscape rush past the window, recalling the original reason for their trip. The fact Olivia sent Nakos to check out potential livestock proved her trust in him where the ranch was concerned. Amy had never doubted that. Besides being friends all these years, Nakos worked hard and knew what he was doing. The men equally respected and feared him. Plus,

128

he cared a great deal, not only about the animals and workers, but the land as well. He took pride in all aspects of his job and gave one-hundred percent.

"Have you ever thought about opening your own ranch?" She tore her gaze from the hypnotic blur of green and looked at him. "You're so good at what you do."

"Never crossed my mind."

"Really?"

He shook his head, gaze on the highway. "Not once. To open my own place would require collateral I don't have, and in this economy, I'd most likely tank in under two years. That's not even accounting for finding workers and competing with farms already present. Besides, Cattenach is home. I grew up there. Everything I know and love is right where I am." He darted her a quick glance. "Why?"

She shrugged. "Just wondering."

He didn't seem satisfied with her response, but he let it go and concentrated on driving while she watched him out of the corner of her eye.

So handsome. He had this quiet, lying-in-wait presence about him that was both appealing and mysterious. Olive skin and lean muscle and perfect bone structure. Such symmetry and strength. His thighs filled denim like the second coming and the way his biceps bulged as he gripped the wheel made her long to be trapped by them again. Like how he'd pinned her to the wall the other night.

The level of desire she felt for him was stronger than it had been with anyone else. He'd claimed all she needed was someone tolerant. As he pulled into the driveway and cut the engine, she couldn't help but think there wasn't a man created more patient than Nakos.

He grinned at her instead of opening the door, grinding her heart rate to a stuttering halt. "Do you kiss on the first date?"

Considering she'd never officially been on one, she didn't know. For him? "Yes."

A groan, and he reached for the handle. He came around and had her door open before she'd extracted herself from the seatbelt. More chivalry. He took her hand and walked to the porch, the calluses on his palms a delicious abrasion against her skin. He didn't try to kiss her, just simply unlocked the door and gestured her inside. Disappointed, she kicked off her flip-flops and made her way to the stairs.

"Not so fast." He spun her around, backed her up, and the next thing she knew, she was flat on the couch with a warm, hard male on top of her. "Much better."

"Uh, hi," she breathed. "Sort of forward for a first date, don't you think?" Not that she was complaining. Their legs were tangled and their hips in alignment, causing every inch of him to be in direct contact with her. His weight was a welcome distraction from her tripping pulse and nerves, and he smelled...so...dang...amazing. Earth mixed with denim.

"I changed my mind. I'm considering Olivia and Nate's wedding our first date. We walked down the aisle together and were the only people in the bridal party." He raised up on one forearm and took his Stetson off, tossing it aside. His gaze roamed her face, stopping at her mouth, and his tone lowered to come-hither. "We've kissed since then, making this our second date."

Okay, she couldn't think, not with ridges of hot muscle pinning her prone and his handsome face right in hers. She could count every one of his short, black whiskers darkening his jaw. Her breasts ached and the apex of her thighs was throbbing to the beat of his heart against her chest. Gone was the stiff, irked man from dinner and in his place was nothing but sheer seduction.

"I adore that look, Ames. The one you get seconds before I kiss you."

"What look?"

"You have it right now." A smile curved his full mouth. "Your pupils blow and swallow all that pretty color, then your lids get heavy." He brushed his thumb across her lower lip, gaze trained on the movement. "You part your lips as if you need more air or you're expecting me and preparing." His eyes shifted back to hers and the heat dialed to scorching. "Utter turn-on."

He dipped his head, and whatever retort she'd had flew out the window. He had the most amazing mouth. Firm yet full lips that coaxed rather than devoured. A slow build of anticipation until need pounded at the door and desire rattled the hinges. He parted her lips with his and his tongue met hers. Shallow strokes and dips. Taunting. Building.

"Put your arms around me. Let me know you're with me, Ames."

And...there. Cold infused her core and doused the flames. Five minutes, and she'd already disappointed him. God. They were still dressed and she wasn't making par. Her sinuses prickled, and she closed her eyes to stave off tears.

He lifted his head. "What happened? Where'd you go?"

Reality, that's where. Hope was a cruel bitch.

"Look at me." He brushed his nose against hers and his fingers wove through the strands at her temple. "Open your eyes."

She complied, helpless to do otherwise, and met his tender gaze. "I told you I was bad at this."

His switch flipped and fury infused his dark depths. A quick adjustment, and he parted her thighs, settling between them. He rocked his hips, ground his erection against her, and she gasped as a tingle shot through her.

"Yeah, *anim*. That's me, liking what we're doing. Very much." He swallowed and his expression eased. "And we're not having sex right now. We're making out. It's too soon for that. I'm not taking you to bed until I know you're ready. I'm just asking for you to be a willing participant."

Her throat closed. She didn't know what the hell would please him, had no clue how to satisfy a man. "What do you want me to do?"

"Whatever you want. Forget what's in your head and feel. Go with your gut. I assure you, I'll enjoy anything you try."

He stared at her, paused for her response, not moving or taking control. She had the impression he'd stay like this all night, waiting her out. And since there was a sense of safety with him, she let her gaze roam over his face, attempting to listen to what her body was saying.

With a trembling hand, she cupped his jaw because she loved the scratch of his five o'clock shadow. It seemed like a good start. His nostrils flared, and he moaned. Emboldened by his reaction, she stared into his eyes. The tenderness and encouragement gazing back at her told her to keep going.

Struggling to listen more intently, she glanced at his hair. She'd always loved the thick, raven strands, even more so now that he'd grown it out a bit. But he kept it in a ponytail at his nape. Rarely had she seen it down and she'd fantasized about running her fingers through it. Using her other hand, she gently pulled out the band and the shoulder-length strands fell around his face.

He kept his gaze on her, but she focused on what she was doing before she lost the nerve. Wrapping her hand around his neck, she slowly slid her fingers into the silky softness of his hair behind his head. His respirations increased, and pride filled her chest to battle with the pleasure already taking up space. She could spend an eternity just like this, and before she realized what she was doing, she shoved both hands into his hair and clutched the strands.

Again, he rocked against her and her breasts rumbled from another of his moans. He lowered his head and spoke against her mouth. "If you think I was turned-on before, I'm out of my mind now that you're touching me." He dragged his lips across her cheek and nuzzled her ear. "Day and night, I want you."

A full-body tremble coursed through her and ignited every nerve along the way. The ache. God, the ache. Between her thighs. In her nipples while their chests bumped. Under her skin, where unimaginable heat burned her flesh. Everywhere. She whimpered, needing something. What, she didn't know. It had never been like this before, and she had no idea how to gain relief from the sweet agony. On instinct, she jerked her hips, causing his thick erection to briefly alleviate her throbbing. It wasn't enough.

He barked a sharp cry of surprise behind her ear. "*Hihcebe, anim.* You learn fast." He traced a path to her neck with his tongue and buried his face there. "Why do you always smell so good?" Moving across her throat to the other side, he nipped her lobe and grazed his teeth along her thumping pulse.

Then, his mouth crashed to hers, and the beast came out of his cage.

Chapter Fourteen

Damaged goods, his ass. All she'd needed was a little encouragement and she'd knocked every brain cell in his head out of whack. His dick pulsed behind his zipper, his heart shoved against his ribcage, and his eyeballs thunked the back of his skull.

The kiss turned brutally punishing and desperate. A battle ensued. Him. Her. Repeat.

So much for her submission, and he wasn't sorry to see it go. Each stroke of her tongue warring with his unleashed something deep inside him he hadn't known existed. Animalistic and raw. Untamed. Gone was any shred of finesse. Forget unhurried seduction. His body wailed to take her. It was all he could do to fight the urge.

Having her beneath him was unadulterated torture. The best kind. He'd gladly bear it every hour on the hour. She had him that enthralled. But he'd meant what he'd said. They weren't going to bed until she was ready. After what she'd told him at dinner, he had a sinking suspicion not only had no man taken time with her, but they'd used her to satisfy a temporary itch, discarding her afterward. That gorgeous body of hers needed to be worshiped, not cast aside after a quick screw.

Damn, though. She was into it. He hated to put a stop to their make-out session simply for the sake of following steps. More than anything, proving to her she was capable of climaxing would only render her readily able to let go when they did come together later.

Her hips moved restlessly beneath him, grinding them together through their jeans, and... Decision made. He slid his hand under her shirt to the warm skin of her belly, keeping the kiss frantic so she didn't lose momentum. Up, he drifted, until he cupped one perfect breast and her nipple beaded against his palm through her bra. She moaned into his mouth, her fingers clenching his hair.

That was the other thing. He never wore his hair down, so the erotic feel of her fingertips against his scalp, her hands buried in the strands, was as new to him as the barbaric urges she brought out in him. Fire licked his skin and need rippled down his spine.

He circled her nipple with his thumb, building her torment, then did the same with the other until that holy-shit whimper arose from her throat again. Testing her, he grazed his knuckles past her navel to the snap on her pants, teasing her skin with brushes above the waistband. Back and forth. Back and forth. She offered no resistance and he flicked the snap, slid her zipper down.

Adjusting his position slightly for better access, he moved over one of her legs, straddling it, and shoved his arm between her and the couch cushion. From behind, with his lips still clinging to her kiss, he tugged her jeans and panties over the curve of her hips and palmed her round, supple ass. She thrust, surprising him, causing his length to grind into her hip.

Hihcebe. She was going to kill him before he ever got to truly touch her. Tearing his mouth from hers, he buried his face in her neck. Which didn't help because all he could breathe was her sultry scent.

Flicking his tongue over her pulse, he cupped her heat before she could see his move coming. If she anticipated his touch, it might pull her from the moment. In time, she wouldn't think so hard or question her body when she was with him. But, for now, it was all about getting and keeping her there. Proving to her she was capable and he knew what she needed, that he could send her off the cliff. Willingly.

And...*yes.* She arched into him, pressed into his hand, silently demanding more. Already, she was more responsive than he'd expected, and he realized it wasn't fear or anxiety on her end holding her back. She craved pleasure, but just didn't understand how to reach for it.

He wanted to maim every guy she'd been with, starting with her ex and working his way backward. How could any man have her in his arms and not cherish her, not relish each moan or gasp? Hell, he could do this all night, whether he received his own reward or not. Just watching her was more arousing than anything.

"Nakos," she breathed, brows pinched tight and eyes shut.

"Shh." He kissed her jaw. "I've got you."

And he'd keep her. Crazy as the notion was, the recognition hit him hard and swift. Without knowing it, she was exactly what he'd been seeking all along. A connection. Trust. Passion as well as comfort. To think, she'd been right in front of his face for twenty years. He'd laugh if the irony wasn't so cruel.

Watching her closely, he parted her folds and groaned at the slickness coating his hand. He slid two fingers inside her wet heat and immediately pressed his thumb over her clit to create pressure, make it good for her.

She trembled beneath him and abruptly turned her head, burying her face under his jaw. "Oh God. I don't...you're..." She rocked her hips, thrusting his fingers deeper. "You're..."

Going to make her come so hard she saw stars, that's what he was going to do.

He'd rather see her face to gauge her reaction, but she seemed to be in her zone pressed up against him and he went with it. Curling his fingers inside her, he flicked his thumb over her swollen little nub and circled, offering alternating sensations to test what she liked.

After a brief moment, she bent her knee and bucked into his ministrations. Panting and gasps followed. Her fingers clenched in his hair, painfully good, and had his own need climbing the ladder of restraint. Her other hand latched onto his bicep, then fisted the cuff of his tee like she needed to hold onto something or she'd spiral.

Keeping rhythm, he stroked the velvet flesh gripping his fingers and worked her clit until his hand started to cramp, then kept going. She shook her head violently like she couldn't take the torment, but he learned that was merely a precursor to her reaching the edge. After he didn't know how long, she tensed against him, her body growing taut in a blink. She sucked in a breath and seemed to hold it a suspended beat.

But, mercy. Then she let go. Quivering, clinging, she cried a pain/pleasure combination against his skin and quaked. Her inner muscles contracted around his digits as she convulsed. Forever, she orgasmed, and he wished he could see her expression as she came. This was about her, though, and he'd have more opportunities soon. It was enough to know he'd given her pleasure, had brought her to release when no one else had been able. Or willing.

A moan, and she went limp, breaths soughing. "Oh my God."

He chuckled and resettled between her thighs. While she was still experiencing aftershocks, he carefully tugged her panties and jeans into place, leaving the snap undone.

Finally, she laid her head back and he looked down at her. Flushed cheeks. Swollen lips. Stubble burn on her jaw. Heavy lids and smiling mermaid eyes. His throat grew tight and his chest pinched. He swore, there wasn't anything more gorgeous than the sight of her right now. Nothing.

And he'd put that awed satisfaction on her face.

Brushing a strand of cocoa hair from her temple, he laid his head beside hers, his nose pressed to her cheek. He attempted to get a grip and couldn't. Two things dawned on him as her breathing regulated and he burrowed into her embrace. In a way, both items went hand-in-hand, and he could kick himself for not noticing sooner.

Matters of the heart were important, but people tended to put too much stock in the particular organ when, in retrospect, it was only tissue. It pumped blood and the body couldn't live without it, sure, but it had no actual bearing on love. The soul was what made a person distinct—the part that lived on after death, how one being connected to another, and what bound essence. To the Arapaho, the soul was of great significance and every living thing had one, from trees and land to animals and humans.

For years, he'd been so focused on the first aspect when he should've paid heed to the second. Olivia may have owned a good chunk of his heart, but Amy was the keeper of his soul. He'd die for Olivia if it came down to it, but that was a result of friendship and genuine affection. Amy was, and always has been, a spiritual connection. If he were to follow the old world culture, or if it was to be believed, he didn't and couldn't exist without her.

It explained the instant bond he'd felt the first time he'd seen her and what kept drawing him back. His protective instinct carried through to both women, but it hadn't been until Amy was put in danger that his world shifted. Or righted, depending on how he viewed it. They were erringly different in many ways yet, together, they created balance. Order.

He toyed with the ends of her hair, sifting the strands, and hoped he wasn't too heavy because he didn't think he could move if the house was burning down around them. And he wasn't the one who'd climaxed. She was awfully quiet, though.

"You all right, *anim*?"

She hummed a sweet little noise and turned her head to smile at him. "My mind is blown. Plus, I'm trying to figure out how to return the favor. I'm not very good with—"

"I don't need anything but what we're doing." Tonight was about her, even though he suspected he might've gotten way more out of the experience than she had. "I proved you wrong. Orgasms aren't a myth."

Her laugh, husky and deep, nailed him right in the breast bone. "I've been known to be wrong on occasion. Tell anyone and I'll deny it."

He grinned, knowing he was sunk. He'd be concerned if he weren't so damn happy. "No one would believe me anyway." After a moment of doing nothing but sharing air, he realized where her hands were and grinned wider.

"Why are you smiling at me like that?"

"Because you're grabbing my ass with one hand like you want a repeat and gently stroking my back with the other as if ready to fall asleep." Always a contradiction, this woman. Before she could knock him out with a verbal one-two, he changed the subject. "What should we do tomorrow for date number three?"

Up went her brows. "Are we keeping tabs?" Yet she rolled her eyes like she did when she was thinking. Or plotting. "Don't know. What do couples do on a date?"

The fact she had to ask broke his heart. It seemed to be an hourly occurrence. "I don't believe there are strict rules on the matter. You haven't been riding in awhile. We could take one of the trails to the creek." They used to do that a lot as kids. He could throw a picnic together or something.

"Okay." She expelled a sigh that shook the heavens. "Nakos?"

"Hmm?" If she kept rubbing his back, he was going to pass out on top of her.

But she didn't say anything and he lifted his head to find out why. She stared at the ceiling, her eyes suspiciously shiny, and her lips pressed firmly in a thin line.

And he understood.

"If you're trying to come up with a way to thank me, don't." Bringing her to climax was only one bar below experiencing it himself. Between the pride inflating his chest and the awe in her eyes, that was enough.

She swallowed and met his gaze. "I thought there was something wrong with me. There's no way you can possibly comprehend what that feels like. So yes, you're getting a thank you."

"Maybe now you'll start believing me and not him."

All she offered was a quiet sigh and an even quieter look that bespoke so much doubt, *he* was questioning his words. He hated that she was hurting, that someone—or a series of someones—had hurt her.

Closing the meager distance, he brushed his lips against hers and groaned when she immediately opened for him. Her kiss was drugging. Of all the women he'd been with, and that list wasn't extravagantly long, Amy alone shoved her way to the unforgettable column. He didn't understand how it was possible for her to be a balm and an ignition. One part coaxing, calling out ingrained instincts to nurture and protect, and the other meant to rile him into chaos.

Her hands settled at his waist and slipped under his shirt. Warm fingers trailed over the dips in his abdomen, and his stomach concaved at her touch. Tentative. Exploring. His erection thickened. He should dial things back, but she hadn't shown much initiative before tonight and he didn't want to deter her from going with impulse.

His breathing escalated as she moved higher. Over his nipples. Swirling her thumbs. Tracing his pecs and skimming back down to his gluts. But then she sent him into cardiac arrest by cupping his length through his jeans.

He broke away and groaned. "*Anim*, I told you—"

She added pressure and he choked. "Can I?"

Again, his heart cracked that she'd felt the need to ask, that she was unsure whether giving him pleasure was all right. Even as his pulse jacked an unfettered rhythm and his dick throbbed, doubt loomed that they might be moving too fast, that she might think she had to reciprocate. But if the goal was to not have her question anything while they were intimate, he had to allow her room to play.

138

"Please," he said, his voice nothing but a rough rasp against her lips. "Do whatever you like."

A second later, he regretted the admission when she unbuttoned his pants, undid his fly, and freed him. The air in his lungs evaporated as her warm fingers gripped his length. One stroke and he was ready to blow. Between her touch, her intoxicating scent, and her supple body beneath his, he was about to lose it. Big time.

"*Hihcebe,* Ames." Brows pinched, he rested his forehead to hers and thrust. Her grip eased, and he wrapped his hand around hers, demonstrating his preference for pressure. Together, they stroked him from base to tip, wracking a shudder from him, and he guided her thumb around his head, over his slit. He jerked as unimaginable heat shot through his body. "That feels amazing."

Encouraged by his praise, she repeated the motion on her own, and he reached up to grab the couch arm above her head for support. And then she did it again with both hands, splintering rational thought into a mushroom cloud and rendering control a distant memory. His fingers dug into the material of the sofa, the muscles in his shoulders knotting.

Slowly—so damn slowly, sweat broke out on his skin—she kept a measured pace. He thrust into her hands, wanting to drive up the tempo, but the unhurried momentum created its own sweet torture that had anticipation almost more rewarding than the result. How funny he was the one needing to rush and it was her showing patience. She had him so fried he didn't know up from down.

Not that he cared. He would rather stay in this suspended state with her than be anywhere else, with anyone else.

She turned her head, caressing his throat with her lips, and he barked a yelp of pleasure. Caging her face with his forearms, he grabbed the couch with such force, he was shocked the frame didn't crack. While he rolled his hips and every nerve in his body misfired, she did something insanely debilitating with her tongue and the tendon in his neck. Tension shot up his spine.

Quickly, he reached behind him and removed his shirt, bunching it over where her hands worked him into delirium so he wouldn't make a mess of her. For a fractured second, she upped the speed, and he blew.

Mouth wide over hers, he came. Pulse after pulse thrummed through him and he bowed, groaning. Dying. Only to return to Earth in the same position. Except her arms were around him and his vision had spots dotting his peripheral.

After a moment, when he could move, he wiped off and tossed the shirt on the floor. Then he kissed her like a man starved. And he hadn't even known he'd been famished.

Chapter Fifteen

Amy hadn't been horseback riding since before the divorce, but her body remembered how and she closed her eyes, tipping her face toward the sun. Leather reins were soft against her palms and the gentle sway of the gelding under her was hypnotic. She breathed in the scent of summer grass and soil, smiling while hooves clomped the earth.

She should be worried about the giddy sensation in her belly, but whatever. Nakos had given her an orgasm last night. If she never had another, she'd carry the memory of that one for two lifetimes. Even better was the pleasure she'd given him. She wasn't sure if it was because she'd been with Nakos or that she'd been coming down off a high, but nothing in her experiences had been so right. No nerves or doubt. They'd been in sync.

Watching his reaction had cemented something in her mind, what he'd been trying to tell her for a couple weeks. He wanted her. Not because Olivia was taken or out of some errant surge of restlessness, but because he genuinely wanted her. Having not been around much encouragement and unused to praise, it was no wonder she had been fighting so hard. It was difficult to trust someone desiring her when all of the attention she'd received had been out of a fleeting sense of lust. Most guys hadn't seen her, but a release.

And she'd been searching, one conquest and mistake at a time, for what Nakos provided. He didn't lie or mislead. That just wasn't his nature. When he looked at her, and how he'd come undone in her arms last night, proved his words. A person couldn't fake that kind of interest. She'd been with enough partners to know. He'd enjoyed, actually enjoyed, the way she'd touched him. She'd…satisfied him.

One of the horses whinnied and the murmur of voices had her eyes opening. Aunt Mae had packed a lunch, and Nakos had asked Olivia and Nate to join them on a ride to Devil's Cross. They came up to the bluff and dismounted. While Olivia tied the reins to a cottonwood, Amy glanced around.

The area was on the far east end of the ranch, pocketed between the northern edge of rocky terrain and halfway to the southern grazing pasture. From this vantage point, she could make out most of the property. The Laramie Mountains were off in the distance and next to their position was a steep incline that dropped to a narrow creek. A set of stone steps led down to the water, roughly twenty feet below.

Nakos and Olivia headed down, but Nate took a seat in the shade of the intermittent tree cover to watch their descent, his jean-clad legs dangling off the side of the ledge. Amy sat next to him, not in the mood for swimming.

Once at the bottom, Olivia skated the pebbled shoreline and kicked a spray of water at Nakos. He shook his head in warning, which amped Olivia's smile. They'd shed their clothes, now littering the stairs, and the sight of Olivia in a black bikini reminded Amy of her inadequacies. Her friend had a slender frame and fair skin, dusted with freckles, and auburn hair that shone like fire in the sun. Amy was all rounded curves with average brown strands that could be found anywhere.

In contrast, Nakos wore red board shorts and was a head taller than Olivia. His natural olive tone bronzed gold in the light, and his coiled muscles shifted in fluid motion when he moved. Lean waist, hard pecs, ripples of abs, and defined biceps. He'd set aside his cowboy hat and had his raven locks in a low ponytail at his nape. His teeth flashed white as he offered a rare grin and stalked closer to Olivia. She squealed, but he caught her around the waist and tipped them sideways into the waist-deep water.

"This reminds me of when we were kids." Amy smiled. They used to come up here a lot to cool the summer humidity clinging to their skin. It had been awhile since she'd seen Nakos drop his guard, let his playful side out. Even as a boy, he'd only done it in their presence. Otherwise, he was all stoicism and quiet observation. "You don't want to join them?"

Nate grunted. "I'm good right here. I could watch her all day." He rubbed a hand over his bald head as if embarrassed by the admission. His tat sleeves were seemingly living extensions of him. "She looks happy, doesn't she?"

"You make her very happy."

He flicked a glance at Amy and back to their friends, shaking his head in disbelief. "That stunning woman is my wife. Still hard to wrap my mind around that. I don't think I ever will."

Surprised by his candor, she leaned back on her hands. "Why's that? You're not exactly an ogre, Nate, and one only has to look at you to know you love her more than anything."

A slow nod. "Yes, I do." His smile softened the longer he gazed at the antics below. "More than air or sustenance or my own life. But you understand, better than most, what it's like to doubt." He shifted his gaze to her, a flicker of speculation in his dark depths. "You and I are a different breed of people."

"How so?" She hadn't had much one-on-one time with Nate but, from the first moment she'd laid eyes on him, she'd felt a kindred connection. Nothing romantic and not at all like the bone-deep tether she had with Nakos. No, it was more elemental with Nate. Guilt recognizing guilt or pain identifying another's pain.

He refocused on Nakos and Olivia, her now on his back trying to submerge him. "I grew up in foster care, never knowing what it was like to matter. You were raised in a house with both parents, yet you weren't taught that basic skill, either."

She leaned forward, wondering how he'd come to that conclusion when this was the first real conversation they'd had. Perhaps Nakos or Olivia or Aunt Mae had said something? But they didn't know the half of it, and why would they bother to mention such a thing to Nate?

"I'm ex-military. I can read situations and people better than the average person." He offered her a half-smile. "No judgment here. I'm simply pointing out our similarities. People like us were never shown love, ergo we don't trust it when it comes along. Now those two?" His chin bumped toward their friends. "They don't know anything else. Their folks showered them with affection and built their self-esteem. They never had to question the basics, unlike us."

"Yeah," she said through a sigh, realizing he was right. "I wonder what that feels like. It must be nice."

"No clue, but it's good to see the flip side to darkness. A relief to know it's there."

143

She nodded, unsure of what to say. In a few short sentences, he'd pegged her to a T, and all because they were the same, her and Nate. "Is there a reason you brought this up or are you just pulling a Humphrey Bogart beautiful friendship moment out of your ass?"

He tipped his head back and laughed. "The girl's seen Casablanca," he muttered. "I knew I liked you for more than your one-liners." He smiled, sobering. "My point is, just because we weren't shown any, doesn't mean we can't love. Or that we don't deserve it. Took Olivia breaching my walls before I realized that. I still wake up every morning needing to remind myself, but the proof is in what she does to me with one smile." He leveled her with a direct glare that brooked no argument. "I love her more than air or sustenance or my own life," he repeated his sentiment from earlier. "And in turn, I'm capable of making her happy."

Dang, he was something. "The bigger they are, the harder they fall. No wonder she's gobsmacked."

Another rough laugh, and he sighed. "So. You and Nakos."

"Ah ha. I see the light." She studied the man in question with Olivia in the creek, having quit their roughhousing and were now talking instead. "Offering advice, Nate, or gathering intel?"

"Both."

Hmm. "Our situation's different." Nate was worthy of Olivia. If there was any doubt, his recent declaration shot it out of the water. Amy didn't deserve Nakos. "This isn't love. We just started...dating."

"I'll bet my right arm and my left nut that you're wrong. You loved each other before you ever acted on it."

"As friends. That's not the same."

Contemplative, he stared at the horizon. "I understand where the lines might be blurred, but you didn't see his expression when you walked down the aisle at my wedding. What was the word you used? Gobsmacked? Yeah, that fits."

Really? That was long before he'd kissed her.

"I tried the love thing once before." She shook her head. "I still have the scars."

"You want to talk scars?" His brows rose in challenge. "Besides, you weren't married to that douchebag. You were married to a concept."

"You think so, huh? Pray tell, oh wise one."

144

His grin was fleeting and, after a beat, he rubbed the stubble on his jaw. "Let's put it this way. Love has many forms, or so Olivia tells me. Multiple meanings. So do several words in the English language. Take 'in' for instance. It's not the most important one-syllable, two-letters, right?" He looked her dead in the eye. "Unless it's thrown in front of the word 'love.' One tiny word changes the whole infrastructure of the other. You may have, in some way, loved Chris, at least the idea of what he could give you anyway. But you weren't in love with him. Just like Nakos wasn't really in love with Olivia."

That was the third time from as many people she'd heard that accusation, and she still wasn't sure she believed it. "I think you're wrong."

He shrugged. "Agree to disagree. I like Nakos a hell of a lot, but do you think for one second I'd let him touch her if he had any romantic notions?" He pointed below.

Olivia had Nakos pinned beneath her, dunking his head. He surged out of the water, her on his shoulders, and tossed her upstream.

"Dude's got his hands all over her. My eye's not even twitching." Nate grunted. "Know why? Because every few seconds, he glances up here to check on you. Wait for it. Three, two, one…"

Sure enough, Nakos looked up, shielding the glare from his eyes with his hand. Rivulets of water trailed over his sun-kissed skin like some naughty version of a Coppertone ad. A beat later, he nodded and turned to Olivia.

"He smiles when you walk into view. Every time. And I don't need to be a mind-reader to pick the thoughts from his head. He's got some dirty fantasies going on in there. It's a guy thing."

She huffed a laugh, but her heart pounded and her skin heated. The longer Nate's words hovered between them, the deeper they sank. Her belly clenched at the possibilities. Perhaps because Nate had no vested interest made it easier to believe him. Or maybe since he had started as an outside party to their unit gave his opinion more merit. Credence.

Whatever the reason, happy was shoving doubt aside. The biggest issue lingered in the fringes of her mind, though. Of all the crap she'd been through, all the horrible things said and done, Nakos leaving her would be her breaking point. No matter how life had tried to decimate her, she'd always gotten back up. A big F-you to the universe. But an end to her relationship with Nakos was the one and only thing that could shatter her for good. Whether as her friend or lover, if they were done, she wouldn't survive.

Olivia and Nakos made their way back up.

He dropped his clothes beside Amy and towel dried before bending over and tipping her head back. He kissed her briefly upside down and smiled at her. "What were you two talking about for so long?"

She glanced at Nate, who had Olivia in his lap wrapped in a towel. "The meaning of life." He winked at Amy.

Olivia snorted. "That's easy. It's chocolate." She dragged the picnic basket closer. "Eh, grapes will have to do." She popped one in her mouth and fed another to Nate.

Nakos sat beside Amy, wrapped an arm around her waist, and plopped her between his stretched legs with her back to his chest. "And what's the meaning of life per Amy? I shudder to ask."

"That's on a need-to-know basis." She reached forward and took a few grapes from Olivia. "Here's a hint. It's not chocolate." She held a piece of fruit over her shoulder, and Nakos took it from her with his mouth.

"Liar. Chocolate is everything." Olivia sighed dreamily, shaking her head at Amy, her gaze glazed over like the sap she'd always been. "Look at you two. Adorable. If I weren't seeing it with my own eyes, I wouldn't believe it."

"Well, start believing," Nakos said around his food. "We're together."

With an I-told-you-so lift of his brows, Nate stared at Amy. Hard. "I think Nakos can be in-the-know."

Yeah, yeah. "I'll consider it."

"Yes, please." Her back pulsated when Nakos spoke. Because he'd put his arms around her. All possessive-like. And it absolutely didn't make her feel girly and gushy. It didn't. "I'm more concerned you and Ames are conspiring." His tone was light, but he was tense against her, making her wonder if he hated the fact she had been alone with Nate. "You're not plotting world destruction or anything, are you? Between your military connections and her evil mind, I'd better start preparing. Right, little red?"

"Amen." Olivia nodded.

"Aw." Amy patted her chest. "You think I'm evil? That's the sweetest thing anyone's ever said to me."

He kissed her neck, shaking his head. "Whatever you say, *anim.*"

Olivia's eyes narrowed. "What's that word mean? It's a new one."

Amy shoved a grape in Nakos's mouth before he could answer. "It means master overlord."

His mouth pressed against her ear, his voice a rasp low enough for only her to hear. "That is quite fitting, actually, since you are master of my heart, my mind, and my body. Shall I start calling you that instead of angel?"

She trembled at the savageness of his words. A beta admission spoken with an alpha growl. Raw sex and promise. No hint of his usual gentleness.

Yet the rest of the week played out like Nakos had something to prove. As if bolstering himself to show the chivalry card, despite the need radiating from him.

On Monday, while Amy was chopping carrots for Aunt Mae's bison stew, Olivia came in the main house's kitchen and said Nakos was looking for her. After drying her hands, Amy made her way to the barn, breathing in early morning dew. She leaned against the doorway and waited quietly for him to dole out ranch assignments to the men.

"One last thing. There's a new development all of you should know about." Nakos turned suddenly and pulled her snug to his chest, stealing her breath. Right in front of all the guys, he bent her over his arm and kissed the daylights right out of her. While she reeled, he glanced at the stunned faces. "Any questions?"

"Holy crap." Kyle shook his head, looking as dazed as her. "You just kissed my sister and you're still standing."

Tuesday morning, Amy woke up to find her bed covered in Hershey Kisses. What had to be at least three bags of the candy were loosely spread around her. On the nightstand was a note from Nakos.

These are a poor substitute. Come downstairs to get real kisses.

On Wednesday, the day they typically left the main house before dinnertime due to light loads, she went outside to take pictures of an impending thunderstorm once they'd returned to

Nakos's cabin. Upon entering the kitchen an hour later, he had supper ready. That he'd cooked himself. With two formal place settings on the table. By candlelight.

Thursday night, he disappeared upstairs as she tidied the kitchen. He hadn't come back by the time she finished. Wondering what he was up to, she made her way to the second floor and stopped short. Two post-it notes were stuck to the floor, one with an arrow pointing forward, and the other a few steps ahead with an arrow aimed at the bathroom.

Hesitant, she walked in the small room to find the lights out, two votive candles glowing on the vanity, and the bathtub full of hot water. Flower petals floated on the steamy surface and a glass of wine sat on the tub ledge. Another post-it was on the tile.

For you. Relax.

By the time Friday rolled around, she was on edge and curious what tactics he had in store next. She didn't know what to make of his gestures, nor had a clue to his end game. He kissed her good morning every day and goodnight before heading to bed, but there had been no more attempts at seduction. No couch romps or orgasms. She swore, his little bombs were like a twisted form of foreplay, except by way of romance instead of the typical methods.

Such as using his hands or mouth or yummy body.

Inside the cabin after the workday, he closed the front door as she glanced around. Nothing seemed out of the ordinary. Regardless, she went into the kitchen, strolled around the living room, and then went upstairs. Nada. Everything normal.

She stood in the middle of her bedroom, hands on her hips, and frowned. She half expected a chubby man wearing a diaper holding a bow and arrow to jump out of the closet and strike her with pointy hearts.

Nakos leaned against the jamb, arms crossed and a smile tugging his lips. "You look confused, *anim.*"

"What did you do today?" She knelt and checked under the bed. No orchestra playing sonnets hiding out. "What surprise is lurking for me?"

He chuckled, darn him. "So paranoid."

"Is there a kitten in your bed? What?"

"Kitten? Why on earth would I—"

"Because I always wanted one and you'd find a way to figure that out. My folks wouldn't let me get one and Chris hated cats. That's not the point. Where is the surprise? Just tell me."

"You're cute when you're flustered." Amusement infused the humor already in his eyes. "Did you not like my little presents?"

She sat on her haunches and blew hair out of her face. "Yes, I liked them." Loved them, was closer to accurate. They made her all discombobulated and gooey. She just didn't know what to do with...nice. He never took their kisses to the hot and heavy point or acted like he expected something out of the kindness. It was weird. Aside from gifts on her birthday from Kyle, Olivia, or Nakos, she rarely got this sort of attention. Okay, not at all. "What game are you playing?"

His expression flatlined. In a move so slow it should've included subtitles, he straightened from the frame and strode over to her. Never taking his gaze from hers, he bent, slid his arms under hers, and lifted her to her feet.

Gaze sweeping her face, he cupped her neck, his thumb idly stroking her pulse. "This isn't a game to me." He stepped flush against her and dipped his head, his lips caressing hers as he spoke. "You're not a toy or a plaything. What you are is someone of importance to me who I care about a great deal." He wrapped and arm around her back, hauling her halfway up his body. "I want you. Badly. But sex isn't the only reason I'm with you. I felt it was necessary you know that before we got any more physical than we already have. Understand?"

Her lungs collapsed and, hand to God, she would've thought she was dying if not for her thundering heart. She nodded, unsure if she could speak around the big ball of emotion in her throat.

"Excellent. Now that we're on the same page, I'll include you in my plans for tonight." He eased back a fraction, determination and heat in his black eyes. "I'm going to make you come like I did a week ago. I can't wait to watch you lose it and I'll love every moment. I've thought about it each waking second since you were last under me. However, this time, instead of my hand, I'll use my mouth."

Chapter Sixteen

Nakos waited a beat until the shock eased out of her expression and for desire to replace it. Cheeks flushed and respirations nonexistent, she stared at him.

Good. She had zero comprehension how hard it had been to keep his hands off her this week. And for her to imply this was all a game to him ticked him off to the point of no return. Some day, some how, he was going to get through to her. He'd probably end up in a padded cell for his efforts, but she was worth every blatant head bashing he was bound to inflict.

Reminding himself undoing thirty years of damage didn't happen overnight, he set her back on her feet. She slid down his body, rubbing against him and upping his need to critical.

"Come take a shower with me?" They'd both been working all day. Besides, undressing her was a fantasy he couldn't eradicate. Getting her wet, in more ways than one, had him thickening with the visual. "Please," he growled.

"Okay." A breathy whisper. Several blinks. "Now, you mean?"

In answer, he crushed his mouth to hers, wrapped his arms around her, and carried her across the hall. He kicked the door shut and cranked the shower faucet, never taking his lips from hers. Desperate noises purred from her throat as he devoured. He could spend centuries on the hot, wet cavern of her mouth alone.

He fingered her white blouse and eased away enough to look in her eyes. "I've been wanting to do this ever since I accidentally walked in on you."

Undoing the buttons slowly, he kept his gaze on hers. Hesitancy and nerves swam in her eyes, and irritation pounded his temples. The dieting? How she wouldn't wear a bathing suit while they'd gone swimming at the creek? He knew it boiled down to the misguided image she had of herself. But he'd show her how wrong she was.

He peeled the shirt from her shoulders and let it fall to the floor. Her eyes drifted closed, but he looked his fill. Showing her he wasn't shying away and that he liked what he saw would hopefully prove to her just how much he loved her body. Her generous breasts were trapped behind white lace, and he freed them with one flick, sliding off her bra to join the blouse. Her panting increased, but she kept her eyes shut like she couldn't handle it if she found disappointment in his.

Never.

Kneeling, he unsnapped her pants, dipped his fingers in the waistband, and skimmed both her panties and the jeans down her legs. Without a word, she stepped out of them. Her arms trembled and her hands fisted as if fighting instinct to cover herself. And still, her eyes didn't open.

On his knees, he set his hands on her hips and took her in. She had curves and softness instead of angles and edges. Something for him to grab onto, not a thin rail with no substance. Her cocoa strands and rosy nipples against her fair tone made his heart pound. Hourglass shape. Long legs. Supple flesh he was dying to sink his teeth into. Breathtaking.

"Beautiful, *anim*." His throat tightened as he glanced up at her.

Finally, her lids lifted to reveal doubt and...hope.

"Beautiful," he repeated and stood. He kissed her gently, taking his time for her to acclimate, and keeping his hands on her waist. Her uneven breath mingled with his, warm, teasing. He swept his lips against hers, coaxing, then licked the seam for entry. She granted him access, and he stroked her tongue with languid brushes and lazy swirls until the stiffness left her frame. "Undress me." Not only would he thoroughly enjoy it, but it would give her some control back.

For that, she wasted no time. Fisting his tee, she dragged it up his torso and over his head. The jeans came next, taking his briefs along for the ride. Then, with pink tingeing her cheeks, her gaze roamed over him. Sparks ignited under his skin the longer she stared. He couldn't recall a woman ever studying him with such precision before. If not for the appreciation in her mermaid eyes, he might've given in to the need to squirm.

Her gaze flicked to his. Held. With one look, she beseeched him to act. Told him she wanted him. Needed to be taken.

152

Picking her up, he deposited her in the shower and stepped in after her, closing the curtain. Steam surrounded the small space, creating a seductive fog just for them. Water trailed down her lush body and...hell. He was going to lick every drop from her skin.

First, he made quick work of washing himself while she watched, then he backed her under the spray. He shampooed her hair and paid extra attention to lathering her body afterward, skimming his rough hands over satin flesh. The build up made her lids grow heavy as he lingered over her nipples, puckered from the stimulation, and between her legs, where he stroked her folds.

Though he preferred taking his time with a woman and patience paid off, he'd never had to put so much energy into foreplay. Not that being with her required effort, but Amy took longer than most to teeter over the ledge. It forced him to cease the frenzy, absorb details, and he found he didn't mind. At all. Hell, it was most enjoyable. There was something oddly arousing about watching her slow climb, focusing solely on her and knowing only he could make her come undone.

Each touch and caress was a roadmap to her emotions, the parts she'd kept contained and dare not let loose. New, yet familiar, and the mystery only added to the punch. Being with her was like discovering uncharted territory and realizing the clandestine terrain was...home.

She grabbed the back of his neck and rose on her toes, her bluish-green eyes round. She stared at him, teeth sunk into her lower lip like she was trying to decide what to do. He skimmed his hand down her drenched hair, letting her work it out, wanting more than anything for her to...

Kiss him. Mouth wide, she plunged. Gone were any reservations and hesitancy as she ate at his mouth. Nips and sucks and thrusts of her tongue meant to have him genuflecting. She pressed against him, skin slick with water and hot as sin.

Hihcebe, yes. Lightning zinged through his whole system, searing nerves and boiling his blood.

Arms around her, he turned them, pushing her spine-first against the tile. Her body was a welcome cushion to his hard frame and they fit. Unerringly right. Like nothing in his life ever had before, they just...fit.

Rootless, fevered need coursed through him and, again, he knelt in front of her. Without wasting a second, he latched onto one of her nipples and sucked it between the roof of his mouth and his tongue while water rained over them. She cried out and he groaned in satisfaction. Shoving her fingers in his hair, she clenched the strands and arched. He moved to the other breast and repeated his motion, glancing up at her.

Damn, but she was something. Swollen lips and flushed cheeks and wet lashes framing lost-to-the-moment eyes. Pride mingled with lust inside his chest, and all his remaining blood supply headed south.

He nipped his way over her stomach and reached around to palm her round ass in both hands. She moaned, trembling in his hold. He traced a path up one thigh and down the other with the tip of his tongue, hoping it would drive her as mad as she was making him. The sharp tug on his hair gave him his answer. Without warning, he buried his face below her small triangle of dark curls.

"Oh God." She gasped, her legs shaking, and he dug his fingers in the flesh of her backside to keep her upright. "Nakos..." She bucked, and he grinned.

He lapped at her wet folds, sinking his tongue inside her, then followed it up with a flick of her clit. One of her arms went wild, slapping the tile, the other nearly jerked his hair from the root. Relishing the slight kick of pain, he went at her again, keeping the rhythm since it seemed to be working for her.

Eyes on her, he had to fight not to stroke his aching, throbbing shaft. It was like watching her peel away layers of accumulated neglect to expose the tender core underneath. The fervor and passion she'd kept buried or, possibly, never knew was there eked to the surface, one lip bite at a time. Hips undulating, head thrown back, eyes pinched tight in a pleasure/pain combo, she succumbed to him and let go.

Her sudden cry and convulsions shocked him into almost dropping her. He hadn't been at it long, and this climax had come in what seemed like way shorter time than when they'd been on the couch. But there she went, splintering in his hands and under his mouth like the gorgeous damn angel she was. Quaking, she parted her lips, and he just about fell apart at her feet.

154

Desire and need battled with affection and tenderness inside his head, his chest, making his nasal cavity sting and his dick twitch. He rested his forehead on her belly after she'd sucked in a breath, needing one himself. Grabbing her waist, he held still, idly stroking her ribs.

After a moment or sixty, she ran her fingers through his hair. When he didn't move—or couldn't—she set her hand under his chin and forced his gaze up to her. "Are you all right?"

There was no way to answer that. No, he wasn't okay. He was coming unglued the deeper they got into this relationship, and he was beginning to realize every second of his life had been leading up to the point where he'd opened his eyes to find her there. And yes, he was more than okay. For the exact same reason.

Rising to his feet, he cupped her jaw. "I think I'm supposed to ask you that."

She grinned. "I'm great."

Satisfaction filled him even as his heart tugged. Instead of wary censure like she had the first time they'd come together, she...glowed. "Yes, you are." He pressed his lips to hers as water beat down and steam plumed.

He went to deepen the kiss, but she...*sank to her knees*. His forehead hit the tile and he slapped his hands there to keep himself standing.

Glancing down, his pulse stroked out at their position. Her, in front of him, mouth inches from his shaft. She rubbed her cheek along the underside. His breaths soughed as he waited, her hair a curtain so he couldn't see her face. Just as he was about to beg, weep, he didn't know what...she wrapped her deft fingers around his base and pumped.

He choked. She'd obviously absorbed his preferences from earlier because her grip was firm and his eyes slammed shut in response. Truthfully, it didn't matter what she tried or how she touched him. He was totally at her mercy. And the fact she'd done this on her own, without cues or encouragement or guidance, only jacked the sensation to holy shit.

His crown was immersed in hot, wet suction and his eyes flew open. She took him deeper into her mouth, fisting his base, and he couldn't drag air into his lungs. Tongue swirling, lapping. Cheeks hollowing. Hand pumping. He groaned from a place so deep in his gut his ribs rattled.

Her name shoved from his lips in a hoarse, long-winded exhale. "So good, *anim.*"

He wanted his hands in her hair, needed to thrust, but he curled his fingers on the tile and locked his legs instead. She never paused or slowed, but when she hummed around his shaft, he lost it. Sensation after sensation flew at him, through him. Blinding heat. Raw desperation. Tension coiled in his back and surged up his spine.

"I'm there." His brows pinched as his mouth opened wide. "Amy, I'm..."

Erupting. From the inside out.

He popped from her mouth, but her hand continued stroking. Tight around his length. Over his head. Back down. The fingers of her other hand massaged his balls, tugged, and he jerked, shuddering as wave after wave rolled through him. A shout raked his throat. Muscles dislodged from bone. Light blasted behind his closed lids.

Mary Mother of God.

She eased up, and he caught his breath. Or tried to. Her fingers trailed over his abs, his hips, and he realized she was rinsing him off. He didn't think he could open his eyes, but he put effort into the task and stared down at her.

Someone looked pleased with herself. And she should. He was even happier, not only because he'd come, that she'd brought him there, but because she was shedding doubt and going with her instincts.

"Come up here so I can kiss you." He didn't wait. Grabbing her under the arms, he hauled her up his body and crushed his lips to hers.

Later, after he'd changed into sweats and a tee, and she'd put on pajamas that covered almost none of her curves, they sat out on the back deck. With her between his legs on a lounge chair, she reclined against his chest and sighed, gazing up at the stars. If he never moved from this spot, he'd consider himself lucky.

Idly, he ran his fingers through her strands and breathed in her sultry scent. Crickets chirped and leaves rustled in the humid breeze, but other than that, her respirations were the only sound. It was so dark the shadows had shadows, the inky sky the only light, but he didn't think he'd ever seen more clearly.

Since they'd met as children, he'd been comfortable in her presence, able to say or do or be anything with her around. But once they'd become intimate, that level of trust turned the tether into a knot. Despite the way she made his heart pound, the nerves fluttering in his gut whenever she was near, he'd never felt closer to someone than he did Amy. It was uncanny, considering he never knew what was going to fly out of her mouth next and half the time he had the strongest urge to bang his head.

Maybe that was the key, though. Balance. He preferred his own company and quiet. She put the "if" in life. There wasn't the slightest chance of things growing stale between them or for him to question whether he was settling. Not with her. Throw in the chemistry, and there wasn't a doubt they were right where they belonged.

Yet there was darkness hiding in her mind, hovering at the fringes. He'd caught it a time or two, and he never measured the depth or how deeply it was embedded until she'd started dropping her guard. A shield he had no clue was even in place. He'd been a part of her life for more than half of his. Learning there were things she'd hidden from him was almost more jarring than the fact they were there. It went beyond basic self-esteem, too. He didn't have an inkling what her secret was, but whatever it happened to be, it kept her from engaging one-hundred percent. She'd been holding back, and he needed to know why. They'd never get anywhere otherwise.

At first, he'd figured she didn't have faith in them in a romantic sense. Possibly even him, to a degree. But the longer he thought about it, he was beginning to realize it was herself she didn't trust. Like everyone else, he'd believed her false sense of confidence. No doubt, she had herself fooled. Her sharp tongue and try-to-stop-me mentality had been so much a part of her personality that it was close to genetic. Yet how much was a defense mechanism and how much was the real her?

Again, he remembered her sitting on the cliff ledge by the creek, talking to Nate. They'd been deep in conversation, and Nakos itched to know what they'd discussed. He hadn't been able to see much when he'd glanced at them to check on her, but he'd caught a few blips of her distant expression. Nate's, too.

Nakos hated to admit it, but the former soldier may be the best person for Amy to open up to. He'd seen and done some unimaginable things in his short thirty years on Earth, and those horrors followed him everywhere. Between Olivia and a lot of effort, he was working past it and moving on. Going after his happy. It couldn't be easy, yet he was trying.

The most gutting part of all was, that darkness he'd seen in Nate's eyes was a mirror to the one he'd found in Amy's. The thought of her in pain, of anything hurting her, stole the beat from his heart.

He rested his chin on the top of her head and banded his arms tighter. As if that would be enough to hold her to him. "You okay, *anim*?"

She hummed quietly in her throat. "You ask me that a lot."

Because he needed a straight answer, even if he didn't necessarily want to hear it. "I worry about you." All the damn time.

Silent for a beat, she traced her fingers over his forearms he'd wrapped around her chest. "I had a crush on you in high school."

What? "I..." Didn't know what to say. He'd had no idea. Shocked didn't begin to cover it.

"It wasn't hardcore or anything. An awareness or attraction, I suppose. I used to pray you'd notice, but you never did." She sighed and turned in his arms, bringing her knees up so that she sat sideways between his thighs.

Resting her cheek on his pec, she went quiet again, but when she did speak moments later, her voice had a distant, melancholy note. "I'm used to disappointment in one form or another. I spent too much time hoping my parents would love me a smidgen of how much they do my brother, but that's never going to happen. Or sitting alone at the kitchen table night by endless night, an uneaten meal growing colder, thinking today would be the day my husband looked at me. Or staring at myself in the mirror, wondering if I'd ever see a reflection that didn't make me turn instantly away in disgust."

He attempted basic oxygen exchange. Impossible. His lungs had seized. A knife dipped in acid and rammed into his abdomen would cause less pain than her admission. Still as stone, gutted, he stared at the horizon, not sure what in the hell to do.

She fingered the sleeve of his tee. "You not realizing I had some stupid crush is barely a blip in disappointments, really, but I don't know how to respond when you want to know how I am. A lot's happened between those idealistic girly years and today. So if we're together now, I'm merely chugging along, waiting for you to call it quits. I keep going back to all those instances I pretended you weren't on my mind, when I didn't look at every couple and wish that was us. Life's taught me dreams are pointless and wanting something doesn't mean I'll ever get it."

She shrugged. "Doesn't matter, though. I'm here, landing on my feet like always, and ready for the next battle where I wind up flipping Karma the bird. So when you ask me if I'm okay, I lie. Because I may not be, but I will soon enough."

Silence hung, and the agony in his chest was so brutal, he glanced down to check if his breastbone had been clawed open. All he found was her thick cap of cocoa strands covering the cavity where his heart used to be. Hollowed, devastated, he buried his face in her hair.

"Bet you're sorry you asked. It's much easier just to say I'm fine."

He slammed his eyes shut, tears burning behind his lids. Breathing through it, he waited until he thought he could speak. He had to clear his throat twice to accomplish the feat. "I'm sorry I hurt you."

"You didn't. Heck, you didn't even know."

Wrong. He may have been blind to her feelings, but he had hurt her. Of the few people in her life she gave a shit about, he was closest to the top of the pile. And he'd unwillingly proved she was of little significance by not seeing what was in front of him. Because of how much they cared about one another, he'd probably done the worst damage.

Chapter Seventeen

At the kitchen sink, Amy rinsed vegetables for tonight's stir-fry and gazed out the window at Nakos's yard while he showered upstairs. Wild and untamed, prairie grass glinted off the sun's rays and swayed with a breeze. Nothing but what seemed like miles of open land with the Laramie Mountains in the vast distance against a cobalt sky.

Since it was the weekend, he'd only been up at the ranch to check on things and tend to the horses. They had the rest of the day to themselves, and anticipation swirled in her belly. Nerves, too.

She recalled her conversation with Nate by the creek, had taken it to heart, and she'd been trying to let go of the past. He'd been right to call her out and lay an emotional gauntlet at her feet. At some point, she had to accept where fate was leading her. Little by little, she attempted to relax and go with the flow. See what happened. Open up. Nakos deserved that much. So hard, she wanted to believe she deserved a chance at happiness also.

Heat blasted her cheeks at the reminder of what she'd said last night while they'd unwound on the deck. Her motto had always been to claim she was fine. There was no sense in upsetting those she cared about by telling them otherwise. It wasn't as if they could fix the damage any more than she could. Nothing but crappy circumstances completely out of their control. And hers.

But she needed to start being honest with him. Relationships were give and take, and if they stood any chance at moving forward, she had to talk to him. Let him in. Nakos had been doing everything in his power to relay to her he was with her because he wanted to be. He didn't lie or mislead or screw around. In fact, if anything, he was too meticulous. Always, he calculated odds and outlooks and angles. No way would he have moved forward based on attraction alone if he didn't truly think the risk was worth the reward.

And yet, guilt was a living thing. It had taken up residence in her subconscious long ago and rarely allowed for progress. Whether justified or not, and that was up for debate, she couldn't help but wonder...if he knew what had been done to her, would he still feel the same way?

Though eighteen years had passed since that awful day, she still felt dirty. Tainted. She may have gotten over it, but she hadn't moved on. Even now, every once in awhile, flashes would slam to mind and she was thrown right back in the alley behind her parents' hardware store.

The brick wall scratching her cheek. Her skirt up around her waist. Panties digging into her thighs as her legs were roughly kicked apart. Tears clogging her throat and fear choking her so she was unable to scream. The sickening stench of Old Spice and sweat. And the excruciating pain of having him shove inside her from behind. It had gone on for what seemed like hours, but was probably minutes. She could still feel the trickle of blood down her leg and hear his grunts in her ear.

Up until that point, she hadn't had much contact with her uncle. He didn't live in Wyoming and had only visited a handful of times. Yet he'd given her the creeps. Even at such a young age, she knew the too-long hugs and lingering pats were wrong. Her first blaring lesson in sex had been a painful eye-opener.

She gave her head a violent shake and focused on washing peppers, resisting the urge to jump in the shower and scrub her skin raw. Repeated bathing hadn't helped back then, nor would it now. It was done. Over with. Except...

The incident had never really allowed her to let go intimately with a man. For whatever reason, the memories didn't invade during intercourse or cause her to freeze up, but she hadn't enjoyed the experiences, either. Like a numb state of autopilot, really. Her first orgasm with a partner had been with Nakos. Last week.

Thirty years old, and she was just now realizing what it was like to be a woman. Sad.

Maybe it was his patience or that she knew him so well, or perhaps the level of trust played a part, but with Nakos, she was helpless to passion. Desire. Need. He wrung her out and brought pleasure she hadn't known was possible. It didn't hurt that he knew what he was doing, too. Every touch and lick and kiss and suck was like detonation. There was no thinking around him.

He seemed equally enraptured. But, again, would that change if he knew? Her virginity had been taken in an alley, next to a garbage bin, with newspapers and refuse littering the way. The potential for her to ever be worthy of a good man wasn't possible. It wasn't just that she'd been violated, rendering her soiled, but the rape had been doled by a member of her own family. By blood. Nakos would be disgusted if he ever found out. As revolted as she had been about herself all these years. She was used goods. Every bit the whore her uncle had grated while he'd…

Footsteps padded behind her and she glanced over her shoulder, bitch-slapping the past away.

In a pair of jeans slung low on his hips, barefoot, and shirtless, Nakos stood on the other side of the counter, his contemplative black eyes on her. Olive skin and six pack abs and corded muscle. God, even his feet were sexy. Heaven help her, he'd left his hair down, too.

She moaned. "Not playing fair, walking around shirtless."

He huffed a rough laugh and rubbed his chest, eyes skimming down the length of her and back.

"Anything wrong?"

He was staring at her like he'd been hit with the stupid stick. That was the other thing. The way he looked at her? For the first time in her pathetic life, she felt desirable. Wanted. Even when he wasn't turned on, his gaze held appreciation and heat.

"Nothing at all wrong. Too right, actually." His hoarse tone had dipped to a groan-inducing rumble like it did when he was aroused or emotional. "You look utterly perfect standing in my kitchen."

Knees? Jelly.

She grinned, shaking her head. "I'm going to pretend you didn't mean that to be as sexist as it sounded." Moving the peppers and carrots over to drain, she started in on the peapods.

He came up from behind and pressed against her, all hot, hard male. His lips skimmed the shell of her ear. "It's not sexist when it's true. And it's not just my kitchen where you look perfect." He wrapped an arm around her waist and flattened the other hand between her breasts, stealing her breath. "My shower." His hand moved up to gently cup her throat and tilt her head back, earning a tremble from her. "My deck." His thumb stroked her jaw, and she whimpered. "My living room or truck or anywhere else. Perfect, Ames."

Water continued to run in the sink, but she couldn't strum up the energy to care. Not with him snug against her or with his hands doing their juju. Heat blasted her from all directions, leaving her damp. Needy.

"Know where else you'd be perfect, *bixooxu?*" His teeth scraped along her neck and she almost slid to the floor in a heap.

"Where?" she breathed. She had no clue what the term he'd just rasped meant, but between his touch and his voice, he could call her a hippo and she wouldn't care. Her breasts ached and her nipples were stiff peaks behind her bra.

"My bed." Reaching forward, he shut off the faucet, only to cup her heat through her capris and grind himself against her backside. "You'll look best of all in my bed," he growled, vibrating the skin along her throat.

Did that mean...? Her eyes flew open, staring unseeing at the ceiling due to the way he held her head back to get to her neck. They'd fooled around and had some mind-blowing moments, but had yet to do the actual deed. She'd wanted to, so badly, yet he never pushed. In truth, she got the impression he'd held off as much for himself as he had for her.

He pressed the heel of his hand more snugly against her mound, right over her clit. She gasped, a full-body tremor coursing through her. Zings rode a current along her nerve-endings. She went from wet to drenched. Panting, she said his name.

A groan, as if he liked his name on her lips, and he was back at her ear. "Yes, I want you in my bed. I'm going to worship every inch of your beautiful body until you can't even think my name, never mind say it. I'm going to taste you and kiss you and elicit pleasure unlike anything you've known or dreamed." He cradled her breast, teasing the nipple with his thumb. "Then, I'm going to make love to you slowly, bury myself so deep a divinity couldn't separate us." He nuzzled his nose behind her ear and spoke into her hair. "Hours, days, years...I'm going to spend on you." A pause. "Please."

Oh God. Time after time, he brought out this whole other side of him. The beast, she often referred to it because that's what he seemed like when turned on. Quiet, contemplative Nakos got knocked aside for his baser self. And if his words weren't enough to send her spiraling, he always threw a "please" after his blatant demands as if seeking permission.

Like she had a choice?

"Yes." She barely got the word past the need tightening her throat. Just in case, she brought her arm back and threaded her fingers through his hair.

He hissed, and the next thing she knew, he'd slipped an arm under her legs and carried her out of the kitchen. She'd never been...swept off her feet before. It made her a little uneasy, but the tension in his expression indicated the strain was sexually related and not from her weight.

As if he'd read her thoughts, his gaze cut to hers while he climbed the stairs. Searing, those dark depths. "Hear me now. This is about you and me. No one else. I know there were others before me and they treated you unkind. I will not do that. Never, will I do that. Your wings will heal, *anim*. I promise you."

Sudden tears burned her eyes and a sob hitched in her chest. How was she supposed to protect what was left of herself after all the slashing previously done if he kept saying things that left her bleeding? "Nakos."

God, she was going to cry. Darn it.

He laid her on the bed and rose over her. "None of that either, *bixooxu*." Brushing his nose with hers, he offered an affectionate smile. "Just you and me. I'm going to make you feel so good."

To prove it, he started with her mouth, and her tears dried before they had a chance to fall. Achingly tender, he brushed his lips with hers and tilted his head. Going deeper, he slid his tongue along the length of hers, swirling the tip and tracing patterns. Whatever strain she'd been holding in her frame suddenly dissolved.

He rose to stand beside the bed and she chanced a quick peek around to calm her nerves. His room was only slightly larger than hers, but the walls were a deep forest green and the furniture a walnut sleigh design. What looked like a dreamcatcher hung over the queen-sized bed. She hadn't realized he had a balcony facing south, and sunlight streamed in, filling the room with natural light. No chance of her hiding her flaws in the dark, that was for sure. The space was warm and masculine like him, with two mountain scenes above the dresser that...she'd taken.

"I look at them every night before I go to sleep."

Her gaze shot to his, her heart turning over in her chest. "Why?"

"Because you took them. And if that's not enough reason, they settle me." With his dark gaze on hers, he unbuttoned his jeans. The zipper came next, and then he shoved the material to his thighs. A couple quick maneuvers, and the pants hit the floor.

She swallowed thickly, keeping her eyes on his face. Though she'd seen him without clothing, this was different. Broad daylight. In his bedroom. And moments from crossing the line. Anxiety clutched her belly, made her tremble. What if she let him down?

He crawled across the bed to kneel between her legs. "Sit up, *anim*." She complied, and he took off her shirt, her bra, and discarded them. "Lay back." With just as much careful consideration, he rid her of her remaining clothing. He offered a reverent shake of his head. "Wanted you like this for so long."

She'd never been comfortable in her own skin, had hated her body and the extra weight that kept her from being pretty. But the way he looked at her left a scorching trail over every inch his gaze roamed. In his eyes, there was no disappointment or displeasure. Only appreciation. Her nerves fled.

Still kneeling between her legs, he gripped her ankles, stroking. His thumbs traced lazy circles and drifted higher to her calves. Yet his eyes remained on her, ever searching, wandering like a heated caress. The longer he stared, the darker his eyes grew until the brown of his irises was swallowed by his pupils.

Breath short, she relaxed and took him in, her gorgeous warrior. His raven strands were loose around his head, long enough to brush his wide shoulders, and had a slight wave to the ends. Thick lashes. High cheekbones. Square jaw dusted with dark stubble.

Tendons in his neck coiled as he moved his hands to the outside of her thighs. His biceps bunched, forearms flexing, and her belly clenched. He had a lean build, more athlete than bodybuilder, with quiet strength under all that hot, bronzed skin. Defined pecs and cut abs. Gluts that made a perfect V to where a thin scattering of black hair left a goody trail.

He wasn't manufactured in a gym, wasn't bulky or intimidating. Rather, he was the delicious result of hard work and

166

years of physical ranch labor. A job he loved and was more play than a profession for him. Sculpted. Toned. Amazing.

His erection was long, semi-thick, and the crown bumped his navel. Shades darker than the rest of his skin, his length was perfect. Protruding veins and moisture at the tip, all jutting proudly from a small thatch of dark hair. She'd had him in hand, in her mouth, and ached to have him buried inside her.

"Beautiful, *bixooxu*." His gaze met hers. He flattened his palms on her breasts, kneading. His throat worked a swallow. "Just beautiful."

She came alive under him, cell by cell, but her mind focused on the word he'd used. He'd said it a couple times today with a possessive note. "What does the term mean?" God, she loved it when he spoke his native tongue. It wasn't pretty or eloquent as other languages, but in his low, deep voice, it sounded guttural. Personal.

He gave a slight shake of his head like he wasn't ready to divulge that info yet, and bent at the waist to replace his hand with his mouth on her breast. A sharp, rapid suck, and he'd claimed the entire nipple. Scorching pressure built in the area and spread everywhere. Before she could rally, he moved to the other one and repeated the motion. Her fingers twitched, so she shoved them in his hair, clenching the strands, holding him to her.

"That's it, *anim*." He groaned as if encouraging her and grazed his teeth on a path to her belly. He swirled his tongue around her navel and a tremor coursed through her. She arched, earning another groan. "That's it right there. Show me you like what I'm doing to you. I'm in heaven."

His gaze flicked to hers as he spread her legs. Feather-light kisses trailed over her thighs. Anticipation flared, fluttered under her skin like razor-tipped wings. She shivered, though she wasn't cold in the least, and bit her lip. His lips quirked in a satisfied half grin, obviously appreciating her reaction. Grabbing her behind the knees, he lifted her legs and situated himself flat on the mattress as if settling in. He set her calves over his shoulders so that his head was locked between her thighs and his face inches from where she throbbed for him.

167

"Do not come." He clamped his large hands on her hips, then dragged them between her and the mattress to cup her bottom. "This time, we do it together. Don't come."

Panting, she stared at him. Every sexual encounter before had been a struggle to feel a measure of what excitement Nakos gave her. Reaching, forever reaching to get to a release, chasing a white light that had never come. The irony was almost laughable because she knew there'd be no effort with him. Not only had he brought her to the cliff edge many times, he'd shoved her over into a freefall. And he wanted her to hold out?

Then he pressed his face between her folds, and she whimpered. He tongued her opening with hot, wet jabs. Invade. Retreat. The motion had lightning flashing through her core, searing nerves at the root. She moaned in frustration, loving and hating the tease. Arching, she closed her eyes, and he rewarded her by flicking her clit. She cried out, fisting the sheets, and he nipped her bud. The breath properly ripped from her lungs.

It seemed every reaction from her, whether a touch or moan or involuntary tremble, earned her more pleasure. His own twisted way of getting her to act on instinct, lose herself in him. Didn't he get it? Any deeper and she'd not exist.

The longer he toyed with her, the more taut her body became, until tingles shot up her spine. "Nakos," she breathed, trying to warn him. He hadn't wanted her to… Oh God. She was so close. She writhed. "Nakos, *please*."

In a blur, he rose over her, their faces close. "Together," he reminded her. He reached over to the nightstand and withdrew a condom from a drawer. Foil ripped. His breathing labored as he rolled the latex down his length. Then he sank in the cradle of her thighs and brushed his nose with hers. "Together."

But he didn't take her. Instead, he kissed her cheek, the underside of her jaw, and nuzzled her neck. His weight was welcome, all his yummy hard in all the right spots but one. He seemed to be waiting for something, yet she had no clue what. She was so wet and ready and out of her mind. More kisses rained over her collarbone as he drifted to the other side, assaulting the nerves behind her ear with his tongue and teeth.

Desperate, she grabbed the back of his neck, and he groaned. The rumble vibrated her breasts. He rocked his hips, rubbing his length between her folds. She gasped and brought her other hand up to sink her nails into his shoulder. This time, he growled, rocking harder and pressing her clit in a slow glide.

Her cry hung in the air. Once her body got over the rapid blast of pleasure, she realized he wanted her hands on him. A part of him *needed* her to show him what he was doing to her, that she enjoyed being with him.

Holding her breath, she skimmed her fingers down his spine, loving the hard muscle over soft flesh. They rippled as if he were an animal being petted. She did it again with her other hand until the fingers of both sunk into his tight ass.

"*Hihcebe*, yes." He panted unevenly, his breath hot. His hips jerked, his erection giving her the pressure she craved.

Without thinking, she spread her legs wider. Lifting her head, she buried her face in his neck, inhaling his scent of male and earth and soap. He rolled his hips, offering shallow strokes and encouraging more. Something wild unfurled inside her. She opened her mouth wide, latched onto the straining tendon in his neck. He panted, pelvis moving faster, and she dragged her tongue along his thumping pulse.

He groaned, hoarse and long and loud. Lifting his head, he looked down at her through half-mast lids. "*Bixooxu* means love." His gaze searched hers, darting between her eyes, while her heart tripped behind her ribs. "My angel, my love."

Before the phrase could fully take root in her mind, he adjusted his hips. The head of his erection brushed her opening, then he penetrated. Slowly, keeping his intent gaze on hers, he pushed inside her, stretching her in a maddeningly delicious invasion. Every inch of him slid along her walls so there was nothing left to feel but him. Only him. Inside her, surrounding her. Everywhere.

When he was as far as he could go, he paused. He said her name on a sigh, rough and like a prayer. "My *anim*, my *bixooxu*."

Her throat closed at the reverence in his tone, in his eyes, but he didn't give her time to react. Tilting his head, he slanted his lips over hers and eased his hips back. At his retreat, she whimpered a protest into his mouth, hating the emptiness he left in his wake. As if sensing what she needed, he cupped her cheek and thrust. She gasped at the fullness, the fit, and tilted her pelvis to bring him deeper.

"Nothing," he said against her lips, his brows pinched. "Nothing feels better than being inside you."

She could trace every red blood cell swimming through her veins. He had her that in tune to her body. Her need. She rolled her hips, restless for him, and he answered by thrusting again.

"Yes." Throwing her head back, she arched. Her arms flung wide, then drifted to the headboard. She planted her palms against the wood, gaining leverage to bear down on him. Lost to what they were doing, she didn't care about what she said or did, how wanton she must appear. "God, Nakos. *Yesss.*"

That seemed to unleash something in him. He thrust harder, faster. Working his arms under her, he caged her against his chest. A desperate rumble, and he nipped her throat. "Never get enough of this."

His hips pistoned while his mouth remained tender. Over her collarbone, up to her chin, across her cheek. Each plunge filled her, again and again, and he ground a quick roll against her clit with every pass. She teetered, so close, knotted with tension.

Removing his arms from around her, he placed his hands on her ribs. The rough calluses grazed her skin as he dragged them over her waist, past her hips, to the tops of her thighs. "Straighten your legs." He pressed down, urging her to follow his order, and stopped thrusting, waiting for compliance.

She'd nearly been there, and he'd...stopped? Torture. She moaned a complaint.

"Trust me, Amy. Straighten your legs for me."

Unhooking her ankles from his lower back, she stretched her legs against the warm sheets beside his. Without preamble, he spread them wider, pinning her thighs to the mattress with his hands.

Oh...*God.* The new position made him feel fuller inside her and rubbed along her delicate flesh to a spot that ripped a violent tremble from her. Her body...*burned.*

"There, *anim.* See? I've got you." His voice was low, cajoling, but carnal arousal danced in his dark eyes. "I've always got you. Now feel me. Feel only me and let go." Hands firmly keeping her legs locked straight, he withdrew and plunged.

Utterly amazing. A careening cry seared her throat. His thickness filled her with absoluteness and he hit so deep her womb clenched. That spot he'd grazed within was stroked again at the same moment his pelvic bone added pressure to her throbbing nub. Wracked with pleasure, she crossed her arms over her face, almost unable to take it.

He paused yet again. "Look at me." He waited until she dropped her arms and their eyes met. "Together, *bixooxu*. Let me feel you come undone."

Her gaze took in his features, and she realized how close he was, too. Tension tightened his forehead, his mouth. His arms shook, and he rasped air like a man dying. Yet he held her gaze with patience and determination, even as need seemed to demand he claim her.

This time, when he pulled out, he watched her as if by no choice of his own. Something connected them, bound them to one another. Stronger than mere desire. Fiercer than a physical joining. And when he drove home, she felt him in every atom of her body.

He plunged into her, over and over, his graceful, fluent motions growing more rigid. And she fell apart under him. Sparks ignited, caught flame, and roared through her in a blaze. She cast a silent scream while she bowed, limbs locking. Convulsing around him, the sweet torment dragged an eternity.

Releasing her legs, he fell on top of her, thrusting through her orgasm and swelling inside her. He brought his arms up, framing her face with his biceps, and rested his forehead to hers. Pain and pleasure twisted his expression. He pumped harder, roared, and shuddered long moments. Then he buried his face in her hair, muttering unintelligible words in Arapaho as his gorgeous body quaked.

He settled as dead weight on top of her, didn't lift his head to look at her, but his hand held the side of her face as if scared she might not be real. Heaving air, ruffling her strands, he finally said something she could understand.

"I was always yours, and now you're mine."

Chapter Eighteen

Nakos had either died or he'd been shot with an elephant tranquilizer. *Hihcebe*, she'd slayed him. Without mercy. Helluva way to go, though.

Face buried in Amy's strands, breaths soughing, he held the side of her face. A part of him was worried she'd evaporate. Sex had never been like that for him. Ever. The connection? The link? The unprecedented amount of pleasure? Nothing like it.

He was probably crushing her, but he couldn't move. Sheer annihilation. Mind and body. Spirit, too. And he wanted to do it again. As soon as he recovered. Which would most likely be a decade from now.

Her light perfume infused his nose, latched onto his skin, and invaded his lungs. The *thump, thump* of her heartbeat synced with his until he couldn't differentiate one from the other. Their warmth mingled, and she seemed to absorb his as much as he did hers. It was as if *his* every inhalation came from *her*, each tremble and moan out of her a direct current through his system.

There was no him. No her. Only them.

He'd heard of this phenomena from his tribe. Old myths and ways proclaimed a mated soul bond could occur for a chosen few. It wasn't always a romantic fitting, either. Sometimes it was a man with the land, an animal. Or, if they were lucky, a woman. He'd like to blame this euphoria on post-coital hallucinations, but he'd felt similar stirrings before they'd wound up in his bed.

Okay, he didn't actually think the universe was at work, toying with him and Amy. And the tribal stories were just that—a means to portray the spiritual aspects of their beliefs. It was more about greater knowledge of oneself and respecting what was around them.

But still, it was like she was inside him, a part of him on a cellular level. Her pain, her joy, her fears, were his.

Idly, she stroked his shoulder, his upper back, her caress delicate and reassuring. "Did you fall asleep?"

"No, but you can stop touching me sometime in the realm of never."

She paused as if processing, and he growled. A throaty laugh, and she continued her ministrations. This time with both hands. He smiled into her hair, content.

"I gotta tell you, Nakos. This animalistic side of you is sexy."

For that, he lifted his head. "What?"

Mermaid eyes smiled at him. "You shift into an alpha when aroused. Growl, take charge, dominate. I had no idea you had this in you. The guy I've known all my life is reserved and contemplative. Mind you, I'm not complaining. It's hot. Surprising, but hot."

Had he been like that? If so, it was a first. He'd always been more about love-making than rough sex. Not that he'd been rough with her, but there had been something...barbaric in the way his body responded. Amy did tend to bring out his baser needs on a gut-deep level.

And he needed to quit crushing her. "I'll be right back. Don't move." He gave her a quick kiss, rolled off her, and padded into the bathroom to dispose of the condom. When he returned, she was under the covers. "You wouldn't, by chance, be trying to hide that beautiful body of yours, would you?"

She offered a lazy smile. "Air conditioning. I was cold without you as a heating blanket."

Easily remedied. He climbed in, dragged her across the sheets, and tucked her to his side. While he ran his fingers through her hair, he thought about what she'd said before he got up. "Animal, huh?"

That husky laugh of hers wrapped around him. "Normal Nakos has returned. No worries. I like both sides."

She leaned over and kissed him briefly on the mouth, then resettled. Her leg tangled with his and her arm draped over his chest. It was the closest she'd come to initiating intimacy, even if it was mere cuddling.

"All this because I was standing in the kitchen?"

He huffed a laugh. "You could be anywhere, Ames. I'd want you regardless."

Setting her chin on his pec, she took in his features. A wrinkle formed between her brows like her thoughts were headed into enemy territory again. "Sex has never been like that for me." She closed her eyes. "That's so embarrassing to admit, but it's true."

"Don't be ashamed. Sex takes two people, and if you weren't fulfilled, it wasn't all on you." He turned on his side to face her and skimmed a hand down the curve of her spine. "The fact that you can talk about it with me is part of the reason why you were satisfied. There has to be some level of trust to enjoy yourself."

"I guess. It still took a lot of work on your part to..." She shrugged.

"You're not work, Ames. You're pleasure. I enjoyed every second." He took in her blue-green eyes, her expression wide open for the first time in he didn't know how long. What he found wasn't exactly settling. She was hiding something, or holding back, and he didn't have a clue why. "Have you noticed you're not taking as long to climax? Each time we come together, you let go a little more. Listen to what your body tells you. Be secure in the knowledge that I adore looking at you, having you against me. Use my actions and words to build the confidence someone took from you. It's freeing, Ames. I promise."

For the longest time, she just stared at him. Nose to nose and sharing air, they lay there while her gaze grew distant. Wherever she went, it wasn't a happy place, and he almost spoke to bring her out of it. But if she was working something out, far be it for him to stop her. He wished to hell he knew what put those shadows in her pretty eyes. He wanted nothing more than for her to believe him. Better yet, to believe in herself. She was getting there. Through every encounter with him, he was chipping away at her walls. He could only pray time would chase away all her demons, whatever the cause.

She blinked as if coming to, her gaze dropping to his mouth, then his jaw and lower. Over his shoulders, across his chest, she roamed, heating his skin more than any touch. The last dregs of darkness receded and her lips parted with shallow breaths. A blush worked up her neck, tinged her cheeks.

"There, *anim*. Right there." It took entirely too much damn effort to keep still, but it was time he made her take action. "What were you just thinking about?" Judging by the heat in her eyes, she was probably conjuring fantasies he couldn't name on his best day.

His shaft stirred, thickening between them. "Show me what you want."

Her gaze shot to his. Tentative. Debating. She was tempted, though. He could tell by the lip chewing and increased respirations.

"Do it, Ames. Show me. Quit thinking. Act."

Her hand lifted, hovering over his shoulder, fingers flexing. She leaned forward and paused, her mouth inches from his neck. A needy moan from her throat sent him from hard to aching without so much as a downshift.

Panting, aroused as hell, he beat back the urge to do this for her. She liked his animalistic side? Well, it was threatening to make another appearance. "Do it," he grated. "Touch me, kiss me, whatever you want. Hell, bite me for all I care. Just do it. *Now...*"

Surging forward, her mouth latched onto his neck at the same moment her hand gripped his bicep. Nails dug into his flesh, and her hot tongue flattening over his tendon ripped a groan from his throat. She pressed against him, her pert nipples grazing his chest. Fingers drifted down his back, scratching, and stopped at his hip. Kissing her way to the underside of his jaw, she threw her leg over his waist and bucked.

His eyeballs thunked the back of his skull so hard they rattled. He shoved his hand in her hair and dragged her mouth to his. Licking his way inside, he plunged, stroking his tongue like he desperately wanted to with another part of him. He worked his arm between them and cupped her mound.

Hihcebe, so wet for him already. He groaned his approval and parted her folds, coated his fingers. Her swollen nub begged for attention, and he pressed his palm there. Circling. Building her tension. Then, he slipped two fingers inside, and her walls immediately gripped them in a vise. Hot, supple velvet. Need shot up several levels and threatened to consume.

As if that was all the encouragement she needed, she drove her fingers into his hair, tugging his head back and severing the kiss. Teeth grazed his jaw. His ear. His neck. A violent quake shot through him. She rode his hand with reckless abandon, nipping his restraint one nibble at a time.

Losing his ever-loving mind, he removed his fingers from her heat and reached for the nightstand, earning a moan of protest. "I'll make it better soon, *bixooxu.*" She could bet her life on it. His hand shook as he tore into the foil and sheathed himself.

When ready, he held her cheek, forcing himself to recall his original mission. "What do you want? How do you want me to take you?"

Eyes pinched closed, she whimpered and rocked her hips. "Nakos..."

"Tell me. Right now." Sanity was this close to taking a permanent dirt nap. "Tell me and I'll make the ache stop."

Her lashes fluttered, and she pinned him with helpless desire wrapped in torment. "Can..." She swallowed. "From behind. Can you—"

Done. He flipped her over, pinning her back to his front. She gasped, sending his heart thundering. Aligning himself, he thrust deep. She went rigid for a fraction of a beat as if he'd hurt her, then relaxed. But it was that split second that shut down all his systems.

"Are you all right, *anim*?" He nuzzled her ear, closely watching her profile.

"Yes, I..." She let out an uneven breath. "I need to do this. Please."

And that stopped his heart. Dead. Her response wasn't exactly a ringing endorsement for their position or what they were about to do. *Need to do this*? As in, to prove something to herself or ...? What, exactly?

Unfathomable conclusions elbowed aside lust, brought on by her and her alone. The way she'd gone stiff just now. Her inability to orgasm with lovers before him. How long it took her to get to the point of no return. And the walls she continuously kept around herself. Like...even he might hurt her.

Was he reading too much into it? A simple sentence? The cold ball of dread in his gut said no. But, as he studied her, he began to doubt his concern. Her brows were furrowed in a frown of pleasured concentration, lips parted like she was struggling to draw air through a haze of lusty fog, cheeks still flushed pink in desire, and...her hips rocked, taking him deeper.

Yet the nettling sensation wouldn't ease.

Gently, he slid his hand up and tilted her head back, exposing her throat and making her position even more vulnerable to him.

"Who are you with right now?" Because he could've sworn when he'd first thrust into her, it wasn't him.

"You," she breathed. "I'm with you."

Warmth pushed out the cold, and he pulsed inside her. "Say my name, *bixooxu.*"

"Nakos." A moan. A plea. "Please, Nakos." She arched, throwing her head farther back against his shoulder and nudging him deeper inside her soft, willing body.

Yes. Mercy, *yes.*

He palmed her breast, kneading, and rolled his hips. "Again. Say my name again."

A strangled sound rumbled through her, into him. "Nakos." Her husky voice was riddled with tenuous tension. "Nakos, Nakos, Nakos," she chanted.

To reward her—or pacify himself—he eased out of her so slowly dots spotted his peripheral. Then, he drove home. Hard. Fast. Her soft, giving flesh cushioned him, cradled every inch of his shaft like a caress. His lungs emptied and his throat burned.

Slamming his lids shut, he pressed his face into the crook of her neck and repeated the motion. Out equaled pain. Back inside was the equivalent of heaven. Torture. Relief. She bore down to meet his thrusts, and the way they moved together was an unbearable graceful dance.

He had her wrapped so tightly in his embrace, there was nowhere for her to go, nothing to feel but her. The backs of her thighs rubbed the tops of his. Her perfect, round ass was snug against his pelvis. The eloquent curve of her spine fit along the contours of his chest like she was made specifically for him alone.

She moaned, trembling, and he realized she was close. He slid his hand to where they were joined, spreading his fingers through her drenched folds and circling her clit with his thumb. Immediately, she clenched around his shaft, and he pumped with all he had left in him. She bowed, but he held her firm. He wouldn't let her escape, would never let her go as long as there was blood in his veins and a beat to his heart.

Fire burned in his gut and spread. His nerve endings sizzled, misfired. He hissed air through clenched teeth as the sensory overload blew him away. He thickened inside her, almost to the brink of release, and his muscles quaked as he tried to hold out.

He pressed his lips to the shell of her ear. "Come, *anim*," he rasped. "Fall apart and take me with you."

She grew taut, teetering on the precipice. He circled his thumb faster, drove harder, and dropped his forehead to her shoulder as a sheen of sweat broke out on his skin. Just as he was about to beg, she let out a short cry and convulsed around him.

He roared against her neck, mouth wide and jaw locked. Though the sound was muted by her skin, it raked his throat and the ferocity misted behind his lids. Balls tight, jet after jet, he came. His bones splintered, only to mesh and fuse back together again while she milked every last ounce of his life from him.

When he came back into his body from wherever she'd relocated him, her arm was bent behind her and she had her fingers buried in his strands. Words and syllables were a long ways off, but he pulled out and turned her so she faced him. They shared a pillow, and he ran his knuckles over the stubble burn he'd put on her cheek.

"You're quiet."

"I'm recovering." Or trying to. He pulled a breath and met her eyes, but he just sunk deeper instead of gathering his thoughts. "I don't know what to say, Ames. I really don't."

Her mouth opened like she wanted to speak, but it was several moments before she did. "That word, bixu...?"

"*Bixooxu*," he corrected, sensing her turmoil now.

"Yeah." Brows furrowed, she bit her lip. "Did you mean that?"

He traced the soft edges of her jaw with his fingertip, gaze following the path. "Would it be such a surprise? I've loved you many years, Amy."

"As friends."

A sound of agreement, even though he suspected it went way deeper all along, and he settled his hand on her hip. "I meant it as more of a term of endearment than a declaration. Love has many forms, but you were always...different. Nothing I can define, and it won't make sense, but I think us, like this, was inevitable. It just took me too long to connect the dots."

"What does that mean?"

He sighed, not sure if that was hope or fear looking back at him. "It means, Ames, that if I'm not already there, it won't be long. Loving you, in any capacity, fills the missing gap I've lived with my whole life. Falling in love with you would seal that fissure." His heart picked up rhythm when that damn doubt crept back into her eyes, and then the beat shifted ribs as uncertainty morphed into what he could only assume was guilt. "Why does that scare you? It's me here, *anim*. Why does the notion of me loving you frighten you so badly?"

"No one ever has, that's why." Her lower lip quivered. "There were people who were supposed to, some that claimed to and didn't, and others who think they may have, but..." She closed her eyes, shutting him out. "If you mean what you just said, you'd be the first."

Hihcebe. If her goal was to gut him, she could consider it a success. He was bleeding out. Pressing a kiss to her forehead, he fought the pain binding his windpipe and let his lips linger. He'd wanted inside her head, had needed to understand her hesitancy, but now he couldn't deal with the answer.

It made sense she'd think this way. Her parents certainly hadn't shown her any support or affection. He hadn't a clue about previous lovers, yet all signs pointed to no. Her ex definitely hadn't given her respect, never mind love. She'd had Olivia, her brother, and Mae, but chances were, years and experience had probably taught her not to trust those feelings.

And there he went. With his chest hemorrhaging and her naked in his arms on a lazy Sunday afternoon, he fell in love with her all the way. No crushing sensation. No fear rising up to choke him. No doubt whatsoever.

His heartbeat leveled as if the organ finally had purpose and ferociously thumped like it wanted to rip through his chest to get to hers. He breathed freely, filling his lungs with her sultry scent, and he let himself savor the peace for just a brief moment. It wouldn't last. This situation may be as easy as him opening his eyes and trusting what was in front of him. Yet for her, it wasn't that simple.

He was in for a long journey ahead. Her mind was a congested freeway, her soul a never-ending stretch of deserted highway, and her heart was under construction, even though her body was a winding, curvy back road he could map with his eyes closed. Nothing worth its weight came without effort or determination. All he had to do was take his time, instill the leisurely pace that drove her mad, and do it as fast as he could before she caught on.

He had to prove to her the destination was worth it, that it was a safe place. A happy one. "I love you, Ames," he whispered against her skin. It was a start, at least. "I love you."

Chapter Nineteen

Just before dawn, Amy slipped out of Nakos's bed and snatched her clothes off the floor. She padded across the hall to her room, changed, and headed downstairs to start coffee. He'd wake up soon for work, but she needed a few minutes to herself.

The past weekend ping-ponged around in her skull as she measured dark roast and filled a carafe of water. Their lovemaking? It may have started off as sex, two bodies coming together in mutual need, but it hadn't finished that way. He'd taken her like a man who'd come unraveled, and she was the only one holding the frayed end to maintain his sanity. Then—*oh, then*—after they'd had dinner, he'd gone slower, worshiping her body like he had something to prove. He'd put the beast back in the cage. Not only had she orgasmed, many times, he'd made the experience all about her. Holding her afterward. Cooing phrases and stroking her hair with endearing tenderness.

And telling her he loved her.

God, the L-bomb. Her throat seized remembering. She and Olivia often did the *I love you* thing. Amy didn't have that kind of relationship with Kyle, but she knew her brother cared. Chris had said it a handful of times, the first being when he'd proposed. Not that she'd believed him. The words had never come off as sincere. Truth was, she'd been so desperate for any sort of attention that she'd latched onto the only guy who'd shown her any. It was better than winding up alone.

Nakos was very different. The way he looked at her, how he touched, and what he said was all unique. She'd stopped wishing for fairy tales and ever-afters long ago. Pithy dreams meant for other people. And then he'd kissed her. The carefully constructed box where she'd stored her emotions in order to survive unlocked when his lips had met hers.

How easy it would be to give in, to just accept the path he was forging, let herself believe she was due for some happiness. Nakos represented every little thing she'd secretly desired and could never have. More hopes she'd locked in her box, now free. When she was with him, she could almost accept the lie.

Until she sucked it up and told him what had happened to her, each moment they were together was merely another shadow closing in. The constant ache in her belly, the knots of guilt, had no chance of dissolving unless she was honest. He deserved to know who his best friend truly was, to know the woman he'd been sleeping with was soiled.

She'd lain awake most of the night, wrapped snug in his arms, thinking of how to go about telling him. Scenarios had drifted in and out of her mind, conclusions a meager theory at this point. If she had any idea how he'd react, maybe she wouldn't be wound so tight, wouldn't be killing herself with what-ifs.

Pouring herself a cup of coffee, she chugged half of it while standing by the counter. She gazed out the window above the sink as pink rays of sunrise split the sky over the horizon. The world began to wake, brushing off twilight and peeking at a new day. Dew glistened on prairie grass and hills were ensconced in golden light. It would make a pretty picture, but her camera was upstairs. Plus, she and Nakos had to be up at the main house for work soon.

Speaking of... She glanced at the clock. Normally, he was up by now. His internal alarm woke him at the buttcrack of dawn, if not sooner. She stared at the ceiling, not hearing the creak of his footsteps or the whoosh of water through the pipes from his shower.

She downed the rest of her coffee, set the cup in the sink, and made her way upstairs. He was still asleep, lying on his stomach, arms and legs spread as if skydiving in dreams. With a smile, she walked to the bed and sat by his hip.

They'd both zonked out naked last night. She didn't know if that was the norm for him, but she could appreciate it. The sheet had fallen to his lower back, was wrapped around his legs, and left his upper half exposed. Olive skin and sinewy muscle. His face was smooshed into the pillow, raven strands spread around his head like a sexy Native American version of an angel. He didn't make much noise when he slept, nor did he move around a lot, but his torso shifted with deep, even breathing. The man was even graceful while sleeping. Didn't it figure.

They'd worn each other out yesterday. She hated to rouse him, but they needed to get going. She set her hand between the sharp blades of his shoulders and frowned. His skin was hot. Nakos had an internal temp that seemed to run warmer than average, at least that's how it felt to her when he'd pressed against her, held her. Like her own personal heating blanket.

Yet this was different. He was really, *really* hot. She brushed the hair off his face and studied his profile. Dark stubble shadowed his wide jaw and he did appear a tad ashen. She pressed her palm to his forehead and winced. That was some fever he had going.

Concerned, she bent and kissed his cheek. "Nakos?"

He grunted, but that was his only sign of life.

"Hey, I think you've come down with something. You're burning up, and the sun rose and shone before you."

"I don't get sick."

Which was true. Aside from a couple sniffles as kids, he rarely got sick. "Well, you were overdue." When he didn't stir, she kissed his cheek again. "I'm going to call Olivia, let her know you won't be in."

For that, he peeked one eye open. "Not sick. I'm getting up." With what seemed like great effort, he rolled to his side, facing her, and muttered a curse. "My bones have melted. And my head's split open. Are my brains spilling onto the pillow?"

Not sick, huh? Since he'd reclosed his eyes and was already asleep again, she left him to it and went into her room to call the main house.

"Hey, Liv. Nakos is sick. He won't be in. If you give me an hour to get him set—"

Olivia laughed. "Is that code for sex? Nice try. Nakos doesn't get sick."

"You're as bad as he is. I assure you, it's not a code. He's got a fever and barely managed to roll over."

Pause. "Hmm. Now I'm worried. Does he need a doctor? Should I call Hank? Because, seriously, he's never used a sick day. Not once."

Technically, Amy was making him use it, but still. "I think he's all right. Just a bug. I'll be up in an hour. Let Aunt Mae know."

185

"No, no." Olivia sighed. "Stay there. Play nursemaid. Men are babies when they're ill. We've got things handled here."

"Are you sure?"

"Yep. Holler if he gets worse, though. I think this might be a sign of the apocalypse, Nakos not working."

Amy laughed and disconnected, then went into bathroom to hunt up Tylenol. Pills in hand, she jogged downstairs, poured a glass of orange juice, and strode back into Nakos's bedroom.

"Hey, I've got some medicine. Can you sit up for a minute?"

Not a muscle twitched, save for that of his mouth. "Not sick. Don't need medicine."

She rolled her eyes. "I have magic candy that'll make your bones stop melting and fuse your head back together."

His lashes fluttered and his lids lifted. Immediately, he hissed and sluggishly dragged his arm over his eyes. "It burns."

She set the OJ on his nightstand and stood. "I see vampirism is a side effect of the illness we shall not name and to which doesn't exist." She closed the drapes, muting the room of daylight, and sat on the edge of the mattress.

"I'd laugh if the effort wouldn't kill me." His words were mumbled since he'd yet to pull his arm off his face. "I might, maybe a little, be sick."

"Uh huh. Lift your head for me. Swallow these and you can sleep."

A world-weary sigh, and he struggled to raise himself onto his elbows. At sloth-speed, he took the pills, downed them with a healthy sip of juice, and flopped onto his back in a heap. "Ugh. The room's spinning." When she rose, he reached out, weakly fingering her pants as if trying to grab hold. "Stay, *anim*. Please."

Oddly touched, she kissed his brow. Chris had never wanted her around when sick. He was a total asshole if not feeling good and usually got meaner. She'd wound up crashing on the couch a number of times.

"I'll be right back." She brushed her lips over Nakos's forehead, earning a weak smile.

Leaving the juice in case he'd want it later, she changed into PJs in her room, seeing as she wasn't going anywhere, and snatched her laptop off the table, then climbed in bed beside Nakos. He was out cold again, so she sat against the headboard and set her laptop on her thighs. She checked her photo site accounts, noting she had a number of downloads and hits. It wouldn't break the bank, but she was earning more revenue than she'd expected.

After playing around for a couple hours, scrolling the internet, Nakos moaned and stirred. She shut off the computer and put it on the floor. His color looked a little better, but he was still very warm.

Idly, she ran her fingers through his hair, massaged his scalp, hoping it would give him some relief. Honestly, seeing him down for the count was more than a little unnerving. He was always so strong, steady. He sighed contentedly, easing into her attention like a cat.

"Ames." Her name was little more than a slur, but the conviction behind his tone made her smile. As if weighed by bricks, he slid his arm over, patting the sheets blindly as if searching. "Ames?"

"Right here." Scooting down, she lay facing him, keeping up with the head massage.

"Feels good." Half asleep, he draped an arm over her waist. "Come here." Before she could move, he snuggled closer and buried his face under her jaw. His frame went utterly lax against her as he settled in, hotter than a furnace. "That's better." His lips brushed her throat as he spoke. "Smell so good. I hope I'm not contagious."

"It's okay if you are. I can take care of myself." After all, she'd been doing it for years. But she held him close, offering the comfort she'd never been given, glad she was here to issue it. Being sick sucked, and she knew what it was like to be in pain or too weak to move, wishing someone would do something as simple as rub her back.

He grunted a sound of disagreement. "Not anymore. I'll take care of you." In seconds, his breathing evened out again.

She adjusted the sheet to cover him and ran her hand up and down his spine. His heartbeat was like a lullaby playing just for her. He didn't stir, but he did seem to slip deeper into sleep. As she held him, emotion once again stalled her lungs.

It seemed silly to get worked up over something so mundane as his behavior when sick. Yet she could no more control her reaction than she could deny him what he wanted. Here he was, feverish and achy, but he still thought of her. Saying nice things, needing her close. He was half-buried in a mind fog, and his first instincts were to cuddle with her, not bark orders or push her away. It cemented her experiences with him as legit, proving he wasn't only saying or doing what he'd thought he should.

They laid in bed all day and evening. In the early afternoon, he'd managed to rouse long enough to eat half a bowl of soup, and sometime around midnight, his fever had broken. He woke up Tuesday morning with the sun, only mildly sluggish for the encounter, and Amy was grateful he was better.

On Wednesday, after they were done with work, he wanted to test out the new horse he and Olivia had acquired, and asked Amy to go for a ride. With her on Pirate, a two-year-old gelding, and him on the new stallion, Brandy, they took off for Dead Man's Pass near the southern pasture.

The twenty minute trek did wonders to clear her head and she relaxed into the gentle sway of her horse. The sun was lower in the sky, but still cast hot rays over the waist-high fields. They had another couple hours of lazy daylight before dusk would settle, and she breathed in the scents of soil and warm fur, cut grass and hay. Sounds of leaves crackling and the creek trickling were a light background to clomping hooves.

They passed one herd of steer grazing in a pasture, and Nakos halted his horse. He dismounted, cooing platitudes to the stallion. "Why don't you hop down? We can rest here a bit."

She obliged, and he tied the reins to a wooden fence post, then gave each of the horses a carrot from the satchel. Grabbing a blanket, he strode over to a lone cottonwood and spread it by the base. He disappeared from sight in the tall, golden prairie grass when he sat.

Curious, she made her way over, finding him prone on the blanket, one arm bent behind his head, and his Stetson tipped over his eyes. A gray tee stretched over the ridges of his pecs, his abs, and his legs were crossed at the ankles, encased in a worn pair of denim.

Lazy, sexy cowboy.

"I really wish I had my camera right now."

He grinned and crooked a finger, summoning her.

Waiting a beat, she chewed her lip. She had an undeniable urge to straddle him, ride him in a more satisfying way than the gelding. Save a horse, right?

And why not? He'd, thus far, enjoyed everything they'd done together and was constantly encouraging her to do what she wanted while they were intimate. They were a mile from the main house and all the guys were done for the day. The area was private, and even if someone did stumble upon them, the pasture would hide their romp.

Smiling, she kicked off her flip-flops and, with her knees on either side of his hips, she lowered herself onto his thighs.

Quick as a blink, he flicked off his hat, grabbed her waist, and lifted his head. A guttural groan rumbled over the call of a whippoorwill as he looked at her. His dark eyes swept over her, met her gaze. The longer they stared, the harder his chest moved air. He seemed to be waiting, albeit patiently, for her to follow through.

"Hell yes, Amy. Come on."

She dipped under his shirt, splaying her fingers over the cut muscles of his abs, and his stomach concaved. Up, she moved, taking the tee on her journey, and when it bunched around his chest, he reached back and jerked it off. His brows rose in a *now what*, but his pupils blew, belying the casual quirk.

God, did she want him. Need him. He'd shown her what true passion was, had given her undeniable pleasure on levels she hadn't known existed. All she had to do was look at him and she wanted. His mouth, his hands, his everything.

Panting, she unbuttoned his fly, carefully released his zipper to free his erection. He wasted no time shoving his pants and briefs down his thighs. She rose on her knees to give him room. Before kicking the jeans aside, he pulled a condom from his pocket, laid it on his chest like a taunt.

Breasts heavy, her panties drenched, she stood and shed her clothing, then reclaimed her position over him. Anticipation buzzed under her skin, fluttered in her belly, and she didn't think. For once, she just went with her gut. Grabbing the condom, she tore into the foil and, watching him, she rolled the latex down his thick shaft. A warm breeze teased her flesh.

He pulsed in her hand and bucked. "*Hihcebe, anim.* Yes." Need had his voice grating like gravel. "Take what you want. Take me."

Rising over him, she swallowed hard. Always before, this position had unnerved her. Wondering what to do, how to move, where to put her hands. Being watched had felt like being judged. Unsettling.

189

But not now. With Nakos's eyes dialed to hell-yes and his respirations cranked to I'm-dying, she didn't pause a beat. She guided him inside her and took him slowly, savoring the stretch and the way he completely filled her. The blessed sweet ache subsided, only to shift that throb to every other part of her body.

He barked a sound of stunned gratification and flung his arms over his head, hands fisted. The deliberate move wasn't lost on her. He was submitting to her, telling her he was at her mercy instead of the other way around. Whatever she wanted to do to him, he was willing. He was hers.

Setting her hands on his chest, she rocked. The slick glide sent a tremble through her entire nervous system. She did it again and, this time, he rolled his hips to meet her.

He thrust his head back, biceps bulging. Tendons strained in his neck. She got so caught up in watching him, his gorgeous body and the way he reacted, she didn't realize she'd paused until he lifted his head and met her gaze with carnal desperation.

A muscle ticked in his jaw. "Look at you." His wandering gaze caressed her skin, even if his hands never sought. Her face, her breasts, where they joined...a scorching trail that had some of the feral animalism draining from his eyes. Wonder replaced everything else. "Look at you, *bixooxu*. The sunlight in your hair, on your skin. How your cheeks flushed when you took me deep. The reckless abandon in your eyes. So fucking beautiful. You have no idea what you do to me. But you? Like this?" He shook his head. "My brave *anim*. Mercy, how I've missed that fire inside you. Show me. Be fearless with me."

As she stared at him, heart in her dang throat, she knew, understood, a flicker of what he'd been feeling. The love he claimed he had, the blinding trust, was all right there looking back at her. It rose inside her, too. Swelled. Warmed her in places that had long ago grown cold. In all her life, she'd never felt wanted, loved. Beautiful. He brought that to her, gave it over as if it were a gift he'd been keeping for the day she'd need it.

"Nakos." God, it hurt. An endearing, heartbreaking kind of hurt that both repaired and destroyed what was left of her.

"There you are." He sat up, cupped her cheeks. "Now you get it, now you hear me. Let me in all the way."

190

As he took her mouth in a slow, drugging kiss, she rocked over him, shoved her hands in his hair to hold on, dislodging his ponytail. He rose up to meet her, pelvis moving in both a restless and refined dance that shattered her. She ground her hips. He thrust. Her breasts crushed against the hard wall of his chest and her legs wrapped around him, as binding as his arms holding her.

They clung, they sought.

And she knew, for once, she finally mattered. If only to him, it was enough.

Chapter Twenty

Leaning against the barn's open carriage doors, Nate crossed his arms. "Things seem to be going well with Amy. Why do you look irritated?"

Nakos gave a last pat for Midnight, their three-year-old stallion, and closed the stall. Unsure how to answer, he searched the expanse behind the ex-soldier as if the land might provide answers.

A front was rolling in, the sky to the west black with ominous clouds. Static charged the humid air and smelled like rain. They'd called it a day just in time to avoid nature's wrath. Nothing sounded better than sinking into Amy's warm body in front of a fire while a storm raged outside.

Except... "She's holding back. From me, from..." He lifted his hand, let it slap his thigh as he dropped it. Frustration pounded his temples. "I don't know. She's stopped fighting me, so there's that. But she's got something in that head of hers keeping her from fully engaging. I wish to hell I knew what. She looks at me like she's gearing her courage to tell me, then clams up." Which pissed him off. When had he ever given her the impression she couldn't talk to him? About anything?

Nate nodded slowly. "Have you asked her about it?"

"No." The situation had been obvious between them, even when all else was smooth sailing. "I'm trying to give her time because whatever it is, it's...dark." Nakos could tell by the shadows in her eyes, the haunted expression. And it was killing him.

"You love her, yes?"

He closed his eyes. "Yeah, that's the other thing. I've told her, repeatedly, and she hasn't said it back." When Nate just stared holes through him, Nakos sighed. "What?"

"It doesn't come as easy for people like me and her. Amy and I? Our situations aren't that different. Remember, it was just a few months ago the roles were reversed. You came to me, laid it out for me about Olivia. I'm just trying to return the favor."

Nate hadn't had any love his entire life. Until he'd landed in Meadowlark and in Olivia's capable hands, he'd wandered from situation to situation like a ghost, repeating mistake after mistake. Nakos didn't understand how there were any similarities between the guy and Amy.

"Think about it." Nate straightened, widened his stance. "Yeah, my life was shit before coming here, but Amy, in a way, had it worse." He removed his black ball cap, rubbed his bald head, and replaced the hat. "I didn't belong anywhere, had no family. Foster care wasn't all warm fuzzies, but I knew my place. Amy grew up in a house with two parents, the very people who created her, and they don't give a crap. You want to talk about a mind fuck? Put yourself in her shoes." He lifted his hand, palm out. "And before you say she had you and Olivia, you need to consider her viewpoint. If her own parents didn't love her, how is she supposed to trust anyone else who claims to? That ex of hers and what he did only locked in that mindset."

Hihcebe, the guy was right. The scenarios had played through Nakos's mind, too. But he didn't know what more to do to prove to her he loved her. He treasured each moment with her, and when they were apart, he felt something akin to separation anxiety. Whatever demons were lurking inside her had their claws in him, as well. He'd be a hell of a lot calmer if he knew what those demons were so he could fight them.

He strode toward the exit and glanced over Nate's shoulder. Up the path, near the mudroom of the main house, Amy's folks stood with a man Nakos didn't recognize, along with Amy's brother and Olivia. "What are they doing here?"

Nate turned his head, scowled, and faced Nakos. "The uncle arrived in town this morning. They came by to visit with Kyle. Olivia's been showing them around the past hour." He paused. "Something's not right about that guy. I told Kyle to stick by Olivia's side so I could get away."

"Where's Amy? Have they seen her?" If they could make a trip to the ranch to visit their son, they sure as hell could check up on their daughter.

"No, they've stuck to outside. Last I saw, she was in the kitchen with Mae."

Which was probably for the best. Nakos ground his teeth. "Let me lock up here and..."

He turned, finding Amy at the rear open carriage doors. She wore her usual casual clothes, a pair of jeans and a peach blouse, but they were wrinkled. Cocoa hair, up in a high ponytail, had wisps messily escaping to frame her face. Her hands were clasped in front of her, the knuckles white, and only one flip-flop adorned a foot. The other was bare, like she'd rushed out and lost one. That pretty mouth was pressed into a thin, distraught line and a sheen of tears swam in her mermaid eyes.

Warning knells clanged. "What's wrong?"

"Can we go home now?" Her voice was brittle and, as he stepped closer, he realized she was trembling. Hard.

He glanced at Nate for guidance, concern ratcheting. But he was focused on her, too, a deep grove between his brows, and he didn't appear to know the reason for her state either, if his expression was any indication.

"Can you give us a sec?"

Nate glanced at him, then back to her. "I'll be right up at the house if you need me."

She nodded repeatedly, the motion frantic. After Nate stepped out, she jerked her wide eyes to Nakos. "Please, can we go?" Her breath caught, and...that was it. He was officially freaked out beyond reason.

He cupped her shoulders and tugged her to him, stroking her back. A leaf dangling from a branch in October high winds had nothing on the way she shook in his arms. Alarm pinched his airway and a cold fist squeezed his lungs. This wasn't her, wasn't his Amy at all. Her take-no-prisoners, hear-me-roar persona had disappeared, and in it's place was a woman he didn't recognize. He tightened his hold, as much for him as for her.

Dropping a kiss to the top of her head, he rested his cheek. "Talk to me, *bixooxu*. What's got you so worked up? Is this about your parents being here?" His heart rate was nearly as hyper as hers, thumping double-time against his chest.

Wrenching away, she cast her watery gaze everywhere but at him. "I want to go. I don't want to see him. I can't deal with him right now. I just can't."

He froze, not only due to her erratic behavior, but her phrasing. She'd said *him*, not *them*. Meaning, her uncle? Why would a man she hadn't seen in years put the fear of God in her eyes, have her trembling beyond measure, and needing to bolt? There wasn't damn near anything that scared her.

Memories flashed through his head, quicker than lightning with twice the voltage. How she'd gone insipidly pale in the tavern when she'd learned the guy was coming in town. The things Olivia had said about him, the way he'd made her uncomfortable as a girl. They'd claimed he was creepy and had stared at them like...

Oh hell. And with his lungs refusing to cooperate, Nakos looked at Amy, at the rabid fear shaking her limbs, the fragile helplessness in her eyes. A frigid ball of dread spread behind his ribs.

No. Mercy, no. "What did he do, Ames?"

She made a whimpering sound and paced, hands on her head. Barely comprehendible mutterings sprang from her lips. "Don't make me relive this...I'm over it...can't hurt me...just want to go home..."

Suspicion mounted higher, ripped the barely beating heart right out of his chest. He was about to lose his shit all over the room. "Ames," he choked. Striding to her, he grabbed her shoulders, dipped to look in her eyes. "How did he hurt you? Tell me," he demanded when she said nothing.

As if traumatized, she merely stared at him with eyes like glass and her lower lip quivering. Hauntingly chilling.

He tried to think. More memories seared to mind. How she'd grown rigid that time he'd taken her from behind. The admission she'd lost her virginity younger than most girls.

Bile churned, rose up his esophagus. Fucking Almighty, let him be wrong.

"Did he...?" He couldn't even say the words. "Did he...put his hands on you?" Say no. Please, say no.

She whined, eyes pleading. Seconds passed. Finally, she nodded.

No, no, no. "Punched? Kicked? Slapped?"

She shook her head, sending what little hope this was a physical abuse situation shattering at his feet.

The alternative was too much to bear. He'd carried her out of this very barn months ago, bruised and broken and bloody, and he'd yet to recover. But...this? The possibility of her having been violated? The end. He couldn't survive it. Not her. Sweet *Hihcebe,* not his Ames.

He was going to be sick. "Worse?" As if the idea of that man hitting her wasn't vile enough. He wanted to die. Goddamn die right now. "Did he do something worse?"

A sob, and she nodded again.

"How much more, *anim*? You have to tell me," he uttered brokenly, eyes burning.

"He did everything," she whispered. Tears clung to her dark lashes, splashed onto her pale cheeks.

And he knew. Before her mouth opened to say the one word that would level him to the ground, he knew it was coming. He tried to brace himself, hold it together, and epically failed.

"He raped me."

Roaring, he held her head in his shaking hands and slammed his eyes shut. Awful, tormenting visions cut through his mind, sliced like a blade. Shredded. Releasing her, he stumbled back, clutched his stomach.

Rage—white hot, sadistic rage—whipped through him. Lashed. Violent in the intensity, it surged as if summoned by the very bowels of hell. Blood boiled and pressure built in his skull, rammed his temples. Someone, that *thing* out there, had dared to hurt his Amy. His beautiful, courageous angel.

A growl tore his throat, and he pivoted. Stormed out of the barn. A quick glance around, and he found her parents, Kyle, Nate, Olivia, and the soon-to-be dead man in the same spot as moments ago. He was going to kill him. Several times. Limb from goddamn limb, he'd tear him to pieces.

Marching up to the group, Nakos zeroed in on the bastard. He had a blip of a second to make out a brown comb-over and fat paunch through a red haze of wrath before he shoved his forearm into the guy's collarbone and slammed him against the side of the house.

197

Nakos reared his arm back, then brought it forward with everything he had. His fist met face. "You." *Punch.* "Sick." *Punch.* "Fuck." *Punch, punch.* Bone cracked. Blood spurt. The guy slid to the ground, and Nakos bent to haul him up again.

Arms wrapped around him, got between him and doling justice, and backed him up several paces. Nate. Had to be with the tattoo sleeves and brawn, because no way was anything but the ex-soldier strong enough to stop Nakos's fury. He shoved, attempted to get free, but Nate held firm.

"Take a breather, friend."

"Let me go." Nakos struggled and got nowhere.

"What the hell, man?" Kyle, kneeling next to his uncle, glared at Nakos.

Mae walked out of the mudroom, the screen door clacking against the frame. "What's all the fuss?" She slung a towel over her shoulder, eyes darting to each of them like she was assessing the scene. "Well?"

"He came out of nowhere and slugged me." Wiping blood from his lip, the uncle looked from Amy's parents to Kyle. "Who is this guy?"

"That's our foreman, Uncle Clint."

Amy's father held out a hand, helped Clint to his feet. "As savage as the rest of his kind."

"How dare you?" Amy's mother looked at Nakos with disgust. "I want him arrested."

Nakos gnashed his molars to dust, his muscles tense as concrete. "Did you know?" He thrashed against Nate's hold, glared at her parents. "Do you know what he did to her? Answer me!"

"Okay, time out." Nate shoved his face in Nakos's. "Explain. I'm assuming the 'he' is Clint and the 'her' is Amy. Now, explain."

Nakos stared at Nate, chest heaving. "He touched her."

"Hey." Olivia, at his side, gently stroked Nakos's arm. "They just got here. We haven't seen Amy."

"He doesn't mean today." Nate, voice flat, looked at him, tension tightening his features. Nakos could all but trace the pattern on the dots Nate connected.

"But, the last time he was here was..." She rubbed her forehead.

"When you were twelve. That's the last time he was in town." Tears stung Nakos's sinuses, formed a hot ball in his windpipe. He had to lock his legs so he wouldn't collapse under the weight of the situation. "She was just a girl, little red. Only a child." Shit. He couldn't take it.

"I don't understand."

He prayed she never would. He looked at Nate, temper threatening again on a low simmer. "He. Touched. Her." He growled, his throat raked raw. "*He...touched...her.*"

Nate's expression went to stone cold steel. His jaw clenched, his eyes narrowed, and he slowly released Nakos. The silent question in the ex-soldier's eyes was directed at Nakos alone, and the underlying savage hint in the dark depths meant he'd already figured it out.

Still, Nakos dipped his chin once in answer, not sure he could speak. His anger was beginning to fade entirely, as if he'd put it all in his friend's capable hands now, and what replaced it was far worse. Realization. Grief. Misery. Remorse.

Sheer annihilation on a bone-deep, visceral, he'd-never-get over-it level.

Kyle turned, backed away from the group. "Are you saying...?" The color drained from his face when no one said a word. "No." Hollow eyes, a more timid shade of Amy's, shifted to his uncle, then his parents. "Mom? Dad?"

Neither Mr. or Mrs. Woods denied the accusations. Most gutting, neither looked surprised or guilty, either.

They'd known. They'd known and had done nothing?

Clint stumbled. "What are y'all blathering about?"

Nate pulsed livid vibes next to Nakos, sucked in a breath through flared nostrils. "You son of a bitch." The barest hint of ink whirred through the air as his fist met his target. Ass over tea kettle, Clint went down. This time, he didn't get back up. "By the way, Wyoming doesn't have a statute of limitations on rape, asshole." He pointed at Amy's folks. "You don't move. You're all under arrest." He flicked a scornful glare at an unconscious Clint. "And assault. I seem to recall he took a swing at Nakos first. That what you saw, baby?"

Olivia, tears streaming down her shell-shocked face, nodded.

"This is ridiculous." Mrs. Woods crossed her arms. "He didn't do anything to my daughter and that barbarian clearly hit Clint first."

"I suggest you utilize your right to remain silent." Nate looked at Mae. "Get the sheriff's station on the phone, would you? Tell Rip I need an assist."

"Sure." Mae, confusion in her eyes, smoothed her white strands and headed inside.

Nakos hit the end of his rope. He pulled Olivia against him, needing the calm she typically brought him. But it wasn't enough. It didn't help the deadening void in his chest or the sickening swirl of nausea in his gut or the erratic thump of his pulse. Nothing would. Noises, awful noises like a wounded animal, escaped his throat. Raked the tissue as they got louder.

He released her, concerned he'd grip her too hard, and grabbed the back of his neck with both hands instead. His legs buckled, and his knees smacked dirt. "*Hihcebe*, little red. I can't...I can't..." Breathe. He couldn't breathe, damn it.

"Kyle, go look for Amy." Olivia knelt in front of Nakos, cupped his cheeks.

Nate muttered something about Amy being in the barn, but it was all a hazy wash in Nakos's mind. Fuzz in his ears. He teetered on a rapid vertigo shift as dots spotted his peripheral.

"Shh." Olivia stroked his cheek, but her scent was all wrong. The touch not right. Not Amy's. "It's going to be all right. You're scaring me, though. I've never seen you this upset. We've got to focus on Amy, so—"

"Ames." Yes, that's what he needed. He needed his Amy. To hold her, to make sure she was okay, to assure her no one was ever going to harm so much as one hair on her gorgeous head again. He surged to his feet, turned as Kyle ran out of the barn.

"She's not there."

"What?" Nakos jogged around him and to the carriage doors. Empty. The sole flip-flop she'd been wearing lay in the dirt. Quickly, he ran to the other side, scanned past the grazing pens to the path she might've taken if she'd hoofed it back to his cabin. Nothing. Panicked, he met up with the others again. "Olivia, search the house. Kyle, check the other barns." He glanced at Nate, who obviously had to stay on Amy's parents and uncle until Rip showed up. "You okay here?"

"Yeah. Go."

Nakos rounded the house and skidded to a stop out front. Thunder boomed, followed by a flash of lightning. He gazed up at the greenish-gray sky and frowned. She wasn't in his truck or on the front porch. Just in case, he ran the length of the driveway, but she wasn't there, either. By the time he got back near the mudroom, Olivia shoved through the screen door.

"No. I looked everywhere. She's not inside. Aunt Mae said she hasn't seen her."

"Shit." He shoved off his Stetson, combed his fingers through his ponytail, then replaced the hat. All he could see were Amy's wide blue-green eyes filling with tears while she'd confirmed his suspicion. The way she'd shook against him. "Shit. Where would she go?"

Nate jerked a chin to his right. "Rip's here. Give me five minutes to get these assholes off the property and I'll help." Taking charge, he turned to Olivia. "Call the ranch hands. Have the men meet in the barn. We'll split into teams." He studied Nakos. "Drive up the main road toward your place. Maybe she just decided to walk."

Leaving the others, Nakos hopped in his truck, turned the engine over, and sped down the driveway. He slowed once he got past the gate despite the thundering race of his heart.

Searching for her, he recapped their conversation in the barn and cursed. He should've stayed with her, should've kept her in his arms and tended to her. Instead, he'd uncharacteristically flipped his lid, and now she was missing. Worry ate away at his stomach lining.

He got all the way to his cabin without spotting her and, just in case, rushed inside to check. Not there. The sky let loose while he floored it to the main house, pouring in horizontal sheets. The wipers barely kept up, and he pictured her in the rain. Alone.

All their men were in the barn when Nakos returned, listening intently to Nate. He paused. "Anything?"

Nakos shook his head. His stomach bottomed out. A needling sense of anxiety itched under his skin. He swore to all that was holy, if she wasn't all right and in one piece, he'd fucking go apeshit.

"Okay, move out. Mic up if you find anything." The guys shuffled out and Nate pointed to an aerial map of the ranch tacked to the wall, then jerked his chin for Nakos to step closer. "Teams of two are going out on ATV here, here, and here." He indicated the three sections of land, the fourth being the main house and barns. "Olivia is with Kyle. They're taking this path south toward your cabin. Olivia thinks she might've gone that way. Mae's staying at the house and will radio if Amy shows up."

Nakos ran an unsteady hand down his face. "Thank you for helping. I'm not thinking straight."

"We'll find her." Nate sighed. "I can't keep her folks or uncle on anything without a statement from Amy about..." He closed his eyes, jaw ticking. "Makes me want to pound on the fucker's face again." Lifting his lids, he rolled his shoulders. "Rip's holding them overnight on bogus trespassing charges until I can talk to her."

"Okay." Damn it all. Where was she? "I can't wait around here. I have to go look."

Chapter Twenty-One

Drenched, shivering, Amy huddled in the corner of Olivia's old tree house and tried to breathe. She hadn't been able to take the emotional assault and just needed to get away. Fast. The frenetic panic had almost been worse than the fear.

After Nakos had stalked out of the barn, she'd gone the long way around so no one spotted her and had stumbled onto their old stomping grounds by accident. A brief storm had come through, but the tree house had no roof, thus she'd been caught in the worst of the rain.

From her perch on the northern side of the main house, she could barely make out the dim glow of lights since there was enough distance to give the illusion of privacy. The small structure was built high in an oak and was roughly seven feet long at most. Old pine boards were scarred, a tad musty, but sturdy. Branches formed a canopy overhead, stars and a sliver of moonlight peeking through the leaves. She hadn't been in here since she was a kid, had forgotten all about it.

It had seemed a good place as any to get her head together, but that had been hours ago. She still couldn't bring herself to move. Dark had descended while she'd cowered and crickets chirped in the night. A soft stirring of grass rustled and an owl hooted. The quiet nature sounds did nothing to calm the frazzled tatters of her nerves.

God, talk about a blow. She'd been washing vegetables next to Mae at the kitchen sink, wondering if Nakos would be interested in a bath together later, and she'd glanced out the window to find...*him*.

Everything had systematically shut down. Kaput. She hadn't been able to think or breathe or so much as form a sentence. There was no way she could've known what seeing her uncle again would do to her. After the...incident, he'd left the next day to go back to Texas and she hadn't seen him since.

Hard, so dang hard she'd worked to build herself back up, put on her big girl panties, and forge her defenses. She'd moved beyond it, had grown stronger, was living a semi-normal life. And one glimpse of that man had thrust her right back to being the helpless girl she'd once been—shoved against a brick wall and crying through the pain.

Alone. Utterly, utterly alone.

A sob hitched her chest for the millionth time. Everyone knew. Judging by the shouting after Nakos had left her standing in the barn, everyone now knew her dirty, shameful secret. She drew her knees to her chest and rested her forehead on them. Mortification stung her cheeks even as the coldness inside her spread. Consumed.

Would she ever be warm again? Did she have any friends left?

Footsteps sounded below, and she tensed.

"Amy? It's Nate." He paused. "If you're in there, I'm coming up. Just letting you know. I don't want to startle you. Here I come."

The floor vibrated as his feet hit the wooden slats of the ladder. His bald head emerged at the opening, followed by his huge inked arms, then a torso in a fitted black tee.

His gaze searched the space, landed on her, and he let out a long-winded gust. "Thank Christ. I'm coming in." He climbed the rest of the way and sat on his haunches, giving her a wide berth. "Are you hurt? Injured?"

She shook her head.

"Good." He pulled out a walkie-talkie. "I'm just going to tell the others that, okay?" He brought the radio to his mouth, eyes on her. "Stand down, everyone. I've got her. She's all right. Head back to base and call it a night."

Nakos, Kyle, and Olivia keyed over one another, their questions a rapid fire.

Nate pinched the bridge of his nose. "Olivia, baby. She's safe. Kyle, head to the main house with Olivia. Nakos, give me five minutes and I'll call you on the satellite phone." He sat against the opposite wall from Amy and stretched his legs out. "That should keep them quiet for a few minutes. We've scoured the entire ranch twice. We were worried."

"I didn't mean to scare everybody. I just...I had to..."

"Run?" He nodded. "I get it."

More like hide, but close enough. "How did you find me?"

204

"I was searching the side of the house again and remembered this was here." As if to give her a moment, he shifted his focus to the cramped quarters, a half smile curving his lips. "The secret place. Olivia brought me up here once, a few months ago. It wasn't entirely a bad experience."

A surprise laugh huffed from her mouth. "We used to hang out in here, spilling our guts. That's why she calls it the secret place. I assume that's not what you two did up here."

"Oh, there were secrets told. She has a way of getting them out." He grinned. "The how was interesting."

Another laugh, and some of her tension drained. "I bet." She shivered, sobered. "I really am sorry."

"I'm only going to say this once, so listen close. You don't have anything to apologize for. None of it. Not one single thing. Hear me?" At her nod, his frown eased. "Good."

The phone clipped to his belt rang, and he glanced heavenward as if seeking guidance. "That's probably Nakos. Do you want him to know where you are?"

She didn't want to see anyone. Couldn't. "Not yet."

He put the phone to his ear, listened a moment. "Yes. No." He studied her, skimmed a gaze down the length of her and back. "I wouldn't lie to you. Trust me on this. She's fine. She's not hurt. I'm not leaving her side until she wants to move. Go home. I'll bring her there when she's ready." He closed his eyes as if in pain. "I know, man. Bye."

Carefully, he set the phone aside, stared at it. "He's out of his mind with worry. And I don't just mean not knowing where you are." He met her gaze, held it with determination. "You didn't see him tonight, Amy, and be glad for that. But understand me. He's a fucking wreck."

Tears, hot and heavy, scorched her throat, fell on her cheeks. She covered her eyes with her hand as pressure built in her chest. "I couldn't tell him what happened. So often, I tried, but... I'm weak. How am I supposed to face him now that he knows?" She wiped her eyes. Sniffed.

"Weak is violating a twelve-year-old girl simply because you can. Weak is having the urge to want to in the first place." He leaned forward. "Strength is getting back on your feet after some jerk took something precious from you. Strength is picking up the pieces when your sense of security, your very trust, has been stolen." His tone softened, and in his golden-brown eyes was an understanding she never thought she'd ever find from another. "You aren't weak, Amy. You're the very definition of courage. Crying? Being scared? Needing to run once in awhile? That's not weakness. That's being human."

"All these years, I was fine. Really, I was. Until..."

"Until the nightmare was shoved in front of you again."

She let out a watery exhale. "Yeah." She met his gaze, hoping to have her doubts assuaged, once and for all. Needed to hear it from a man. "What if..." She swallowed thickly, pressing a hand to her belly to stop the churning riot. "If it was Olivia, would you look at her the same? Would you still...want her?"

"Yes. Hands down, without a doubt, no thinking required, *yes*." He rose, scooted to the spot next to her, and leaned against the wall so they were shoulder-to-shoulder. "She'd still be the sweet, stubborn, bleeding heart I married and can't live without. Just like you're still the same sassy, strong, talented, and independent woman Nakos fell in love with. Scars and history don't change that."

"Really?"

"Swear to God." He tilted his head. "Now, if it was Olivia, I would, however, hunt the asshole down and beat him within an inch of his life. Which, by the way, is what Nakos tried to do until I held him off." He scratched his jaw. "Kinda sorry I stopped him."

"He did not. Nakos?" Then again, now that her head was a little clearer, he had seemed...well, out of his mind when he'd left her in the barn.

"Totally came unglued. Clocked your uncle three times before I got in there."

"Huh. Wow. He's always been level-headed. Meticulous, honestly. Drives me nuts sometimes."

"Take it from a guy. Men in love? We don't know our asses from our elbows. Threaten our women, and we lose it." He turned his head and looked at her, their faces close enough she could see some of the shadows still lurking inside him. "Let me ask you this. If it had been Olivia, like you said, would you consider it her fault? Would you agree with her if she blamed herself?"

Okay, fine. She got the point. It was hard to erase years of ingrained thought mentality, though. "You know I wouldn't."

Empathy shone in his eyes, and it changed the whole big bad wolf persona he had going for him, showed the heart under all the brawn. "I'm going to be blunt. You were raped. You were violated. You had no say in the matter or control over what happened. I think maybe it's time you realized you were a victim. And it might be a good idea for you to take some of that power back."

Tears threatened again at his tenderness. "How?"

"For one, talk about it. With Olivia, with Nakos, with the dog. Doesn't matter who. Six months ago, there's no way I'd admit that, but there is something oddly liberating about voicing the ugliness."

She didn't know if she'd ever get to a stage where she could, but if Nate thought it was a solid start, she'd consider it. "What else?"

"Press charges." He shook his head when she opened her mouth to argue, and took her hand in his. "We've got him locked up, just waiting for your statement. I'm not claiming that retelling what happened will be easy. Flat out, it's going to suck. I'll be right there, not judging, along with Olivia and Nakos, if you want to go that route. The asshat will probably fight the charges and there will be a trial. I'm not going to lie. That'll suck, too. And there's no guarantee he won't walk. But it'll hold him accountable for the sick thing he did, and perhaps the process will give you closure."

He squeezed her fingers. "Victim doesn't equal weak. Regardless of what you decide, remember that much. You are ten times stronger than he is, and he'll never touch you again. You have my word." He suddenly looked a little distressed at her new stream of leaking tears. His eyes widened and his brow furrowed. "Or I could just kill him. Nakos told me once he knew where to hide a body so it'll never be found. Of course, he was threatening me at the time."

Laughing, she dropped her head on his shoulder. "I'll think about it. The pressing charges part, not murder."

"Open offer."

She laughed again, then sighed as they slipped into a comfortable silence. Animals scurried in the night and leaves crackled. She breathed in heavy humidity, the scent of wet grass and fertile soil, feeling calmer. A damp, rain-tinged quality hung in the air, and it had a strangely cleansing effect. Or maybe it was the company.

207

"You're a good guy, Nate."

"Didn't used to think so, but I'm a work in progress." He patted her leg. "The stuff I told you tonight was all a variation or another of what Olivia and Nakos have reiterated to me. Must be true, right?"

Smiling, she lifted her head. "Must be."

He studied her face. "Since we're here in the place of secrets, I have one for you. Olivia's pregnant."

On a gasp, she straightened.

"Yep. About six weeks along. She wants to wait a couple more before telling everyone, so act surprised when she does." He paused, staring ahead as if lost in thought. "We all get scared, Amy. Right now, I'm fucking terrified."

"Don't be." At his grunt, she squeezed his arm. "That's the best news. Consider it a fresh start. A clean slate. You're going to be a wonderful dad."

"If I don't royally screw it up."

"Not going to happen. You have all of us to help steer you in the right direction and you, of all people, understand what going without is like. Those instincts to protect are ingrained in your DNA. Plus, you love Liv so much. A baby is proof of that love."

A laugh, and he swiped a hand down his face. "No truer words." He sighed. Stared at her. "What about you? Gonna tell Nakos you love him? Put him out of his misery?"

She should've a long time ago. His giving heart, his unyielding patience, his strength? All root deep and part of the beautiful man she never thought she could have, nevertheless hold on to. The passion alone would keep her warm for the rest of her life. And for some reason, he wanted, loved, her above everyone else.

She'd work on believing she deserved him. Because Nate was right. It was time she stopped giving shame and fear the reins.

"I do love him."

"No kidding." He grinned and glanced around. "So, can I give you a lift home or is this your new pad?"

She lumbered to her feet and stretched. "Home, please."

Taking her offered hand, he stood as well, pretending to let her assist. No way she'd really budge him. "You sure? An inflatable mattress over there. A chair in the corner. You could be pretty solid here. Except for the leaking roof. That might be a problem."

"I'll have to bring it up with the landlord."

"Be happy to help. I hear she's a hot redhead."

"God." She laughed until her side ached. "Definitely a great guy. Come on. Take me home."

"Good choice."

They climbed down and strode over damp grass flickering with fireflies toward the driveway, where his Harley and Olivia's truck were parked. He opted for the truck, she assumed, because she was wet from the rain.

Once they were headed for the gate, he broke the silence. "Do me a favor. I'm going to talk to them when I get back, but come up to the house tomorrow and have a chat with Olivia and Kyle."

"I will." In fact, she pulled her cell out of her back pocket, relieved it turned on considering how drenched she'd gotten. She shot off a quick text to Liv, copying the same message for her brother.

I'm all right. Talk to you tomorrow. Love you.

She re-pocketed the phone as Nate cut the headlights and bumped up Nakos's driveway. He put the gear in Park and glanced at her in the truck's dim interior.

Anxiety twisted her belly, banded her lungs. "Is it stupid that I'm nervous as hell?"

"No." He rubbed his jaw. "Love has a way of bringing people like us to our knees. If you weren't nervous, I'd say there's something wrong with you. You're going to be okay, Amy."

A nod, a weak smile, and she stared at Nakos's cabin. Two stories of cedar with a wrap-around porch. No frills, just a couple rocking chairs, but she'd come to think of the place as home. Truthfully, she'd been more comfortable here than anywhere else. She'd never felt welcomed or wanted growing up in her parents' house, and the little ranch she'd had with Chris had seemed more like a weigh station for passing time.

Nakos had opened not only his cabin, but his life and heart to her. No hesitation. He'd given her the safety and security and love she'd been missing, that she'd so desperately craved and hadn't trusted. Which, she realized, had been wrong on her part. Understandable, but wrong. She should've believed in him.

The proof was right in front of her. Every light in the place was on as if he'd kept the torches burning for her safe return. Emotion squeezed her throat, put a sheen in her eyes.

"I am." She tore her gaze away from the house and looked at Nate. "I am going to be okay."

He flashed her a grin. "Damn right."

Exiting the vehicle, she strode up the porch steps and eyed the door. Taking a deep breath, she turned the knob.

Nakos sat on the couch, elbows on his thighs, hunched over with his head in his hands. His feet were bare and he wore a pair of loose gray sweats with a forest green tee. His raven strands were out of the band and in chaos as if he'd repeatedly fisted his hair. The rigidness of his frame was stiff with tension, and her heart lurched. Turned over in her chest.

As she closed the door, his head jerked up and his red-rimmed midnight eyes met hers. Wide. Frenzied. Disbelieving.

Oh God, he'd been crying. She opened her mouth to say something, but he shot to his feet, swept his gaze over her. Once. Twice.

Then, he made a choking sound and stalked to her. Ate the distance between them like the beast had total control of his body. He cupped her face, pressed her back against the door, and crushed his mouth to hers.

Chapter Twenty-Two

With violently shaking hands, Nakos held the gorgeous face he feared he'd never see again and kissed her with all the pent up, avid torment he'd had gutting him for hours. When that wasn't enough, he kissed her eyes, her forehead, her cheeks, and pressed against her, trapping her to the door.

"*Hihcebe*, I was scared to death." Unimaginable things had scowered his mind. All the scenarios she might've been in. Or done. After revealing such a horrible memory, he had no clue where her head was at, what she might do in the wake. His ribcage had been pried open by steel claws and his insides shredded until there was nothing left. *For. Hours.* "Scared to goddamn death, *anim*."

He'd barked orders at the men. Had ridden on horseback to every place he could conceive she may have gone. Stood helpless in the rain, searching, searching. Each second had been an eternity. And then Nate had radioed she was all right. But Nakos hadn't seen with his own eyes, touched with his own hands to gain proof. So he'd climbed the walls at home, waiting, praying she'd return before his head exploded or he tore the place down to the studs.

Still jacked and busting apart at the seams, he took her mouth again, somewhat more gently, and repeatedly told himself she was here, she was home. She wasn't bleeding out somewhere or in that bastard's hands or aimlessly wandering around, wondering if she had anywhere to go. He had her, was holding her. She had a heartbeat, breath in her lungs, and tangible form.

"I love you." He pinched his eyes shut, pressed his brow to hers. There wasn't enough space in his chest for how much love he had. He might kill her for doing this to him, though. "Love you, love you."

Her cool fingers settled on his neck, and they were like ice. She shivered, and he eased away. Goosebumps skated her arms and her lips were slightly blue. Her clothes and hair were...drenched. Pretty mermaid eyes stared at him, a little dazed. She searched his expression, parted her lips to speak, but he snapped. For the three-million and ninety-seventh time tonight, he flipped his lid.

In a surge, he swept her into his arms and hauled ass for the stairs. He needed to get her dry. Warm. Safe.

"Nakos, what are you doing?"

Her voice. Shit, that voice. He never thought he'd hear that again, either.

Saying nothing, as he wasn't in a rational frame of mind, he climbed the staircase and pivoted for her room. Depositing her on the side of the bed, he moved to the dresser, opened and closed drawers. Shoved items around.

Flannel pants. Yes, those would do. Sweatshirt, check. Wool socks. Perfect. He froze at the colorful array of panties, then snatched a random pair and rushed back to her.

Ignoring her round, questioning gaze, he fisted her wet blouse and pulled it off. It hit the floor with a *thwap* and her bra followed. He tugged the sweatshirt over her head, manipulated her arms into the sleeves.

"Nakos, I can do it."

"No, I..." Had to get her warm and safe. He'd failed before. She'd been alone. In the dark. In the rain. Scared.

All his fault. He'd just...left her there. In the barn. *Left her there.*

He pushed her shoulders until she laid back. Fingers bumbling, he stripped off her jeans and underwear, tossed them aside. Lifting her ankle, he put one foot, then the other into the fresh panties and flannel pants, and yanked them over her hips into place. He slipped the socks onto her feet while she sat up.

And because visions of her in the dark, in the rain, alone and scared filtered to mind, he dragged the comforter over her, too. Squatting in front of her, he wrapped his arms around her waist and dropped his head in her lap.

He sucked oxygen for the first time all evening and wound up breathing her scent into his lungs. Tentative fingers stroked his hair, his shoulder. He cinched his arms tighter, wanting to crawl inside her. His sinuses stung, and he almost wept. Again. Or still.

Her quiet sigh filled the space between them. "Nate said you went a little crazy, but I didn't believe him."

"Crazy doesn't cover it." His words were muffled by the blanket, but he couldn't move. She was in his arms and he wasn't letting go. "Love you, *anim*."

"Look at me." She held his jaw and forced him to meet her eyes. "I love you, too. So very, very much."

Hell, she was killing him. Over and over, minute by minute. Killing him.

Heat filled the frigid corners inside him her absence had created, spread warmth throughout his chest cavity until his blood sang and his limbs quit shaking. Tender endearment looked back at him and, for the first time, it wasn't clouded by guilt or pain.

There she was, his Ames. There was the place he'd been trying to reach.

He rose onto his knees until they were eye to eye. Cupping the back of her head, he pulled her to him and pressed his lips to hers. Gentle sweeps and tender strokes. He allowed the feel of her against him to unfurl the tension clamping his muscles, loosen the stronghold of concern and fear.

"I'm sorry I scared you."

He rested his cheek to hers. "I'm sorry I handled things so poorly. I should've stayed with you."

When he thought he could move, he picked her up and carried her into his room, hit the wall switch with his elbow to cut the light, and settled against the headboard, her straddling his lap. She snuggled into him, face buried in his neck, and he held her. Just held her like he'd been needing to do since that awful moment in the barn.

They stayed like that for he didn't know how long before she drew a breath, let it go in a ragged exhale. "It happened in the alley behind my parents' hardware store."

He froze as it dawned on him what she meant. Her voice was quiet, calm, belying the harsh slap it had to bring her to remember the...rape. Damn it all. Just the word incited rage and anguish in every atom of his body. His heart stopped and his hand faltered over the curve of her spine. He swore, he didn't know if he could handle hearing the details. But this wasn't about him. It was about her, and she seemed ready to tell him.

"Nate says I should talk about it, that it might help me get closure."

Then, somehow, he'd get his shit together. In answer, he wrapped one arm around her lower back, silently letting her know he had her, she was safe. The other he slid into her hair, threading his fingers in the strands.

"We'd just gotten back from church. I was wearing this horrid pink sundress my mother made me put on, and I just wanted to take it off. But one of my chores was emptying the wastebaskets in the shop, so I grabbed the bag to take the garbage out to the dumpster. He surprised me from behind."

Nakos slammed his eyes shut and gnashed his teeth so his jaw would stop trembling. He focused on his breathing when he wanted to yell.

"He pushed me up against the wall. He..." She trembled and he hugged her harder, fighting the threat of angry tears. "It was over quickly, but it didn't feel that way. I didn't scream or say no. Too scared. It...hurt. Bad."

A sob cracked his chest, and he gave up. Choking on tears he refused to let fall, he hissed, fought for air. Bringing his knees up, boosting her a tad higher, he buried his face in her hair.

"Stupid things ran through my head when he was done. How I'd be in trouble for getting my dress dirty. What would I say if I was asked about the blood on my underwear. Was I supposed to help with dinner when I could barely walk." She went quiet a beat. "I showered afterward, scrubbing my skin raw. I told my mom that night, who told my dad, and neither of them believed me."

Her face was still pressed to his neck, her body limp against his as if she'd resigned herself to the inevitable outcome. Meanwhile, he was goddamn dying. And useless. Unable to do anything to help her while every instinct railed at him to fight. Protect. The attack may have happened years ago, yet for him this was new. Occurring now.

But, *Hihcebe*. That part of her, that sweet heart of hers she almost never showed to anyone except him, seemed to understand his distress. Her fingers stroked his jaw, an affectionate caress, like she was attempting to prove *to him* all was well.

Silence fell, and he eventually settled enough to speak. "This was what you've been trying to tell me. I understand why you had a hard time with the decision, but I don't want you to think you can't talk to me."

214

Slowly, she straightened and looked down at his chest, hesitation written all over her. "I thought..." She bit her lip and closed her eyes. When she opened them, misery clung to the tears pooling. "I was worried you wouldn't want me anymore."

As if that declaration didn't slice through muscle, artery, and bone, she kept going with the verbal assault at a speed he could barely track.

"I felt soiled and dirty. You're a knight, Nakos. Everything good and kind and honest in this world and I was...*tainted*." Tears spilled at an alarming rate and her voice raised several octaves, bordering on hysterical, taking his pulse along for the ride. "Finally, you looked at me and, for a moment, I had what I always wanted. I was so scared you'd be...be...disgusted."

Oh, fucking hell. "Stop." He grabbed the sides of her head, desperate himself, and gave her a little shake. "Please, stop. I can't take anymore tonight. I can't." How could she ever think that's how he'd react? Worse, what did it say about him that she'd jumped to that conclusion?

"Look at me, in my eyes, *bixooxu*." He waited until she did. "The act, what that man did to you, was disgusting. Not you. Understand? You are not tainted or dirty or anything else. I love you. No matter what, I love you. That's not going to change."

She nodded, a frantic assurance to the quickness of the gesture, but the tears were drying and she began to breathe with less hyperventilation. "Nate said you'd say that. Do you mean it, though?"

He was going to buy Nate another Harley to say thank you. Scratch that. Two Hogs. "Yes, I mean it. With every cell, Ames." He dragged a pull of oxygen. "There's no extracting you from here." He took her hand, set her palm over his heart. "I wouldn't want to even if I could. You make me happy."

"Because of you, I know what happy means." Her lips made a pout as she wiped her cheeks.

He was about to beg her to shut up until sunrise, just a few measly hours to give his shattered heart a reprieve, but she opened her mouth first.

"Will you go with me to the police station tomorrow?"

Stunned stupid, he stared unblinking.

215

"To give an official statement so they can hold my uncle on charges. Nate said he'd be there the whole time, but I want you with me, too. Please?"

"Yes." Was she kidding? "Of course, I'll go with you." He always knew she was brave, fearless, but he'd underestimated her level of courage. And damn, he was buying the whole auto lot out of motorcycles for Nate. Seriously, no lie. "I'm debating whether we should have us surgically joined. It might be my only peace of mind."

She laughed, and nothing sounded sweeter. "How about I promise to love you forever instead? Less awkward than going under the knife and we wouldn't have to get insurance involved."

In answer, he sealed his lips to hers, sank deep with a slow glide until he was under the influence and she contentedly hummed. His world righted and his lungs inflated and his heart rhythm finally waved a white flag.

They were going to be fine, the two of them. Just fine.

When he pulled away, he brushed his nose with hers and smoothed her hair from her face. "How would you feel about getting married again, this time to the right guy?"

Blink, blink. "Was that a proposal?"

"Not yet. Answer the question." He nibbled his way down her throat.

She tilted her head. "Well, if Charlie Hunnam asked, I wouldn't say no. I'm—"

He smacked her ass. Hard.

"Okay, okay. And rawr for Alpha Nakos." She sighed. "I would feel favorably about the situation."

Good. He was already plotting as he traced her cheek with his fingertip. "Promise me something. No matter what, we'll have no more secrets. You and me, Ames. Nothing between us."

"Deal." She gave him a brief kiss and smiled against his lips. "For the sake of honesty, I need to tell you something. It's important." Her expression grew stoic.

His pulse tripped. "What?"

"I'm very, very overheated in this outfit you put on me."

He narrowed his eyes.

"I mean, I know my clothes were wet from the storm, but I was only a little chilly stepping into the air conditioning."

Tongue in cheek, he cleared his throat. "You were shivering."

She gestured down at herself. "Hello, overboard. And, wow. You just tossed those wet clothes aside. It reminded me of when I try on an outfit and it doesn't look good on me. I throw it on the floor and say, *no, you don't deserve to be hung up. You sit there and think about what you've done.*"

"Are you making fun of me?"

"Just a little." Sexy impish grin. She'd pay for that in a second.

He flattened his lips to avoid a smile and almost failed. "I was this close to needing a straightjacket and a padded cell, and you're teasing me?"

"This close? Nakos, they have you scheduled for basket weaving on Tuesday." She patted his shoulder, placating. "It's the middle of summer. I look like I'm ready to climb the Laramie. In January."

Grabbing the hem of her sweatshirt, he jerked it over her head. "Better?"

"Getting there."

It would take the rest of his natural life and hers to keep up with her. And he was very much looking forward to it. He laid her out on the bed, stripped off her sweats and panties. "How's that?"

She held up her feet, covered in wool socks.

A hearty sigh, and he pulled them off by the toe, flipped them over his shoulders.

Stretching out in all her naked glory, no hint of her previous shyness, she grinned. Arched her back. Bit her lip.

Gorgeous. And his, heaven help him.

"You're overdressed, too."

He took care of that problem quickly by shedding his clothes, then rose over her. She accepted him in the cradle of her thighs as he lowered himself to her. The skin-to-skin charge was both a jolt and a welcome home.

"Anything else, *anim*?" He kissed her neck, loving the blush that started at her collarbone and infused her cheeks.

"Just one more thing." Her heavy-lidded gaze met his. "Don't let go."

Hands buried in her hair, he stared at her—those amazing eyes framed by thick lashes, her lush mouth, her dark strands spread over the sheets. She'd said the same thing all those months ago when

217

he'd carried her out of the barn. The day his world stopped on its axis. She may have been bruised and bloody, but he'd been the broken one. That terrible moment had begun this wonderful path for them by kick-starting his heart when, in truth, it hadn't beaten until she'd given it reason.

She owned him, all of him, and probably always had. Always would.

"Never," he said, feathering his lips over hers. "I promise, I'll never let go."

Epilogue

One Month Later...

In the main house's kitchen, Amy flipped through the pictures she took last week, Olivia next to her at the island looking on. They had plans to take a ride up to Blind Man's Bluff as soon as Nakos was finished with the horses.

It was a gorgeous Saturday, the sun bright and warm, and Amy was looking forward to enjoying it. The past couple weeks had been rough between the trips to Casper for pre-trial hearings and retelling the rape to a bunch of strangers. But her friends had been beside her the whole time, a silent show of support.

Aunt Mae set her tea on the table where she'd been watching them. "So, Clint took the plea bargain."

"Yeah." Amy put the photos back in the envelope. "The district attorney called yesterday. I'm shocked, actually."

There was no physical evidence to credit her accusations against her uncle. They'd both taken lie detector tests, which wouldn't hold up in court, but it had given authorities something to go on. She'd passed. Her uncle had failed. And when her parents had admitted, under oath, she'd told them about the assault the day it had happened, Clint's lawyer had pressed him to plea out.

Olivia frowned. "Two years in jail, likely out in months, isn't near enough."

For Amy, it wasn't about the length of his sentence. It was about standing up for herself and getting the closure Nate had suggested. He'd been right, too. Every day got better and she'd been able to shed most of the doubt she'd lived with all her life.

"I'm just glad it's over." She hugged Olivia, smiled at Aunt Mae.

"Amen to that." Olivia eyed her. "You and my husband are spending a lot of time together. I'm really grateful you guys are so close."

Rehab, they'd named it. Wednesday afternoons, Nate and Amy would climb up to the tree house and "talk" for an hour. He'd opened up and mentioned quite a few awful things from his past, and she'd done the same. It had been...expunging. Olivia and Nate had great communication, as did Nakos and Amy. But sometimes dark called to dark, needed someone who understood. It had been exceptionally therapeutic for them both.

"I'm grateful, too." Amy sighed and knelt at Olivia's feet. Her friend wasn't showing yet, but Amy liked to talk to her belly anyway. If she was going to corrupt her future niece or nephew, she had to start early. "How's my favorite fetus doing? I bought you a ton of new toys. I'm hiding them until your mommy's baby shower. Loud, obnoxious toys."

"Great." Olivia rolled her eyes and grinned. "Where's Nakos's meticulous control when I need it?"

"In my defense, I was left unsupervised in the store." Amy shrugged and straightened as the back door squeaked.

Kyle poked his head in from the mudroom. "Nakos is looking for you in the barn."

She blinked at her brother. "Why?"

"I dunno." With that blinding insight, he ducked out again.

"Well," Mae rose from the table, "let's go see. I could use some fresh air."

Mae and Olivia in tow, Amy walked across the gravel-strewn path toward the three barns. They bypassed the first two and zeroed in on the third where the horse stalls were located. A whippoorwill cooed and cicadas buzzed. It was going to be a hot one today, but a nice breeze relieved the heat and brought the scent of grass and hay.

Amy jerked short in the doorway and glanced around.

What the hell? The ranch hands were all lined up on both sides of the barn's interior, in front of the stalls as if forming an aisle. At the back, standing between the open rear carriage doors, was Nakos. Slightly behind him and off to the side, Nate grinned.

"Are you practicing military training, Nate?" Amy eyed the workers, her brother included, with their hands behind their backs, eyes on her. "Because, uh, you're retired, you know."

Nakos, smiling, crooked his finger, beckoning her. Wearing cowboy boots, faded denim, and a black tee snug enough to trace all the coiled muscle underneath, how could a girl resist?

She stepped closer, taking in his black Stetson, his low ponytail, and the dark dusting of stubble on his jaw. So sexy. Add in his bronze skin, and her knees weakened. She stopped in front of him, wondering what was going on, and sent him a questioning glance.

"I love you."

A flutter pinged her belly, just as it did every time he said those words. "I love you, too."

"I wanted to wait until all the ugliness was over before doing this. And now that it is, we have nothing in our way, *bixooxu*." He dropped to one knee, his midnight eyes on her.

"Oh God." She gasped, clapping a trembling hand over her mouth.

He held out a ring on his palm, his gaze solemn. Through a watery haze, she glanced at the square princess cut diamond in a heavy gold band before he started talking and drew her attention back to him.

"I loved you as a boy and fell in love with you as a man." He fisted his hand over his heart. "You're in here so deep that there is no you, no me. Only us. Marry me, *anim*."

"Yes." God, like there was even a need to ask. "Yes!"

He flashed a wicked grin and stood, wrapping his arms around her. Her feet left the floor as his lips crushed hers. Cheers erupted behind them, and she laughed against his mouth.

"That was really romantic." She sighed dreamily, hardly able to believe this amazing man was hers.

"You haven't seen anything yet." He set her on her feet and slid the ring on her finger. After a kiss over her knuckles, he gripped her shoulders, turned her around, and swatted her butt. "Go get ready."

She whirled back on him. "For what?"

"Our wedding." He winked, then pointed to Olivia. "One hour."

"I'll have her ready. Count on it."

"What?" Amy dug in her heels, but Olivia tugged her by the arm toward the exit. "I can't get married today. That takes planning and—"

"He's got it covered."

Shocked silent, she glanced over her shoulder as she was maneuvered out of the barn. The guys stood around, talking and smiling. She caught Nate pulling Nakos in for a hug and bromance back slap before she was dragged out.

"Liv, seriously." Through the mudroom, past the kitchen, to the stairs they went. "Today? There's no time to invite guests or get flowers." All the things missing from her first mistake of a wedding. This was supposed to be her second chance, the start to her ever-after. She'd wanted, so badly, to have the day done right. Up the staircase to Olivia's third floor suite they continued. "I don't even have a..."

Amy halted in the kitchenette. Stared straight through the open floor plan to Liv's small living room. Stopped breathing. Grabbed her chest.

"A dress," she whispered.

She gazed at the white gown, hanging on a curtain rod in front of the window. Sleeveless, it had a fitted bodice that flowed into a loose skirt, which looked to hit maybe mid-calf. As she walked closer, she realized the material was satin, but it had a very light mesh overlay with tiny pearls sewn into the hem to give the simplicity a hint of elegance.

It was...beautiful. She didn't care for big, foofy dresses or all the layers typically found in bridal gowns.

"Aunt Mae made it." Olivia set a soothing hand on her back. "You shouldn't be too warm in it and you'll look amazing."

Trembling, Amy blinked at Liv and realized Kyle had followed them up. He stood next to Mae, a sheepish smile curving his lips.

They had a dress, a beautiful one, all ready for her. A survey of the room showed a pair of ballet flats in an open box by the couch and two bouquets of flowers on the coffee table. Bluebells and white lilies. So pretty. There was even a navy blue sundress with spaghetti straps, she assumed, for Olivia, which hung in the doorway to the bedroom.

"I really am getting married today."

Mae walked over, rubbed her arms. "You're really getting married today. Everything's being seen to outside. You, sweetheart, just have to show up."

"Thank you for the dress. I love it."

"The groom didn't give us much time. Go figure, considering he takes forever to do everything." Olivia took Amy's hand, guided her to the kitchen island, and had her sit on a stool. "Welcome to my office. Lay your hands flat. We'll do a manicure first."

While Liv began filing, Amy dazedly looked at her brother as he plopped on a stool beside her. This couldn't be real. The whole thing was a dream.

"I'm going to give you your present now." Kyle pulled an envelope out of his back pocket, flicked his gaze to Olivia bent over Amy's hands, and shrugged. "Guess I'll open it." He slid out a piece of paper, unfolded it, and held it up for her to see.

The letterhead had the logo for the consolidated loan company she used for the bills her ex had accumulated. She skimmed over the numbers, not understanding, until she got to the bottom.

Balance = $0.00

"What?" She went to reach for the paper, but got her hand slapped by Olivia.

"Hold still. I'm polishing."

"Calm down, Amy." Kyle, his expression dialed to an unusual tone of serious, looked Amy dead in the eye. "I've worked on this ranch for going on ten years and haven't paid a dime in rent since I live in the quarters. I built up a lot in savings and—"

"Kyle, God. No, I can't let you—"

"You can and will. Shut up and listen to me. I wasn't there for you when I should've been, didn't see the pain and heartache you were dealing with. I never got involved in the crap with Mom and Dad when I should've stuck up for you." He sighed. "That denial ends now. You will take this gift and get your fresh start. I will walk you down the aisle and give you away to our broody foreman who loves you so much, and you will cooperate with a smile on your face. Got it?"

A sob hitched her chest, and she stared at her brother, normally so laid-back and carefree, looking at her like he was ready to battle anything in his path. "Are you sure?"

"Damn sure."

"Get the crying out of your system now." Olivia blew on Amy's nails, painted a delicate shade of iridescent white. "Makeup is next and you're not botching the job once it's done."

Amy took several deep breaths and thought about what Kyle had said. "Are Mom and Dad coming today?"

They'd told the truth when questioned about the details of her assault, but they hadn't made any attempt to mend fences. She suspected they'd cooperated because they were under oath, not out of any sense of loyalty. They hadn't believed her as a girl, what made her think they'd believe *in* her as a grown woman?

"No. I'm sorry, sis." Kyle frowned. "Rid them from your mind. They're not worth it. And, if it makes you feel any better, they're as disappointed in me as they are in you." He paused. "I came out of the closet, told them I was gay."

"What?" Amy straightened on the stool, mindful of her tacky nails. "You're gay?" What next? Olivia's Loch Ness Monster showing up to serve cake?

He nodded. "Kept it private a long time. Being raised by two God-fearing people had me afraid to tell anybody. You gave me the courage to...you know. They called me a heathen, said I was going to roast in the bowels of hell."

"Oh, Kyle. That's not true." Jeez, their folks were such assholes. "I'm proud of you, and I love you."

"Love you, too." He sucked in a breath. "So, we can be sinners together."

"Darn right."

"Do the guys know?" Olivia set a cosmetics bag on the counter. "The other ranch hands? Have you told them?"

Kyle nodded. "Told them yesterday. They were pretty cool about it. I got the *as long as you don't hit on me, we're good* speech from a few, but they were okay."

"If that changes, you let me know." Olivia pointed at him. "I mean it. I won't tolerate hate on my ranch."

Before Amy knew it, she was in makeup, dressed, and standing in the pasture at the end of an aisle. White folding chairs lined both sides, where some people from town and the ranch hands stood waiting on her. Nakos's parents smiled and waved encouragingly.

Olivia faced her from the makeshift altar and nodded, but Amy couldn't take her eyes from Nakos very long. In place beside Nate, he'd left his hair down, raven strands stirring in the breeze. He'd worn a suit. *A suit.* Charcoal gray with a navy blue tie. Lord have mercy, he dressed up nice.

He pressed a hand over his heart, watching her ascend with Kyle, as if he was trying to keep the organ from pounding out of his chest. Love shone in his eyes, telling her everything she needed to know. When she made it to him, Kyle kissed her cheek and sat by Mae.

"You're breathtaking, *anim*. Gorgeous."

"Thank you. So are you."

She smiled, still stunned over all of this, and feeling like she'd been plunked into some fairy tale version of a life that wasn't hers. But it was. This was her man and these were her people. The ones who mattered.

They did an Arapaho ceremony first. They were directed to sit on a bench, shoulder-to-shoulder, then they were covered with a cloth. A member of his tribe chanted words in his native tongue she couldn't understand, and incense was involved. Lots of incense.

Afterward, Rip presided over the nuptials and, in a daze, she repeated what the sheriff told her to.

She snapped to somewhere between Nakos kissing her to seal the deal and applause loud enough to have the nearby horses whinnying. They took pictures and chatted with the guests, and then Nakos tucked her to his side.

"You ready to dance with me, wife?"

Giddy, and not caring how girly she probably seemed, she grinned up at him like an idiot. "I'm ready for anything."

"Good." He stripped off the tie and jacket, earning a laugh from her as he rolled up his sleeves. He swooped her in his arms and headed for the first barn. "I hope the reception's to your liking. I want you to be happy from now on, *bixooxu*."

"I only need you for that."

"Careful, Ames. You're going soft on me." A wide grin, and he pressed a quick kiss to her mouth. He jerked his chin toward the carriage doors. "Behold." Carrying her, he stepped inside, and her lungs collapsed.

"Oh my God."

Round tables with seating for guests were placed along the left and right walls. Tea lights and bluebells were on the white tablecloths. Up front, by the open rear doors, was a little area reserved as a dance floor. But what was above them had her heart tripping and her throat tight.

Strands of white lights rained from the rafters. Between them, attached to tiny clips hanging by thin string, were photos. Hundreds of them, twirling in the cross-breeze. And they all seemed to be pictures she'd taken. Nature shots. Ones of Nakos. Selfies of both of them. She stared up, in awe, while he walked deeper into the barn.

He set her on her feet up front, pulled her to him. "I love you."

"God, Nakos." She could hardly breathe. Was there such a thing as being too happy? If so, she'd gladly perish from it. "I love you, too. I love this. It's amazing."

It's exactly how she would've planned the day herself. Better, actually. Simple elegance, intimate setting, and rustic-chic. Personal touches.

A song she didn't recognize started to play, and he wrapped her in his arms. "No, my *anim*, my *bixooxu*. You've got that all wrong. You're amazing. This is just paper and decoration."

She danced with him, with his father, with Nate and Kyle and all the ranch hands. She drank champagne with his mother and Olivia and Mae, laughing until late into the evening.

And when all the guests had gone home, Nakos walked her across the grass, cool under her toes in the night air, and up the hill to the oak tree. Crickets chirped and fireflies blinked and stars shone through an inky sky.

He grabbed the rope of the tire swing, gave it a meaningful glance. "It all started here." He chuckled as if surprised. "Hop on."

She did, hiking up her dress and sliding her legs through the opening. She held the rope, rough against her palms, and he placed his hands over hers.

"It all started here," he repeated. "Do you remember the first thing you said to me?"

"Boys are stupid?"

Tilting his head back, he let out a low laugh. "No, but that does sound like you." His expression sobered, yet amusement still warmed his eyes. "Mae and my parents left you and me and Olivia here to get acquainted while they went off to talk business."

He set the swing in motion with a gentle push. "I was struck stupid by her hair, all that red, but I noticed you first. Those damn expressive eyes that were like a mermaid call. Bluish-green and glinting with sunlit mischief. Olivia asked me questions, and I was too shy to answer. I hadn't spoken at all, actually. For some reason, I kept going back to you, to your eyes, even though you had yet to engage me in conversation."

Touched, she smiled at him, encouraging the rest. She had a vague recollection of their first meeting, but his memory was obviously more indelible.

"After Olivia wound down and stopped trying to badger me with kindness, you studied me with this little frown line of concentration right here." He stopped the swing and pressed a fingertip between her eyes. "You said, *hello, friend*. That's it. Nothing more. Two words that bid me welcome and gave me a title. *Hello, friend*."

He kissed her forehead. "I needed that, I think. I needed the direction after the culture shock and to know my place." His eyes narrowed. "Of course, then you stole my hat and climbed up the tree. And thus began our relationship—you accepting me, just like that, while simultaneously making my heart pound in worry with a side of teasing me to death."

She grinned and slowly shifted to stand on the swing.

"Don't you dare, Ames."

Her grin widened. "Think I can climb a tree in a wedding dress?"

She reached above her head, but he wrapped an arm around her waist and hauled her over his shoulder. He stalked away, carting her.

"*Hihcebe*, woman. You can't even cut me a break on our wedding day."

Since she had a great view of his ass from the position, she didn't complain about the barbarian treatment. Gotta love Alpha Nakos, anyway. "Where's the fun in that?"

"Never a dull moment with you."

"Get used to it." She bobbed while he carried her toward the barns, most likely heading to his truck in the driveway. "Hey, I have something that sounds better than *hello, friend*."

"I shudder to ask, but okay. What could possibly be better than that?"

"Hello, husband." She paused as his steps faltered. "Maybe tonight we could start trying to produce a little person that'll someday say, *Hello, Daddy*."

He stopped, slowly let her slide down his body, and before her feet could touch the ground, he kissed her. Long, lazy, and with so

227

much sentiment, she was dizzy. He pulled away and smiled, emotion shining in his eyes.

"You're right. That is better. In fact, it sounds perfect."

Read more about Nate & Olivia in REDEMPTION.
Available now!

Turn the page for more great books...

Want to help an author? Please consider leaving a review and tell others about the great romance you just read!

Redemption

Redwood Ridge

Covington Cove

Counter balance

exposure

The disfunctional Test

www.AuthorKellyMoran.com
Enchanting ever-afters...
Sign up for Kelly Moran's newsletter and get a FREE eBook!

ABOUT THE AUTHOR:

Kelly Moran is a best-selling & award-winning romance author of enchanting ever-afters. She is a Catherine Award-Winner, Readers' Choice Finalist, Holt Medallion Finalist, and a 2014 Award of Excellence Finalist through RWA. She's also landed on the 10 Best Reads and Must Read lists from USA TODAY's HEA.

Kelly's been known to say she gets her ideas from everyone and everything around her and there's always a book playing out in her head. No one who knows her bats an eyelash when she talks to herself. Her interests include: sappy movies, MLB, NFL, driving others insane, and sleeping when she can. She is a closet caffeine junkie and chocoholic, but don't tell anyone. She resides in Wisconsin with her husband, three sons, and her hound dog. Most of her family lives in the Carolinas, so she spends a lot of time there as well.

She loves connecting with her readers.

Made in the USA
Columbia, SC
12 August 2017